40 HOURS
THE UNBOUNDING

A southbound ride to the Edge of India
An unravelling he never saw coming

Yuvaan
books

An Imprint of Unbound Script

40 Hours : The Unbounding

First Edition : January, 2026

Written by Vineet

ISBN : 978-93-47125-91-1

Publisher : Unbound Script
2/41, Ansari Road
Daryaganj, Delhi-110002

Website : www.unboundscript.com
E-mail : books@unboundscript.com
Phone : 011-35807601

Printer : Yash Printographics
Noida, Uttar Pradesh

Price : ₹ 349/-

40 HOURS
THE UNBOUNDING

A southbound ride to the Edge of India
An unravelling he never saw coming

VINEET

Yuvaan
books

CONTENTS

*To those who taught me that becoming
is not an escape from where you begin,
but a patient return to your capacities*

Where This Journey Will Take You

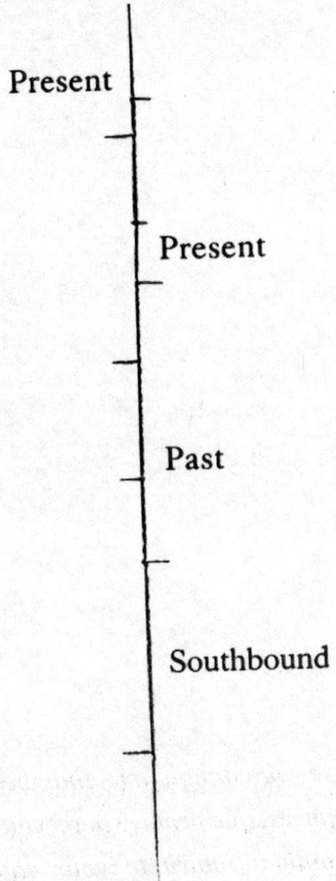

People You Will Meet on This Journey

<table>
<tr><td colspan="2">Tarun Jayadevan (TJ/ "Average Bittu")
The narrator. A scientist, a son, and an ordinary man carrying an inherited past he does not yet understand.</td></tr>
<tr><td colspan="2">The Childhood Circle (Pantnagar)</td></tr>
<tr><td>Adrien Chadha
A celebrated illusionist. Moves instinctively between art, intuition, and wonder.</td><td>Shiva Mehra
A scientist. Restless in both thought and ambition.</td></tr>
<tr><td>Chandra Prakash (Chandu)
An engineer. Notices patterns long before they become obvious.</td><td>Ishan Mathur
A medical doctor. The quiet conscience of the group.</td></tr>
<tr><td colspan="2">Unexpected Outsiders</td></tr>
<tr><td>Kai
Introduced through Ishan. Observant. Fragile. Not entirely from here.</td><td>Zeilo
Seen by few. Believed by fewer. Kai's own.</td></tr>
<tr><td colspan="2">The State and Its Shadows</td></tr>
<tr><td>Trishulin Jayadevan
An intelligence operative. A man with answers TJ did not know to ask.</td><td>Shukla
An operative. Easily overlooked. One of the fantastic fours.</td></tr>
</table>

Fellow Travelers	
The Fantastic Four-Shukla, Verma, Sahoo, Ganesh Strangers met on a train. Their conversations linger longer than expected.	**Vajpai Ji** An older traveler whose words carry more weight than they seem to.
Mrs. Gupta Warm, talkative, unmistakably ordinary.	
Quiet Anchors	
Benjamin A roommate from Lucknow. Helped TJ understand belief without preaching it.	**Professor John Elrond** A legendary scholar whose ideas leave TJ quietly "un-Johned."
Family and Absence	
TJ's Parents Their past casts a longer shadow than their presence ever did.	**Ira** A name that still echoes.

PROLOGUE

FORTY HOURS.

That was all it took for my world to come apart, and reassemble into something I no longer recognized.

I boarded the Nauchandi Express from Bulandshahr as one man, unaware that the version of myself I knew was already on borrowed time. The train was crowded, loud, and chaotic. On it, I met four strangers who called themselves the Fantastic Four. At the time, they were nothing more than fellow passengers, voices in the noise. Only later would I understand what those hours with them quietly set in motion.

Twelve hours later, I was in the air, headed for Bengaluru, sitting across from Trishulin Jayadevan. By then, my past had already been pulled apart. My parents, long gone, were no longer who I believed them to be. Their lives, their deaths, carried consequences I was only beginning to grasp.

The journey didn't slow down. It accelerated.

Within hours, I was back on a train, the Nagercoil Express this time, moving steadily toward the southern edge of the country, toward a place where land ends and the sea begins.

Somewhere between stations, I realized I had crossed into something I could no longer step away from. A mission. Though I still didn't know its shape.

By the time dawn broke over the ocean, one thing was clear.

Whatever I thought this journey was about, I was wrong.

The real danger wasn't where I was headed.

It was already elsewhere, moving quietly, unseen, toward the world we take for granted.

Part A:
TRAIN TO JOURNEY WITHIN

Chapter – 1

The Briefing

The rhythmic hum of Anand Mishra Ji's auto-rickshaw was a gentle counterpoint to the cacophony of Lucknow's morning traffic. I leaned back, letting the early sun rest on my face. The Charbagh station, a monument to my past, receded in the side mirror.

And with it, a chapter of my life felt like it was finally, truly, closing. The passage on the Nauchandi Express from Bulandshahr had been a crucible, forging new connections, resurrecting buried truths, and leaving me with a fragile sense of peace I hadn't known in five long years.

My mind drifted back to the journey– the chaos of the general compartment, the strange camaraderie with the "Fantastic Four," the haunting story of Bhartu, the quiet wisdom of the veterinarian. That journey had felt like a careful dismantling of my own defenses, forcing me to confront ghosts I had kept locked away for years.

For the first time since losing Ira, since losing my parents, I felt unburdened. Free from the weight of a past I couldn't change.

I had even typed a note on my phone:

A Train to My Journey Within: Bulandshahr to Lucknow.

Lucknow was in bold.

A story for myself, perhaps. A way to anchor the maelstrom of emotions.

I was still miles from my modest hostel room, yet a part of me already felt… different. Lighter. The weight of "Average Bittu" had loosened its grip, replaced by a budding, unsettling understanding of who I– T. Jayadevan, son of heroic Indian spies– might actually be.

My phone buzzed in my pocket.

An unknown number.

I almost ignored it, wanting to hold on to the stillness a little longer. But some instinct, a faint echo of the urgency that had defined the last few hours of my train journey, made me answer.

"Hello?"

A pause, then a voice, crisp and familiar, a voice that had sliced through my reality only hours before near the train lavatory. "TJ?"

My breath caught. "Trishulin Sir?"

"Yes. Listen carefully. You're in. But don't go to your hostel. Plans have changed. I need you at the Lucknow Command Center. Now." There was no room for argument in that tone. It was the voice of a man who moved worlds.

My mind raced. In? In what? Command Center? The auto suddenly felt too small, the city sounds too loud. "Sir, what's going on?"

"No time to explain over the phone. I'll send you a location pin. Get there as fast as you can. It's… critical." The line clicked dead.

Anand Mishra Ji, still humming *Deewana Hua Baadal*, glanced at me in the rearview mirror. "Sab theek hai, Sir Ji?"

I stared at my phone, the blank screen reflecting my own stunned expression. The fragile peace of the morning had been shattered. Critical. Command Center. The words echoed sharply, dragging me out of reverie and into something cold and immediate. Shukla's face surfaced in my mind. The whispered truths about my parents. About the Indian Institute of Foreign Particle Research. About programmable explosions.

"Uncle Ji," I said, my voice strained, "change of plans. I need to go to this new location. Urgently." I showed the driver the pin that had just arrived– a nondescript point on the map, somewhere in the heavily secured cantonment area.

Anand Mishra Ji, ever obliging, nodded. "Ji, Sir Ji. Jahan app lejaieya vahi chalengey." The auto veered, joining a different current of traffic, heading towards a future I couldn't begin to imagine.

The Command Center was nothing like I'd expected. Hidden behind the facade of an old colonial-era administrative building, it was a hive of hushed activity. Men and women in crisp, unmarked uniforms moved with quiet efficiency through corridors lined with doors that bore only codes, no names. Escorted by a stern-faced guard who had met me at a discreet checkpoint, I felt I'd stepped into a different dimension.

Trishulin Jayadevan was waiting for me in a sparsely furnished briefing room. He looked tired, older than he had on the train, but his eyes held the same intensity. And beside him stood Shukla, one of my "Fantastic Four," no longer in his casual train attire, but in a functional, unmarked uniform, with his grim expression. This sight confirmed the illusion of the past few hours.

"TJ, thank you for coming so quickly," Trishulin said, gesturing towards a chair. "Things are moving faster than we anticipated."

As I sat, my mind flashed back to the moment on the train when the truth had first surfaced. The conversation near the lavatory. His apology. The revelations about my parents. About controlled nano-explosions. About my mother's brilliance and my father's pursuit of justice.

I remembered asking him just one thing in return.

Get me in.

Now, looking at the holographic display that swirled into existence, showing equations and geographical data, it was clear that my plea was being answered, whether I was ready or not.

"The incident at Moradabad," Trishulin began, his voice low, "the one involving your parents and Ira, was not an isolated event."

My pulse quickened.

"We believe the technology– or a variant of it– is active again. Or, more accurately, someone is attempting to activate it."

"The nano-explosions?" I asked.

"Precisely," Trishulin confirmed. "Two days ago, there was a minor, localized event at a laboratory, in Bengaluru– IISc, to be exact. It was officially reported as an equipment fire, a small chemical combustion. But our deep-space monitoring network, the one we use to scan for foreign particle energy signatures, picked up something else. A ghost in the machine."

He magnified the wave pattern on the holographic display.

"Every explosion leaves a kind of fingerprint," he said. "Most of the time, it's the same. Heat. Light. Force."

He zoomed in again and shook his head.

"But this one isn't."

He pointed to a sharp bend in the pattern. "When certain materials react, like the ones used in your parents' explosion, the blast doesn't just disappear after it's over."

He looked up at him.

"It leaves behind an echo. A trace of energy that shouldn't be there. And once you know what to look for… you can't miss it."

"Think of it like a scream at the smallest possible level," he said. "Something the world has never heard before."

"For five years, we've been listening for that exact echo. Scanning wherever we can, waiting for it to appear again."

He paused.

"And two days ago, it did."

"For the first time since Moradabad."

He adjusted the holographic display.

"Our systems aren't advanced enough to monitor every location on Earth at the same time. So we work with a rotating watch list, a limited set of places we track closely each week."

"This time, purely by chance, IISc was on that list."

He added, almost as an aside, "My son studies there."

He looked up again.

"If IISc hadn't fallen into this cycle, this signal would have passed us by completely."

He let the weight of this information sink in between us.

"Someone inside that lab has already tested it," he said quietly. "On a very small scale. Just enough to prove it works."

"They have everything they need, the raw material, the trigger, the binding agent, and the catalyst that sets the reaction in motion. And now they know it can be controlled."

His eyes returned to me.

"Your specific area of research– green synthesis of nanomaterials, and their controlled reactivity, it suddenly matters a great deal."

He hesitated.

"We haven't had anyone with that kind of expertise since your.... mother."

The room felt tighter.

"This knowledge is far too valuable to be entrusted to someone new."

"There's something else. We could be wrong, but part of the signal from this test doesn't match anything we've seen before."

"It behaves almost... alive."

"The reaction lasted longer. It held together. Adapted."

"It's like throwing an intelligent bacteria into a fire, one that multiplies to survive but only aids the burning."

He paused, choosing his next words carefully.

"We may be looking at a hybrid weapon, a fusion of nanotechnology and some kind of an advanced bio-chemical energy."

Biochemical energy.

The phrase struck me with the force of a physical blow. A face flashed in my mind– young, intense, surrounded by bubbling beakers and complex diagrams, even as a teenager. A memory from Pantnagar.

"Shiva…" I whispered, a name tasting alien on my tongue, carrying all the youthful memories. "My friend… he was always working on bio-chemicals… He's in the UK now, doing his Ph.D."

Trishulin and Shukla exchanged a look.

"Your friend…" Trishulin said slowly. "That's not the kind of coincidence we like"

The display shifted again.

"We need you, TJ," he said. "To understand this. And to stop it."

"We're leaving for Bengaluru immediately."

He held my gaze.

"Are you with us?"

The question was heavy with implication. This wasn't just about understanding my parents' past anymore. This was about the present, about a tangible threat. It was a call to step out of the shadows of 'Average Bittu' and into a world he was only beginning to comprehend. A world where my "average" knowledge might, just might, make an extraordinary difference.

I thought of the train journey I had just completed, of the faces of Ganesh, Sahoo, Verma, and the quiet dignity of Bhartu. Even Shukla, who seemed like a nobody until a few hours ago, was part of a far wider web than I'd imagined. That journey had been about understanding where I came from.

This one would be about what I did with it.

I looked at Trishulin, then at Shukla. I took a deep breath. "Yes," I said, my voice clearer, firmer than I thought was possible. "I'm with you."

Shukla stayed at the Lucknow command and Trishulin Sir and I left for the military airbase.

On the flight to Bengaluru– a sterile, pressurized cabin speeding through the stratosphere– the present felt thin and unreal. The mission briefing echoed in my head-chatter; anomalous energy, nano-signatures. But the name that truly resonated, the one that pulled me back through time, was Shiva.

My mind, reeling from the implications of Trishulin Sir's words, suddenly found itself drifting, pulled by an invisible current back to the mists of Pantnagar. Perhaps it's how we cope, how we ground ourselves in the face of the unimaginable, by seeking the familiar echoes of our past. The Command Center, the sterile jargons of nano-explosions and bio-chemical warfare; all of it seemed a world away from the boy I once was, the 'Average Bittu,' navigating through the simpler yet no less formative landscapes of my childhood.

It was a baffling feeling to be suddenly ambushed by memories that were once my entire world, yet had remained dormant and unbothered for the last six years. The thought snagged on Shiva and the gang from Pantnagar– the keepers of my childhood– and the last link to my life where the memory of my parents was still alive. And just like that, another thread led back to Benjamin, my roommate from the early Lucknow days. Losing touch with him, I realised, was like losing a thread. The thread which connected me to Ira, who had been my anchor after my parents were gone.

In the relentless forward march of the last six years, I hadn't just lost touch with my past. I'd let my anchors slip, one by one, and only now, in this sterile room, did I truly feel the drift.

In the early nineties, Pantnagar was our universe. The sprawling university grounds, the residential colonies that felt like self-contained worlds, the untamed fields brushing against the Terai forests– it all seemed to hold a certain magic. Even for a boy like me who usually aimed for the middle ground, there was a sense of boundless possibilities in that magical world. Most families were associated with the university in one way or the other, so focus on education remained an integral part of all our lives.

Even then, there was a quietness about me, a way I had of watching the world from a slight remove. I wasn't unfriendly, just… quiet; though not out of calmness rather to conceal myself, my full identity. Shiva, in his infinite capacity for bluntness, had coined the nickname 'Average Bittu.' It wasn't malicious; it was just how I seemed to navigate life– always the middle option– never too loud, never too visible. I carried an invisible weight, a shadow in my eyes that my friends, in their youthful carelessness, never truly questioned. My father, a Subedar in the army, was often away. My mother, a gentle, intelligent woman, was the still point in my often-moving world. Looking back, I wonder if my 'averageness' was a carefully constructed shield, a way to avoid the sharp edges of a life I didn't fully understand.

Shiva Mehra was anything but average. Brilliant, restless, he perpetually challenged the status quo, whether it was the rules of a neighborhood cricket match or the established laws of physics. Science wasn't just a subject for Shiva; it was a living entity, a puzzle box he was determined to unlock. He'd dismantle radios, concoct strange-smelling potions in his makeshift 'lab' (a corner of his father's garage), and dream of harnessing the power of lightning. He was driven by a fierce, almost untamable energy, a need to understand the 'why' of everything.

Adrien Chadha was our resident charmer– the artist, the performer. Born to a French writer father who always seemed to be chasing the ghosts of a bygone literary era, and an aspiring Hindu scientist mother, whose brilliant mind sometimes wrestled with its own complexities, Adrien grew up in a crucible of contrasting ideologies. He unintentionally interbred these two different worlds, and even then, he had an uncanny ability to read people.

To understand the unspoken currents of emotion in a room. He had this strange habit: whenever his then young mind deciphered something new, he'd frame it as a scientific law, organizing his thoughts like they were universally acceptable. His early 'magic tricks' were less about illusion and more about connection. His empathy was profound, a quest to make everyone happy that would later define his unique path.

I remember one particular discussion about the peak moment for a singer when Sunidhi Chauhan came for a live performance in the university grounds. Adrien, with that thoughtful smile of his, suggested, "I think that 'high' lies between the moments the artist words out her last sound and when the crowd knows it's time to go all mad, cheering up… yeah, it's always in-between those moments when the action is made and its fruit is awaited!" He called it the "Law of In-Between," and even back in 2005, I could sense the stirrings of the Romantiologist he would become.

Chandra Prakash, or Chandu as we all called him, was the pragmatist– the voice of reason. If Shiva was the wild idea and Adrien the emotional resonance, Chandu was the one who'd quietly figure out if any of it was actually possible. He had a knack for gadgets, an early fascination with computers. He was methodical, logical, and possessed a dry wit that often caught us off guard.

And Ishan Mathur. He was another quiet one in our group, but also a keen listener. He wanted to be a doctor driven by an inability to bear seeing suffering. Adrien once helped Shiva (and by extension me and Ishan) understand "Law of Reality-Balance"– a term coined by him. Shiva was incensed when a neighbourhood boy had supposedly insulted his mother with abuse. Adrien calmly pointed out that Shiva's mother, visible across the field, seemed perfectly fine. "So, is it you who is hurt or your mother?" The question, simple yet profound, made Shiva falter. It made me ponder too. I recall Adrien also speaking of the "Law of Masters and the Slaves" when Shiva was fuming about their maid who didn't show up the previous night, and Shiva had to do the dishes. Adrien gently countered Shiva's assertion of dominance, saying, "You all seem to be the slaves to these thoughts of you being the masters here… I think what's missing here…is this love…companionship."

The tapestry of our Pantnagar days continued to be woven with shared laughter and individual anxieties. I remember Adrien explaining his "Law of the Creator and the Created" when we were discussing Chandu's father, a self-made businessman, who wasn't keeping well due to some illness in his mid-life. Shiva had remarked on how hard Chandu's father worked to create his destiny, his factory, spending his days and nights there. Adrien drew a circle in the dust: "First, he created something, his factory", he explained, "and then that something affected him, his very existence, and in turn, created him with his illness… It's a never-ending loop! We all get recreated by what we create."

The years in Pantnagar, like all childhoods, eventually drew to a close. Higher studies beckoned. Shiva aimed for the top science institutes. Adrien, defying both his parents' hopes yet somehow embodying both, chose psychology and theatre arts. Chandu enrolled in engineering. After my mother's passing and my father's subsequent transfer, I found myself in Lucknow pursuing Chemistry. Ishan headed off to medical school.

Our goodbyes were not dramatic. We were setting off on our individual journeys, unaware that sixteen years later, those threads would be pulled taut, drawing us back into an orbit none of us could have ever predicted. The kaleidoscope of our destinies had been shaken, and the new patterns were only just beginning to form.

Chapter – 2

The Romantiologist

The Indian Air Force transport plane jarred to a halt at the Yelahanka airbase with a jolt that perfectly mirrored my own frayed nerves. As we were driven in an unmarked car towards the sprawling IISc campus, the urgency was palpable. Trishulin, his face etched with worry, was on a secure satellite phone, his conversation curt and coded. I stared out at the unfamiliar cityscape, my mind a whirl of scientific theories and the raw, recent memories of my parents' true legacy.

The campus, when we arrived, was an oasis of green tranquillity, a stark contrast to the tension humming in the car. But as we neared the main administrative buildings, my attention was caught by a vibrant splash of color against a notice board– a large, glossy poster. My breath hitched.

"An Evening of Enchantment! The Grand Illusionist ADRIEN CHADHA presents THE SUNLIGHT WEAVERS!"

Beneath the flamboyant title was a picture of Adrien: older, more refined; but with the same charismatic spark in his eyes that I remembered from our childhood. He was dressed in a sharp, modern magician's attire, a stark contrast to the makeshift capes he used to fashion from bedsheets in Pantnagar. The show was scheduled for that very evening, part of IISc's annual cultural festival, 'Pravega.'

"Adrien…" I murmured; a wave of disbelief surged through me. My childhood friend, Adrien Chadha, a famous magician, is performing here, now? The coincidence was too profound.

Trishulin Sir followed my gaze. "This young chap has become quite the sensation. He is from your childhood, right?"

"You know him too?" Surprised, I asked.

"Well, who doesn't!" Trishulin Sir exclaimed. Apparently, his blend of illusion and… well, 'Romantiology,' has a massive following. Some call it pseudoscience, others swear by its therapeutic effects. Looks like he is the star attraction in this fest today."

Romantiology. The name itself felt like Adrien, a blend of his French writer father's romanticism and his Hindu scientist mother's analytical mind. It seemed he had made a career of a philosophy born on that drunken teenage night.

"Sir," I began, an idea forming, "could I… could I possibly have a few minutes? His show… it might be a coincidence, but…"

Trishulin Sir studied me for a moment, then nodded. "Alright, TJ. We have about half an hour before our briefing with others who are on their way. But be quick. And discreet."

I hurried towards the auditorium where a large crowd was already gathering. I slid into a spot in the back just as the lights dimmed. A single spotlight hit the stage, revealing Adrien. He owned the stage with an easy grace, his voice amplified, possessing the same warmth I remembered. After a few dazzling introductory illusions, the main event, 'The Sunlight Weavers,' began. An intricate network of delicate glass tubes formed an abstract sculpture on stage. As Adrien brought a sleek, handheld light generator near them, the tubes came alive, a luminous substance flowing within.

He engaged the audience, finally selecting a "random volunteer" from the crowd. The moment the student volunteer touched the tubes, an image began to form, a luminous three-dimensional portrait of the volunteer, timed perfectly and glowing with the same moving substance inside the tubes. The crowd exploded.

"The true magic isn't in making things appear or disappear. It's in seeing the light that already exists within each of us, and finding ways to help it shine a little brighter. That's the heart of Romantiology.", Adrien said softly as the applause subsided.

I then understood why Adrien was so loved. But a new thought pricked me– how did the tubes glow like that? It wasn't simple fiber optics. There was something inside them, like thousands of fireflies moving at the speed of light, only controlled by Adrien. As he took his bows, I felt a complex mix of pride and unease. My friend was a star. And I was an operative, hunting a ghost.

The applause for Adrien's final illusion was still echoing through the auditorium when I felt a tap on my shoulder. I turned, half-expecting one of Trishulin's security personnel, but found myself face-to-face with a figure both familiar and changed. Thinner, perhaps, with an academic intensity in his eyes that hadn't been there in youth, but unmistakably…

"Shiva?" I breathed, stunned.

Shiva Mehra's sharp features broke into a rare, wide grin. "Bittu! I thought that was you lurking in the back! What in the world are you doing here?"

The years dissolved in an instant. As we patted each other on the back, my mind flashed back to Pantnagar, to Shiva's radical kite design: 'Vajra' that had outlasted all others, a perfect symbol of his brilliant, unconventional mind. He explained he was here for a PhD delegation.

"Can you believe it? Adrien Chadha, the grand illusionist!" Shiva shook his head in awe. "Who would've thought our kite-flying, potion-making Adrien would end up captivating thousands?"

Just then, another voice cut in. "Well, if it isn't the prodigal scientist himself! And Average Bittu, no less! This is turning into a regular Pantnagar reunion."

Chandra Prakash– Chandu– stood before us, a little rounder, dressed in the smart casuals of a tech professional. He was working for an AI startup in Bengaluru.

"What on earth, all of you, here?" We all stood stunned, unable to comprehend what was happening. Apparently, it was Adrien who attracted us all from our usual mundane life like a living, charming magnet. Everyone thought they were coming to see only Adrien, but who knew this was going to be a reunion of all, including Ishan, that would change our lives forever.

Shiva, Chandu and I just stood there, a nexus of shared history in the bustling present. Before we could make plans, a slightly flustered figure approached. It was Ishan Mathur, the quiet empath of our group. He was a doctor now who was in town with a patient. "A new friend, Kai," he explained. "He's been suffering from a very unusual ailment. He's quite taken by Adrien's work, finds it soothing."

Just then, Adrien, having extricated himself from a throng of admirers, spotted us. His face lit up with genuine delight. "My God! The whole gang! This… this is unbelievable!" He strode over, embracing each of us in turn. "Tonight, my friends," he declared, "the universe has given us a gift. We are celebrating."

"And No excuses, TJ!" I had always been the one ruining their plans in our school days.

All five of us. Together again. The air hummed with unspoken stories. I looked at their faces, and it was as if our entire childhood was laid bare– Shiva's restless brilliance, Chandu's pragmatism, Adrien's artistic soul, and Ishan's deep-seated compassion. And me, the quiet observer, now harboring a secret that dwarfed all of ours combined.

My phone vibrated. A message from Trishulin Sir.
Main Lab. Urgent.

The weight of my new reality returned in a crash. I looked at my friends, their faces ablaze with anticipation. How could I explain?

Chapter – 3

The Alien Among Us

“Adrien, guys, I… I really can’t,” I said, stopping myself halfway through.

“It’s work. Something came up.”

Shiva frowned. “Something came up five minutes after we met?”

Adrien didn’t smile. He studied my face instead.

“Nothing in science happens that fast,” he said quietly. “You’re not being called into surgery.”

“I know,” I said. “It’s not like that.”

Shiva chuckled, trying to keep it light. “Still the same, Bittu. Always disappearing when things get interesting.”

“I’ll try to catch up later,” I said, already stepping back. “It was good seeing you.”

The words sounded wrong the moment I said them. Too neat. Too distant.

If this were anyone else, they would have laughed it off. Maybe cursed me under their breath and gone back to their evening. That's what happens when years have passed and lives have moved on, when restraint is mistaken for maturity.

That was never the way we learned to be.

Even through long silences, even without calls or updates, something between us had held. Not loud. Not sentimental. Just present.

They had seen my face like this before. The kind of quiet that didn't belong to inconvenience or work, but to something giving way underneath.

So it didn't strike me as strange that they didn't let me walk away.

If anything, it would have been stranger if they had.

Adrien noticed.

"You don't say that to people you haven't seen in years," he said.

I didn't answer. I gave a quick, awkward wave and turned away, heading toward the corridor Trishulin Sir had indicated.

I was almost there when something felt off.

Footsteps.

Not close. Not hurried. Just… there.

I glanced back.

All of them were behind me.

Not following exactly. Just not leaving either.

Kai walked beside Ishan, half a step behind the rest, quiet as ever. Chandu lingered near the back, hands clasped, scanning the corridor with open curiosity. Adrien and Shiva walked together, exchanging a look I couldn't read.

"You're headed somewhere specific," Adrien said.

It wasn't a question.

I stopped.

"You should go back," I said quickly. "This isn't– "

"This is IISc," Shiva cut in, gently. "People don't rush off like that unless something's wrong."

I hesitated. Just long enough.

Adrien met my eyes.

"You don't have to explain," he said. "Just don't lie."

That surprised me more than it should have.

The doors slid open behind me.

From the inside, unprompted.

The sound cut cleanly through the corridor, sharper than it should have been. Our voices suddenly felt too loud, too exposed, for a space that clearly wasn't meant for hesitation.

Inside, people had already turned.

A cluster stood around a bank of monitors, their attention fixed not on the screens now, but on us. No confusion. No chatter. Just silence.

Two of them were in uniform. Military. Not security.

Adrien noticed immediately. So did Shiva. Chandu stiffened. Ishan's hand drifted instinctively toward Kai's shoulder, then stopped.

Before I could step back, before I could say anything, Trishulin Sir moved forward.

He didn't look annoyed.

If anything, he looked mildly amused.

"Ah," he said easily, as if this interruption had been expected. "You've brought company."

His eyes passed over all five of them, polite, curious, measuring without showing it.

"Please," he added, already gesturing inward. "Come in. You're just in time."

I opened my mouth to object.

He didn't look at me.

"It's better this way," he said calmly. "I was about to improvise anyway, especially with these two ." He gestured towards Adrien and Shiva.

Adrien hesitated, then stepped forward. Shiva followed. Chandu and Ishan exchanged a glance before moving in. Kai came last.

The doors slid shut behind us.

The lab was quiet. Sterile. Too controlled.

Monitors flickered with erratic patterns, sharp spikes, uneven traces. Trishulin turned back to the room, his tone warm, conversational.

"Gentlemen," he said, nodding once toward the uniforms, "consider this an unscheduled demonstration."

A faint smile crossed his face.

"Sometimes," he added, "the universe insists on an audience."

Before I could step forward and apologize, he spoke.

"Mr Chadha," he said, turning toward Adrien. His tone was polite, almost curious. "Earlier… those lights of yours. The glowing tubes."

Adrien shifted. "It's just a performance piece," he said. "Nothing scientific."

Trishulin smiled. "Of course," he said easily. "And I wouldn't dream of asking a magician to give away his secret."

Adrien blinked, caught off guard.

"I'm not asking for the secret," Trishulin continued, lowering his voice slightly. "Not today."

There was a pause. The faint hum of the lab filled it.

"I'm only asking if you'd be willing to show us what you already have," he said. "The way it behaves. Nothing more."

Adrien hesitated. His eyes flicked briefly to the monitors, then to the two men in uniform. He slipped a hand into the inner pocket of his jacket and drew out a small, compact device, no bigger than a torch.

"This stays controlled," he said carefully.

"Always," Trishulin replied without missing a beat. "I can explain more later. For now… "

He smiled faintly.

"Let's just say your motherland is calling."

Adrien exhaled. Slowly.

"All right," he said. "Just one."

From a side pouch of his backpack, he took out a single sealed glass tube, already familiar to him, already warm from being carried around. He rolled it gently between his fingers, as if reassuring himself it was intact.

"They're tiny," he said, almost absently. "Living things that glow under certain light. Harmless. Self-contained."

He glanced at the tube again, then continued.

"This wasn't something I planned. About six months ago, I had a setup like this at home. Just a glass tube near a window. Nothing special."

He lifted the tube slightly, angling it toward the light in the room.

"One afternoon, I noticed something inside. Not one insect, but a few. Almost invisible. They kept drifting toward the side where the sunlight hit the glass."

He shook his head faintly.

"I tried to get them out. Couldn't figure out how they'd even gotten in. The tube was sealed."

He paused, as if replaying it.

"When I came back later that evening, they were gone. I thought that was the end of it."

He adjusted the grip on the device in his other hand.

"But when I switched on my sunlight-spectrum lamp," he said, quieter now, "the tube lit up. And I could see them again. More than before. Moving inside, like they'd been there all along."

He glanced up, half-smiling, half-uneasy.

"For every show, I carry a few with me. Under the light, they multiply. That's all there is to it."

Adrien thumbed the switch.

The torch– like generator came alive, and the tube in his hand began to glow with its soft, ethereal light.

Then something went wrong.

The sealed tube in Adrien's hand shimmered, just for a second. The glow inside flickered unevenly. Adrien tightened his grip instinctively, and that was when the seal gave way with a faint crack.

A pinpoint of light slipped free.

It was tiny, almost nothing, like an insect made of glow. It shot through the air, too fast to track, straight toward Kai.

No one had time to react.

The light touched Kai's arm and vanished.

Just like that.

Adrien stared at the tube. Then at his hand.

"That's… impossible," he said, his voice unsteady. "They're sealed. They've never done that before."

Kai swayed.

"I… I don't feel well," he whispered, clutching his arm where the light had disappeared. He looked at Ishan, his eyes wide, searching, afraid.

The monitors stayed quiet. No alarms. No spikes. Nothing to suggest anything unusual had happened at all. Trishulin Sir and everyone now knew, those insects weren't responsible for the energy signals. That made it worse.

"What was that thing?" one of the scientists demanded, turning on Adrien.

Adrien shook his head slowly. "I don't know," he said. And for the first time, it sounded like the truth scared him.

Kai's breathing grew shallow. A cold sheen of sweat appeared on his forehead.

Ishan was at his side instantly, his hands steady even as his face betrayed him. "Kai, look at me. Stay with me."

Kai's legs buckled.

Ishan barely caught him before he hit the floor.

Everything after that happened too fast.

"Hospital. Now," Ishan said, his voice sharp enough to cut through the room.

Trishulin was already speaking into his secure comms, his tone calm, controlled. Arrangements were made quickly, quietly. A stretcher appeared. No questions were asked.

The scientists watched in stunned silence as Kai was wheeled out.

The rest of us followed in a separate vehicle, no one speaking. The quiet between us felt heavier than anything we could have said.

The hospital was colder. Brighter. Not exactly a regular hospital; ordinary in plain sight but more like a multi-functional covert ops building, standing hidden on Bengaluru roads.

Kai lay unresponsive in a diagnostic suite filled with machines I didn't recognize. Ishan stood close, answering questions, watching monitors, waiting for something to make sense.

It didn't.

Tests came back inconclusive. His vitals refused to stabilize. His body temperature rose and fell without pattern.

"His cellular metabolism is abnormal," one of the senior physicians said, frowning at the screen. "It's as if his cells are fighting for energy, but something is blocking them."

Chandu stood near the glass, eyes darting between machines. "This is a mess," he muttered. "They're looking at everything separately."

Before anyone could stop him, he moved into the control room, already pulling a cable from his backpack.

"You've got three different systems," he said quickly, plugging in. "Blood chemistry, energy output, brain activity. Each one's talking to itself."

A stunned technician stared at him.

"I need them talking to each other," Chandu said. "Patch me into the server."

Trishulin Sir hesitated, then nodded once.

Desperate to find answers, another physician authorized an emergency MRI.

The images began to form on the screen Chandu had linked to his tablet.

The room went still.

Kai's body was mostly familiar. Mostly.

But not entirely.

His digestive tract was simpler. Shorter. His lungs larger than expected. And beneath his skin, faint, thread-like networks appeared, especially along his arms and face, delicate and unmistakable.

The senior physician lowered his voice.

"He's… not entirely human, is he, Dr. Mathur?"

Ishan didn't answer.

Kai stirred.

His eyes fluttered open, unfocused at first, then suddenly clear. He saw the faces through the glass, the screens, the quiet panic.

With a strength that came from nowhere, he tried to sit up, pulling against the restraints of the MRI table.

"Kai," Ishan said urgently, moving toward him.

The machines began to protest.

"No… stop…" he rasped, his voice barely there. "They… they must not know…"

His eyes fluttered. Then he went still.

The medical team moved quickly, voices low, hands steady. They managed to stabilize him, but Kai did not wake again.

Later, after he had been moved to a private, secure room, Kai regained consciousness.

Ishan went in alone.

We waited outside. No one spoke. Minutes stretched into an hour. Every now and then, a nurse passed, avoiding our eyes.

When the door finally opened, Ishan stepped out slowly.

His face had drained of color. Not fear exactly. Something deeper. Awe, maybe. Or shock that hadn't yet found words.

He gathered us into a small consultation room and closed the door behind us.

"His name is not Kai," he said quietly.

No one reacted.

"And he is not from Earth."

The words hung there, unreal.

What followed sounded less like a confession and more like a memory he was still trying to understand.

"He told me where he comes from," Ishan said. "A planet called Sone'Vora. It orbits a distant star."

He paused, pressing his fingers together.

"They are far older than us. Far ahead. Over generations, they learned to live differently. They learned to draw energy directly from their sun."

"He called it 'growth,'" Ishan continued, his voice tightening. "A way to transcend their biological limits. They bio-engineered their bodies, altering their digestive systems and there was no need for food; it became obsolete. They even dismantled their borders, creating a single, unified world, believing it was the pinnacle of evolution."

He swallowed.

"They were wrong."

"Sone'Vora… is dying," Ishan continued, recounting Kai's words. "For three years now."

A silence followed even in our breaths.

"A sickness spreads across their world. They grow weak. Their light fades. They die."

Their scientists found no cause. No cure.

"So he was sent here as a last resort," Ishan Said. Being the last of his kind to undergo the process of eliminating the need for food, Kai was sent here to learn from their 'past' civilization, to see if our world held a forgotten key, and if we still carried something they had lost.."

"He chose Earth carefully," Ishan went on. "And India deliberately."

Kai had learned our languages. Our customs. He wanted to live among people who still believed in balance, in coexistence, in living with nature instead of mastering it.

"That's how he found me," Ishan said quietly. "He was looking for those who studied life in equilibrium."

"My way of treating illnesses!"

He took a breath before continuing.

"The insect from Adrien's show," He said, "When it touched him, he felt the sickness return.

He looked at Adrien now, not accusing. Just afraid.

"It could be the source."

We sat in silence.

An alien. A dying world. A disease carried by something that glowed gently inside a glass tube.

It was too much. Too unlikely. Too vast.

And yet, nothing about Ishan's voice sounded imagined.

If Kai was telling the truth, then the fate of two worlds might depend on understanding something so small we had nearly missed it.

A tiny, glowing insect.

The thought settled uneasily.

But one question refused to leave my mind.

How had Adrien ever come into possession of them?

We sat in the sterile quiet of the hospital's consultation room, the weight of Ishan's words lingering between us.

He is not from Earth.

An alien.

A dying planet.

A plague.

The ideas felt too large, too distant, almost unreal against the ordinary hum of the hospital around us.

Ishan watched our faces, then drew a slow breath and went on. Not because he wanted to, but because stopping seemed worse.

"His planet," he said, choosing his words carefully, "Sone'Vora… it isn't just a place."

He looked down for a moment.

"It's a living organism in itself."

He explained that the Sonvorans believed their world and its people were part of the same living system, driven by a single need. Growth.

"Not growth as an idea," Ishan clarified. "A physical requirement. Like breathing."

Their body cells became coded to expand, to adapt, to keep becoming more. To stop was dangerous. "They call it The

Stillness," he said quietly. "When growth slows, the body begins to fail. It's a slow decay. Always fatal."

Ishan rubbed his hands together, as if grounding himself.

"They don't age the way we do. No wrinkles. No visible decline."

He hesitated.

"Kai described fine, glowing lines across their skin. Bioluminescent patterns. He called them linae vitae, life lines."

As a Sonvoran learned, created, or changed, those lines grew more complex. More intricate.

"That's how they measure worth," Ishan said. "Not by wealth. By what they call virescence. The richness of those patterns."

Their entire civilization was built around it.

Nothing was ever finished. Cities were designed to be added to endlessly. Art was meant to evolve. A symphony was never complete, only passed forward for others to continue.

"To finish something," Ishan said, "was considered a kind of death."

For a long time, he told us, even with the threat of The Stillness, their world held together.

Then their leaders intervened.

"They decided growth could be perfected," Ishan said, his voice tightening. "They initiated a planet-wide program. Genetic refinement. A process that would allow them to live on sunlight, water, and air alone."

A pause followed.

"In trying to free themselves," he said, "they changed something fundamental."

The very process that promised endless efficiency made them vulnerable to an unknown sickness. Something their science could not identify. Something that turned their source of life into a slow poison.

Ishan looked up at us.

"Kai believes the organism carried by that insect may be connected."

The room went quiet again.

"Kai was the last to undergo the process twelve years ago," Ishan added. "And three years later, the plague began."

The timeline settled heavily between us.

"When he came to Earth," he said, his voice softening, "he first landed on a small island off the coast of Puducherry."

He paused, as if picturing it.

"He felt better almost immediately. He told me he would sit outside restaurants and watch people eat. Just watch. He wanted to remember what hunger felt like. Taste. Mess. The ordinary discomforts of being alive."

Ishan looked down.

"He missed the simple biological experiences his people had engineered away."

From there, Kai travelled quietly. Always observing. He already knew our languages and customs before he arrived. Eventually, he reached Bengaluru.

"In a city park," Ishan said, "he saw me leading a group through breathing exercises."

A faint smile crossed his face.

"He noticed how people listened. How they trusted me. He followed me to the clinic and booked an appointment."

Kai had told him a story. The orphaned son of an Indian mother and a Japanese father. A young man with strange symptoms no one could explain.

"I believed him," Ishan said simply. "And when the tests failed and nothing made sense, I didn't send him away."

He hesitated, something tightening behind his eyes.

"Now I wonder if those tests were ever real."

We looked at him.

"He would never have gone to a proper lab," Ishan continued. "Someone would have noticed. Asked questions."

A quiet exhale.

"I think he brought reports that were convincing enough. Or altered just enough to keep me looking elsewhere."

There was no anger in his voice. Only clarity, arriving late.

"He needed to stay close," Ishan said. "And I let him."

A friendship formed. Slowly. Naturally.

As he spoke, a strange sense of recognition crept over me. Something aligning itself without warning.

I looked at Adrien. He had been sitting very still, his face pale.

"Puducherry," he said suddenly. His voice sounded far away. "Three years ago."

We all turned.

"I was there," he continued. "At an artist's residency."

His eyes unfocused, caught in memory.

"The gallery had these hollow glass tube installations. Beautiful things. One afternoon, I noticed something inside one of them. Just a flicker. A speck of light."

He swallowed.

"It kept drifting toward the sunlight coming through the window."

Adrien told us how he had closed the windows. The light disappeared. Later that night, he returned and switched on a spectrum lamp that was part of the installation.

"The speck came alive again," he said. "Moving inside the tube. Like it was following the light."

"I was mesmerised," he admitted. "I managed to isolate it. Trapped it in a smaller tube."

Over the next three years, he experimented. Carefully. Quietly.

"I learned which frequencies made it multiply," he said. "How to guide its movement."

He looked up at us then.

"That's my show. The Sunlight Weavers."

His voice dropped.

"They're not just a trick. They're Kai's plague."

No one spoke.

The silence was complete.

In that moment, everything aligned. My secret mission. Shiva's research. Adrien's art. Ishan's patient who had become a friend. We just didn't know it yet.

None of it had been accidental. Our reunion was not a coincidence. It was a convergence.

Each of us, in our own way, had been walking toward the same point. Now we were standing inside it.

And somehow, impossibly, the fate of two worlds rested in our hands.

Trishulin Sir had been listening quietly until then.

He looked at each of us in turn, not studying, not judging, just taking us in.

"Stories like this," he said at last, "don't gather people randomly."

He gestured lightly, as if the room itself were part of the thought.

"You. Your paths. Your work. The timing."

He shook his head once.

"I've learned to pay attention when the universe insists on being heard."

A faint, almost tired smile crossed his face.

"And today, it's speaking very clearly."

He straightened.

"It's telling me that all of you are connected to this in ways we don't yet understand."

The words settled heavily.

"So be prepared," he said. "You're all in."

A pause.

"And it's going to be a long night."

With that, he turned and stepped away, already speaking into his secure line.

Another operative took his place and began explaining what they knew. Or what they thought they knew. Names, locations, fragments of intent. Too much information arriving too fast, with no clear edges.

None of us spoke.

We just sat there, absorbing it.

The weight of it.

The absurdity of it.

Only hours ago, we had been living ordinary lives. Arguing, creating, researching, drifting.

Now we stared at one another, sharing the same unspoken thought.

What exactly had we fallen into?

Chapter – 4

The Great Indian Trains

The quiet of the hospital consultation room pressed in on me. Too clean. Too still.

An alien plague. A glowing insect. A dying world.

My mind struggled to hold it all at once.

The others had already started speaking in low, urgent voices.

Plans for Kai. What could be done, what couldn't.

I barely heard any of it.

Trishulin Sir moved through the room, speaking to each of them in turn. Briefly. Calmly. As if taking stock.

I stayed where I was, still trying to catch my breath. Then, when I wasn't paying attention, he touched my arm and drew me aside. His expression had changed. The warmth was gone. What remained was focus.

"TJ, I need you to move," he said quietly. "Now."

Something in his voice cut through the fog.

"We've just had confirmation," he continued. "There's chatter around tonight's Nagercoil Express. It leaves Bengaluru Junction in less than an hour. Heading south, toward the tip of the country." He spoke calmly, but the words came fast.

"Coach S10, S11, and B1. You'll be booked across them. We've secured S9 and B2 as buffers, front and back. Move freely. Blend in."

A brief pause.

"Some interested parties are expected to board at Salem."

Before I could respond, Chandu appeared at the doorway, breathless, already halfway into work mode.

"Sir," he said, "your instincts were right." Trishulin didn't turn.

"Bookings at Nagercoil," Chandu went on, "carry the same digital residue as the shell firms that funded the Bengaluru accounts. ATM withdrawals too. Same pattern. Machines near the IISc campus."

The room seemed to tilt slightly.

When Chandu stepped away to relay more details, my thoughts finally caught up with my pulse. "What kind of chatter," I asked, keeping my voice low, "are we talking about on the Nagercoil train?"

"Nothing specific. Just… interest. Too much interest from the wrong people. This is usually a task for Shukla, simple observation, but he's back in Lucknow. I need a set of eyes on that train, someone who can blend in with no known background in the intelligence unit, and someone with a curious mind who knows what to look for when something comes up. This is your first official assignment, TJ. Board that train, and become a ghost. Just watch, listen, and report."

He stopped to take a breath and continued.

"We need to figure out this serendipitous encounter with our new friend, Kai, which I really don't know how to digest and report about, and to whom. It's going to be a circus, trust me."

"We have to understand what happened in that lab and if not those insects then what caused those energy signals at an educational institute like this. We'll join you directly in Salem."

My first assignment. The words landed with a strange blend of dread and thrill. There was no time to process, no time for doubt. A car was already waiting. Tickets and some money were handed so smoothly as if nothing new had happened. As I left my friends to grapple with a cosmic mystery, I was dispatched into a terrestrial one, a solitary operative hurtling into the unknown.

5:10 PM. Within an hour, I was on the Nagercoil Express, Coach S10, the train carrying the same Indianness as Nauchandi Express. I had found my seat, a side lower berth, and melted into the anonymity of the carriage. The train was a world unto itself, a river of humanity flowing through the evening of Tamil Nadu. Families settling in for the night, vendors hawking their wares, the low murmur of a dozen different conversations. It was all so normal, so mundane, yet my senses were on high alert. Every passenger was a potential threat, every piece of luggage a possible secret. I casually walked to all three compartments, the same side lower berth in all. Nothing worth paying attention to. After roaming around, I settled inside S11 even when I had access to B1, probably due to the old sleeper-class habit.

And within a full sweep of the clock's hands after learning about my first assignment, my new life as an operative had begun. As I settled into my side lower berth on the Nagercoil Express, the clatter of the wheels became a hauntingly familiar drumbeat.

A group of men in the next cabin were loudly debating politics, their voices rising with confident cynicism. I could only understand it through the little bit of English two of them used every now and then. The sound was so familiar that it acted as a key unlocking memories from just the day before.

Until the team could join me, my orders were to do nothing but observe. But with hours to kill, the quiet and the steady motion of the train began to work its insidious magic. Staring out at the fleeting landscape, my mind, unmoored from the immediate crisis, began to drift. The haunting symmetry of my situation, alone on another train within 24 hours, was too powerful to resist. The past day had been a whirlwind, but it was my journey from yesterday that had started it all, the one that ended just this morning with this call from Trishulin Sir, that came rushing back to me, not as a single memory, but as a living, breathing presence. I wondered how all these events from today would have been different if I had missed my Bulandshahr– Lucknow train yesterday...

BULANDSHAHR → HAPUR → LUCKNOW
(DAY 1, NAUCHANDI EXPRESS)

It felt cold, the bench, cold as a politician's promise, even though the sun was still out there showering its proud and flashy rays all around on the Bulandshahr railway platform.

Maybe that's the beauty of these December rays. Or maybe it was those winds to be blamed, those painstaking, non-visible, cruel, winter witches, stealing away all the due credit for my lovely and striking sun-rays. Well, winters in North India are a deceptive beast; the days could fool you with their warmth, but the nights and the shadows bite with a vengeance.

I deserved all the warmth of my darling rays until this fatso, this roly-poly, muffin-top lady asked me to shift my bum to make some 'space' for her towards the part of the bench that came under the shadow of a non-fruiting mango tree.

"Arre beta, are you boarding this train too?" she asked, her voice booming over the cacophony of honking rickshaws and shouting vendors. She didn't wait for an answer before she elbowed me to clear even more room on her side.

This bench, one of those utilitarian monstrosities made of perforated metal, was designed to accommodate a maximum of three people, or perhaps two generously proportioned ones. She alone herself clocked in at a solid one point seven five, maybe two. And though she arrived alone, a woman being a woman, invited reinforcements: two more aunties, each armed with opinions as sharp as their tongues, to discuss what they called, 'life.' It mostly involved complaints about their husbands, daughters-in-law, and the rising prices of tomatoes and onions.

Inch by agonizing inch, I was forced to cede territory. My buttocks performed a slow-motion dance of retreat towards the edge of the bench. My bottom stubbornly rested on the air. Finally, my center of gravity gave up the ghost and almost relocated to the hard-packed earth beneath. I felt robbed, plundered, violated even. I wanted to curse them, hurl them all onto the tracks, but some useless morality showed up to say "hi" at the same time. Instead, I relocated to the base of the mango tree, shuffling my gaze between the coven of aunties and the random chaos of the railway platform.

My eye snagged on my left shoe, where two defiant rays of sunlight pierced through the skeletal branches above. I looked up, imagining this place during monsoon, when the tree would groan under the weight of ripe mangoes, and this very lady would nudge children out of the way to claim her share, all for a bit of mango achaar she'd make from her grandmother's recipe. She definitely was one of those achaar-loving ladies.

"Here" she said suddenly, producing a small packet of homemade sweets from her bag and offering it to me with a smile that suggested she was used to being both generous and demanding. "Take one! It's good for your health."

"Thanks," I mumbled, accepting the sweet reluctantly while trying not to think about how many hands had touched it before reaching mine.

The slanted light rays shone resplendently on parts of the railway track for as far as I could see, turning the steel rails into molten gold. It dazzled. For a moment, I was transported. I was no longer on a dusty platform in UP, but by the ocean; the tracks mirroring the sun's rays like water.

I had lost track of the arrival and even the departure of my train; gone astray staring at the blazing railway tracks. It was her voice, cacophonous yet somehow kind, that snapped my reverie. "Arre beta, Sonny! Are you not coming?" She stood shouting at the door of her air-conditioned coach, opulent and gleaming, a stark contrast to my humble sleeper-class. Her name was Mrs Gupta, I later learned, on her way to Barabanki to visit her daughter, a doctor, and show off her new silk sari; her daughter, who apparently had no time to visit her.

The train had already begun to stir, protesting with a series of metallic groans. I hadn't even noticed. "F*!*" I responded, a heartfelt expression of gratitude and panic. With a burst of adrenaline, I sprinted, barely managing to grab the railing at the back of the compartment.

"You wanted warmth, here it is!" I imagined Mrs Gupta smirking. Our paths wouldn't cross again until Lucknow, if at all.

Half-exhausted and panting, daring to catch my breath, I clung to the side-bar, one foot on the floor, the other dangling precariously. The gateway of the sleeper compartment was a seething mass of humanity. "Excuse me, sir! Thoda sa... just a bit..." I squeezed through, ignoring the glares and muttered curses.

You usually encounter such scenarios in General compartments, where people are forced to fill up the space like herds of sheep. And although my sleeper compartment and the adjacent AC coaches were 'reservation-only', till Hapur Junction, the train looked like a Khurja-Hapur General Passenger one. It was an informal truth everyone was aware of. So most of the people there were free-loaders, i.e., ticketless travellers.

The interior was a revelation: a cave teeming with life. The God, it seemed, had sent a curated selection of his creations; from wide-eyed children to wizened ancients, all crammed into this metal tube hurtling towards Lucknow. There were animals too, some born that way, others working hard to achieve it.

God fashioned such a beautiful species– Homo sapiens– but there, why was everybody trying to shift to the Animalia kingdom or Canis genus?

A high-pitched voice, shrill as a rusty hinge, sliced through the chaos. It belonged to a girl named Sheetal (yes, I eavesdropped shamelessly), who was holding court with two friends. Her boyfriend, Rahul, was apparently a canine. "A BAD BAD DOG!" she declared, her voice laced with such venom that I feared Rahul might spontaneously combust wherever he was.

Sheetal, I later learned, was a law student in Bulandshahr, dreaming of becoming a judge. But her current preoccupation was the treachery of one Rahul Verma, her now ex-boyfriend.

"He promised me a trip to Nainital, and then he took that Sonia! That Sonia from his office!" Sheetal wailed while her friends clucked sympathetically.

"Men are dogs, yaar. All of them.", one of her friends, a girl with eyes to kill, announced with the gravity of someone revealing the secrets of the universe. This was Priya, a medical student with a cynical streak and a sharp tongue. The third girl, Neha, was quieter and more observant– a budding journalist who scribbled furiously in a notebook.

Rahul's transgression, it seemed, was not just infidelity but also a lack of wisdom in meeting this girl in the first place. Mathematically inclined as I was, I couldn't help but wonder how Rahul would approach his new epithet.

As I moved deeper into the compartment, the cacophony grew. Vendors hawked their wares ("Chai garam! Garam chai!"), children shrieked, and the air hung thick with the smell of sweat, spices, and unwashed bodies. Reaching my seat, somewhere in the middle of this mobile anthill, was going to be a Herculean task.

They say reaching Kailash-Mansarovar is no piece of cake; with snow, hail, rain and mountain-monsters troubling every other pilgrim! But reaching your seat is quite a Herculean task in the Indian trains, especially when the train is passing through a remote stretch in West UP city, Bulandshahr-bound, where no one gives a duck to your reservation. You must cross borders, sometimes mountains of luggage, and if you're super lucky, you might need to pass through the ego of your fellow travellers, which, by the way, is the most difficult part. You encroach; that is how you could feel, through the aisle of a sleeper class compartment.

They consider themselves rightful heirs and rulers of their own; owned-seats, never caring or being compassionate about how much they are troubling others by encroaching on someone else's share of space.

As if the luggage is not sufficient for some people, they bring their honoured presence down to the floor in the form of sitting; and some would simply lie down on the floor, with no hesitation or care for a thing in the world. Lying there is their fundamental right; no one can deny or snatch it from them, and to get in the way of these soulful people is nothing short of a sin.

There, I could also see other simultaneous events taking place. Two kids were crying, yelling, and screaming, almost shouting for a cheap, sugar-coated candy: Chooran Goli, which a vendor of approximately their age was selling. On the next seat, a pair of young love birds were twittering, touching, giggling, and what not, inconsiderate of the presence of a single person around. The girl had covered her face with the dupatta. The guy seemed to be from one of those well-to-do houses of the town that cannot afford to lose their honor in the face of this patriarchal society.

There was also an old man sitting beside, staring at the girl with eyes of disgust, as if he himself was her father. His name was some Sharmaji, as the TT would announce later. Perhaps he was just jealous because he could never enjoy his younger days like that couple, and go on a trip with his girlfriend when he had time. But did the term girlfriend even exist in those times?

The next cabin was full of local milkmen; I could see their traditional cylindrical milk cans in every nook and corner and some hanging by the windows outside of the train. They would bring milk all the way from their villages to the city, and then travel back home, hundreds of kilometers every single day, to and fro, just to find a market for their product. These milkmen would leave early in the morning and return late at night, making this their daily routine to earn a proper living for themselves. I felt a deep respect for those people, for their hard work and dedication toward their family. They made me forget about my struggle to reach my seat, though only ephemerally.

So, it's true; motivation is really real, but see, then life happens.

The next cabin was the most remarkable one in this journey so far. Four men were there, describing the condition of our country, India, with great enthusiasm. It was a scene from a cheap Bollywood movie, only this time, with better content. They were enjoying the taste of crisp peanuts while throwing the peels on the floor and pitying how the basic facilities and hygiene were surprisingly absent from the Indian Railways, compared to the European system, as one of them recalled his recent journey from Paris to Budapest a few days back from his honeymoon. He seemed to be the only one married amongst them. The other three lacked that mannerism garb, commonly found on the shoulders of the wedded one, especially the newbies. Okay, I lacked that garb too!

“The problem just doesn’t stop at the lack of hygiene or unemployment. It’s everything: the population, the corruption, the government! The condition is deteriorating more each passing day, I tell you”, one said, adjusting his underwear. He was full of opinions and unshakable in his conviction, like a once fiery activist during his teen years, now acting like a disillusioned cynic.

“Yes, the economy is in tatters, the Japanese fever is taking lives, the poor are famished… if the same situation prevails, the day is not too far when this country will disintegrate into several smaller countries for better administration of its territories,” the other seconded the first one, welcoming a mild burp as the peels of the peanuts touched the floor.

“Well, I do feel,” pausing and humming with the sound of munching, the third one continued, “after fifty years or so, every city in itself will become a country in their own way.” Now, this was a biggy for me too, as I tried to pull my thoughts to understand how they reached from cleanliness in the trains to the disintegration of India. This guy looked like those artists who play guitar in the metro hoping NOT that someone gives them money, but rather a girl just smiles their way into his eyes.

My heart poured with love for all of them. Even Mahatma Gandhi and Sardar Vallabh Bhai Patel would have saluted them.

As I followed the directions towards my seat, a drunk man appeared from nowhere and fell on another man who was resting on the floor. I could tell from his clothes and unkempt beard that he’d seen better days. He was clutching a half-empty bottle of country liquor.

"Arre bhai!" the man on the floor shouted, pushing the drunk away. He was thin, wiry, with calloused hands, likely a farmer from a nearby village.

"Sorry, bhai!" the drunk mumbled, the rest of his words slurred.

The drunk opened his eyes and took a look all around. To my amazement, he passed a smile and closed his eyes soon after. Resting quietly, he provided everyone with a theme to re-focus their thoughts.

The ones lying on the floor abused the drunk, while the seated-ones cursed them both. Maybe he would be abused until people were given another reason to talk about. The fantastic four resumed the debate on whether it was the alcohol that had ruined the country. If they had said it a day before, I would have believed them; however, despite being a teetotaler, I hesitated to believe whether it was the alcohol impeding the growth of our beloved country, India. Maybe it was something more. I had no clue of that 'something more' though; I'm no economist.

I peeked at the expression of every person sitting there. Pity was all I could see on their faces for how they needed something from the outer world to keep them full, except for my dear, drunken man. He just rested there, devoted loyally to his alcohol, wearing a diluted smile on his face and eyes shut, completely unaware of the jinx that people were showering upon him.

On turning back, I noticed those two children crying for the Chooran Goli were, in fact, still crying. I witnessed the mother offering slaps to their cute little cheeks. An old woman, perhaps Sharmaji's wife and quite younger than him, groaned seeing the way she treated her children, and the children kept turning towards the chooran goli vendor while screaming at the top of their lungs. They could be held responsible for driving the attention shift from that wise drunk man towards themselves from our cave community.

This dramatic episode lasted for about twenty minutes, and my ass still coveted my right, my reserved seat. In those action-packed twenty minutes, I witnessed almost every single emotion listed in Book II of Aristotle's "Rhetoric."

Perhaps this emotional resilience is a trait of the Indian middle class, a knack for not dwelling on one emotion for long. Maybe that's why boredom is rare, or why disputes are fleeting, maybe we just create new ones to keep life interesting. Or maybe…that's just life!

Overcoming pan-Indian diversities, I finally managed to make a touchdown. Seat number thirty-nine it was, the side lower berth. It was beyond the periphery of existing words to express how it felt like an achievement in that very moment.

But the next moment was similar to what we see in the movies: a beautiful piece of music to set the mood and then, a discordant sound to announce the arrival of an opposite emotion. Often, it's for the audience's laughter. Now it was my turn.

It was the side-lower, adjacent to the cabin of those fantastic four. Their faces brought an unrest, a prophecy of endless chatter filled with shit, while I craved silence. Disappointed, I aimlessly peeped out of the window.

The start of my journey was thus 'awesome', overflowing with a cacophony of voices and cramped spaces, and the unshakable prophecy that these 'fantastic four' would talk nonsense all night long. I managed a place for my luggage, my bum, and an ego that had accepted its fate. What else could I do?

Chapter – 5

Between Stations

As the Nagercoil Express rattled on, my memory, now a current of its own, pulled me deeper. The faces of the strangers on the Nagercoil Express blurred, replaced by the chaotic, vivid theatre of the Nauchandi Express just the day before...

BULANDSHAHR→ HAPUR → LUCKNOW
(DAY 1, NAUCHANDI EXPRESS)

As the train finally lurched into motion, I couldn't help but think of Mrs. Gupta's booming voice urging me to board on time. If only she were here now to silence these fantastic four.

Barely a minute had passed, and they were off, spouting opinions like a broken water tap, fuelled by their Pan Masala and boundless self-confidence. Craving silence, I tossed and turned, battling the urge to unleash my inner Hulk and smash their peanut-shell-strewn corner into oblivion. But no, I was a civilized man. A mostly civilized man. Instead, I burrowed deeper into my side-lower berth, pulling earphones into my ears like a shield against the cacophony. The universe, it seemed, was a comedian with a penchant for bad jokes. Could there be a better time for my earphones to be on a dead battery?

Just as I was contemplating whether those earphones were a legitimate form of self-defense, one of the fantastic four pulled out his phone. Oh great, I thought, "here comes the onslaught of WhatsApp forwards and conspiracy theories!"

He brandished the device like a newfound treasure. "Arrey bhai! You HAVE to see this," he announced, his voice buzzing with manic energy.

He blasted the phone volume, unleashing the shriek of a sensationalist news channel. The anchor seemed to audition as a supervillain, and the 'news' paraded as reality TV for conspiracy lovers.

"Doston!" the anchor bellowed in a nasal Bihari accent. "You've heard of the man-dog, the killer pigeon, the bloody witch … but brace yourselves! We now present… The Indian Blue Monkey!"

I rolled my eyes so hard I thought they might get stuck. "Seriously? Blue Monkey? Is this what passes for news these days?"

The video displayed shaky footage of what appeared to be a monkey, but its fur was dyed an unnatural shade of electric blue. Patches of gold shimmered in the sunlight, like a poorly executed Bollywood special effect.

The reporter shoved a microphone in the faces of bewildered villagers.

"He was blue, completely blue, like Bhagwan Krishna!" one old woman exclaimed, her eyes wide with reverence. "And it shone like sona (gold) in the sun! I greeted him, and he returned my greetings! I talked to God, and he talked back, in my own voice!"

Another villager chimed in, "He touched my bald head, and look! Now I have hair!"

A third man declared, "He touched my barren field, and now my crops are overflowing with tomatoes!"

"Yeah, right.", I thought, stifling a yawn. "And I'm dating Julia Roberts." So, this is where we are now? Worshipping blue monkeys and getting our lands fertile from celestial primates?

I wanted to laugh, but the sheer absurdity of it all was more irritating than amusing. It was like watching a train wreck in slow motion, knowing you couldn't look away.

The fantastic four were captivated. One declared, "This is proof! India is a land of miracles!"

The link to the video spread like an outbreak in the cabin. I could hear devices playing the same video and getting all those creatures temporarily involved.

As the video continued, a self-proclaimed guru seated across the next cabin suddenly perked up, "Aha! The Neel Bandar! It is a sign! The gods have sent him to cleanse our nation of corruption! He has come to guide us towards enlightenment!"

A vendor, smelling rupees, suddenly materialized. "The Blue Monkey charms! Get yours now! Protect against bad luck, cure baldness, and guarantee a seat on a Rajdhani Express! Only fifty rupees!" He hawked cheap plastic monkeys, painted a shade of blue that would make Yves Klein blush.

A child tugged at his mother's sari. "Amma, will we see the Blue Monkey? Will we? Will we?"

His mother, a harried-looking woman with tired eyes, sighed. "Chup kar! Be quiet! There's no such thing as a blue monkey. Yeh sab bakwas hai (It's all nonsense)."

The compartment transformed into a circus. Sometimes I wonder if there's a secret agency dedicated to spreading nonsense like this 'Blue Monkey' story, keeping us distracted from real issues with tales of celestial primates. Arguments erupted between believers and skeptics. Someone started playing a blaring bhajan about Hanuman, convinced that God was somehow involved. With the volume in the compartment steadily rising, I felt a headache brewing behind my eyes.

"Okay, I've had it. If I hear one more word about this mythical blue primate, I'm going to snatch peanuts from the fantastic four's bag and start flinging them at everyone.", I declared to myself.

Desperate to escape the madness, I grabbed my ass and wormed my way down the aisle. Of course, there was no escape. A card game was in progress, accompanied by the usual shouting and accusations of cheating, the usual commentary on politics, cricket, and the sorry state of our beloved nation. A baby wailed like a banshee, its mother singing a lullaby that sounded suspiciously like a dying cat. And a man snored with the force of a thousand monsoon clouds colliding.

"Fine, universe." I thought, sinking into a nearby seat. "You win. I surrender. I'm officially embracing the madness, along with those fantastic four as my new neighbors.. Bring on the blue monkeys and the tomato-blessing primates. Maybe they're the only ones who can make sense of this country anymore."

Welcome to India, I thought wearily, where logic is optional, miracles are commonplace, and blue monkeys might just be the sanest thing you encounter all day.

The train rattled on, a small slice of India hurtling through the Uttar Pradesh winter evening. Outside, the landscape blurred; inside, the human drama unfolded. Blue monkeys, political chattering, crying children– it was all part of the same tapestry. I closed my eyes, finally surrendering to the rhythm of the rails. I knew this was just the beginning. The blue monkey might fade, the fantastic four might tire, but something new would inevitably take its place. Because on the Great Indian Train, there's always a new story waiting around the corner, a new character to meet, and a new absurdity to embrace.

Lucknow, here I come... and God help us all!

The train sped on, a dark blur against the Tamil Nadu landscape. I remained on my side-lower berth, a solitary ghost suspended between two journeys. The present was a low hum of potential danger, the faces of my fellow passengers on the Nagercoil Express a sea of unknowns. But the past was a vivid theatre, replaying itself with relentless clarity. The absurdity of the Blue Monkey, the cacophony of the Nauchandi Express– it all felt more real in this moment than the cold steel of the window I was leaning against. Hapur Junction loomed, welcoming a brief respite from the cacophony and chaos that had defined the journey thus far. As the train screeched announcing a halt, I felt a primal urge to escape– to breathe fresh air, stretch cramped limbs, and perhaps find a moment of lucidity amidst the madness. Little did I suspect that the railway platform held even more surprises in store.

Hapur was the last local station on the remote stretch. My sleeper compartment and Mrs. Gupta's AC coach would be cut off here, from this passenger coach, and will be reattached to this special train, Nauchandi Express. It also meant that the journey for all those creatures, the unauthorized ticketless travellers, ended there. May they never see the light of tomorrow!

Suddenly, long queues started forming outside the toilets as the train started to slow down. Some strange power induced the ammonia mixed liquid inside their body, urine we call it, to put pressure on their bladders and they all 'had to go' before the train completely stopped.

Finally, the train came to a halt. The winter air was crisp as I stepped out and made my way to the crossover bridge, hoping to find a cold drink that wasn't just water with a fancy label.

Beneath the staircase, a group of children played, their laughter bright against the backdrop of rust-streaked clothes and dusty concrete. Their joy felt out of place, yet oddly comforting.

Descending on the other side, I nearly missed it– a splash of color on the left-side wall. A breathtaking graffiti mural stared back at me, arresting my steps. My eyebrows lifted involuntarily. It wasn't just art; it was alive, though something about it felt… unfinished.

"What's missing here?" I murmured to no one in particular.

Maybe science guys don't have a thing for art, my heart whispered mockingly. I liked calling myself a 'science guy'– it gave me a sort of quiet pride, especially when I was alone in my thoughts.

I was on the verge of accepting defeat, resigning to never solving this peculiar puzzle. Disappointment curled in my chest as I prepared to move on. My brain sent the command; my muscles obeyed. My right foot lifted, ready to carry me away– but fate wasn't done with me yet.

From behind, a sudden burst of maroon sprayed across the wall, the scent of paint– sharp and electric. The final strokes filled the empty patches. And in that instant, the image revealed itself: a map of India, complete, with PoK still on our side.

A grin tugged at my lips, pride swelling in my chest. I had cracked the code, deciphered the art's unspoken message. The mural wasn't incomplete– it was waiting for that last, defiant flourish.

And maybe, just maybe, science guys can appreciate art after all.

I heard the word 'Saary' (sorry) from a gentleman as he brushed against my left shoulder. 'Vary saary again,' he added, his voice muffled by the paan he was still working through. He spat the leftover juice near the platform's edge, unintentionally shaping Sri Lanka in red. 'I couldn't control it, very sorry, again,' he repeated, spitting the last bit onto the railway tracks.

'It's okay,' I replied, calmer than even I expected. After all, how could he know he'd unintentionally helped me complete my great art-mystery?

'One pistachio-flavoured milk, please,' I said to the shopkeeper. Two younger guys beside me turned to stare, their expressions twisted in disgust, as though I had ordered something shameful. They proudly flaunted soda bottles in one hand, unlit cigarettes in the other– symbols of their rebellion, I supposed.

I didn't care. I wasn't one for over-hyped soft drinks. Not for any health reason, mind you– I just didn't like them. I couldn't even remember the last time I willingly bought one. Honestly, I'd probably had more beers than sodas in my life, and yeah, that felt like something to be proud of.

'Kids,' I conveyed through a deliberate, exaggerated blink, raising my glass bottle of cool, sweet pistachio milk like a trophy. The cold weather made it taste even better. Savoring the sweet, nutty flavor, I was reminded of the milk my mother used to prepare, especially during the winter. Well, after you lose a parent, maybe this is how you want to remember them, liking flavoured-milk over sodas. And before a feeling of self-pity and disgust could pinch in, I moved on, throwing the bottle in the dustbin, still half-filled.

On my way back, I passed the 'graf-spit-ti' again. A couple of chewable tobacco pouches had joined the scene, scattered near the wall art, their wrappers displaying grotesque images of cancer-ridden mouths. God bless these humble, down-to-earth artistic souls.

Back on the bridge, midway again, I watched the sun kiss the horizon. Since mine was a special train from a remote area, I had the luxury of wasting time– nearly an hour until departure.

From my vantage point, the rails stretched endlessly, meeting at a vanishing point. It reminded me of a painting my elder cousin once had in her room. As a child, I would ask her where those rails led. 'Very far,' she always replied. Back then, I thought 'Very Far' was an actual place– some distant, magical land waiting at the end of the tracks. That childhood innocence had vanished over time.

I took in a panoramic view of the platforms. To my right, the evolving graf-spit-ti carried on. More people had gathered, contributing to the mural in their own messy way. By now, the map of India was nothing but a giant red wall, a horrendously maroonish-red splotch, shouting at all the visitors that this is the shit we all live with, eating poison and pooping it out of our mouths.

To my left, something else caught my eye, a different kind of energy. People moved with some restless urgency, swirling around someone. It took me a moment to realize they weren't just passing by– they were converging. Someone important, or at least desperately sought after, had arrived.

Pushing through the crowd, I finally reached the source of all the commotion: the TTE.

The first thing that caught my eye wasn't his face– it was his shoes. Ugly, blue-and-white sports shoes with stars stitched into the stripes. The exact kind my parents forced me to wear as a kid. And the exact kind I hated with every fiber of my childhood soul. Paired with loose black pants, the combination was so jarring it made me judgmental, instantly and apologetically.

Even before I saw his face I had a vivid picture in my head: a pale, bloated man with a long, dark-red vermillion mark on his forehead and a wad of betel leaf stuffed in his cheek. The type who'd lean on a roadside stall, ordering samosas with a smug, greasy grin.

My assumptions weren't far off. His stomach strained against his pants, held in place by suspenders– a style straight out of some medieval English portrait. His black overcoat shifted back and forth as he repeatedly scratched his left armpit with his right hand, the motion rhythmic and almost hypnotic. It wasn't just the outfit that felt out of place– he himself seemed like a relic from a different era, trapped in the wrong century.

So, at the heart of the growing circle stood the undeniable centerpiece– the great Indian TTE (Traveling Ticket Examiner). Neither a TC (Ticket Collector) nor a TT, as many affectionately call them. No, this was a full-fledged, uniformed, clipboard-clutching TTE. It struck me that this was the first time I'd seen one arrive before the train itself.

Back to reality– his obnoxious aura became unbearable, forcing my eyes to find a safer, more pleasant escape. That's when I spotted them: two puppies, curled up together, their little bodies pressed close for warmth. They seemed to be in the middle of an intense, high-stakes discussion in their squeaky puppy voices.

I must've stolen their attention, though– one of them snapped its head toward me, flashing a tiny warning snarl. The other followed.

They exchanged glances. One said, 'Bow, bow.'

'Boowww,' the other replied, as if confirming a strategy.

Then, in unison, they barked at me– a coordinated effort.

'Oh, so that's what this whole meeting was about,' my heart chuckled. 'Planning a two-puppy intimidation strike, huh?'

'Alright, little warriors,' I murmured, amused. 'You've awakened the beast within me now.'

I took a playful step forward, ready to reclaim my dignity from these pint-sized guards– and that's when their backup arrived. Another dog, a bigger one, burst onto the scene with a wagging tail, launching into a full-on, sloppy, unsophisticated licking assault on the two little ones, before they all started barking at me.

"Alright, I forgive you today," I telepathized to the barking trio in front of me, "but next time I hear a single word– mind you, one word– I'll slaughter your whole breed."

"Grrrrr, bow, bow…" The big one led the chorus, unfazed.

"I meant next time when I visit here again, not like... next-time-of-today," I corrected myself, my inner voice wavering.

"Waauf. Wauuf…" the third responded softly. I translated that as, "Okay. Get lost now."

Obediently, I retreated and found an old man sitting about twenty meters away on a half-broken bench. We Indians are masters of adjusting when it comes to sharing government-provided amenities.

From a distance, the dogs seemed different– cheerful, lovely, even beautiful. My irritation melted into fondness. Satisfied with my defeat, I let my gaze wander to the train that had stopped on platform one while I'd been busy negotiating peace with the dogs.

An anxious mother stood by, seeing off her daughter– a beautiful one, or so it seemed from my half-seated perch. The wheels rolled, the engine hissed, and a shadow of despair crept onto the mother's forehead. I felt it too, that pang of separation. I wanted her to stay, maybe even remembering someone of my own.

A man, perhaps the father, though younger-looking than the mother, emerged, handing a water bottle to the girl. She looked even more graceful as she unfolded and refolded her hands in thanks.

The train picked up speed, and tears spilled from the mother's eyes. The father turned away. Men don't cry– especially not in front of their daughters. The whistle blew harder this time, and so did the mother's sobs. The father quickly waved and returned to his stoic stance. Maybe it was the mother's knee pain or the father's pride, but neither ran alongside the train as I'd hoped.

Suddenly, the train halted again– perhaps for a signal. The parents' eyes lit up. Sharing a look and a few hurried words, they dashed towards their daughter for an unexpected bonus round of goodbyes. The father took the lead, gesturing urgently for the mother to hurry. She gathered her sari in one hand, her left knee struggling to keep pace, but her heart outpaced them both.

"C'mon, aunty ji," I whispered, rooting for them.

The daughter, oblivious to it all, was already glued to her phone. Boys like me on that train were probably devising their own strategies to woo her before nightfall.

The train started moving again, slow but relentless. The daughter's window slipped out of reach. The old couple slowed, their hope fading. They watched the train disappear, shrinking into the evening sky.

I felt something shift inside me. Was it longing for my mother, or the girl who reminded me of someone with whom I had shared a parcel of my life? I didn't know. The orphan inside me longed for its parents, a loving mother, and a father to take care of inconsequential and trivial things like a water bottle with an urge as if you were leaving for a desert. An unusual feeling for me these days, remembering my past!

My eyes drifted back to the dogs, now part of a larger pack playing on the tracks– the same tracks that would take me to Lucknow, a few hundred kilometers away. No one waited for me there, except an old room, a few books, a black backpack with a Superman logo, a faded lucky charm keychain, and my lab.

Chapter – 6

My Maternal Uncle

The Nagercoil Express pushed steadily south, its motion a constant, rocking cradle. The usual, average chatter in my coach formed a stark contrast to the storm of memories brewing in my own mind. My thoughts were still at Hapur Junction, walking the platform, a boy untethered, grappling with a world that felt both alien and achingly familiar. I was a ghost on this train, but I was a ghost haunted by another...

BULANDSHAHR→ HAPUR → LUCKNOW

(DAY 1, NAUCHANDI EXPRESS)

Still sitting beside the old man on that half-broken bench at Hapur Junction brought me life's biggest irony. Two men, generations apart, one with a world of notifications on his phone, the other with a world of memories in his eyes, found themselves searching for the very same thing in the distance: a sign of the train's arrival.

A long sigh escaped his lips, a sound that carried the weight of a harvest lost or a son settled too far from home. I recognised its echo in the silent sigh caught in my own throat, one that tasted of loss and hollowness. We were both experts in the great Indian art of jhelna– of enduring. We spoke of the Decembers which no longer were cold, the late train, and anything under the world but the real weight we carried. We were both playing the same game, known to everyone here, i.e., how to use a smile to hide a tired heart. His tiredness was from a life fully lived; mine was from a life being lived too fast. In the end, it was all just baggage, a shitty shit baggage, just a little heavier than the bags at our feet.

In less than fifteen long minutes, we ran out of all the words we could share with each other. How long could one walk the shallow talk anyway? Finally, honesty found its way. And we sat there in silence.

I casually walked towards the end of the platform. The sun had already set, but the sky clung to life in the far west, crimson patches battling the encroaching grey clouds. Incredulously, the day seemed to linger longer than usual. It was the kind of sky that people would rush to capture on their phones, eager to post it to their families and friends and lovers and haters with a profound caption about life and endings. Such losers!

Witnessing rather a slow, passionate dance between day and night, their intimate union left me envious. Their embrace would've shamed all those longing for their lovers. Happily jealous, I returned to sit beside the old man.

A distant memory surfaced: a book cover I once glimpsed through a Delhi bookshop window while visiting with my aunt. The cover depicted a boy under a tree, beneath a sky where moonlight met the fading sun's rays. One side of the cover was painted crimson red while the other was black and scattered with silver stars. Two moons hung in the scene: one among the stars, the other reflected in a lake far below. The boy's silhouette faced upward, probably gleaming with the same wonder now filling me– 'where did I belong?'.

The moon dimmed again, and exhaustion settled in my bones. I watched how clouds overtook the moon's youthful glow and the sun's dying light. I also witnessed how, moments later, the moonlight stabbed the belly of a cloud, after much struggle, splitting it in half while the wind was its accomplice in the crime.

Then I thought about my bond with the moon. It always absorbed my unspoken feelings, amplifying memories of better times, often sending flutters of joy through me. As I adjusted my bottoms on the bench beside the old man, the moon peeked through the flying clouds, resembling a chooran goli– reminding me of the little boy who never got one. The moon, unchanged for centuries, still appeared different each night. A moment later, it looked like a bowl.

My relationship with the moon– India's universal maternal uncle– went back to childhood, when it was just a geography lesson. My teacher explained its changing phases. After a brief rebellion against my conscience as a kid, I accepted it. A decade later, the moon was no longer my uncle or a celestial fact. It had become a part of me– a biological phenomenon, tangled with my heart and soul.

Last month, at my aunt's place in Delhi, I stood on the balcony past midnight, wrapped tight in winter clothes, coffee in hand. The full moon hung above, glowing coldly. Not a wisp of wind could touch me.

My cup emptied. On my way to refill it, I glanced at my laptop– "GOOGLE" stared back. It hit me how nothing escapes Google's gaze. Ask for anything– knowledge, places, even dreams– and it delivers. You can see everything, touch nothing.

I imagined a "Google Cup": type in your coffee of choice, and voilà: latte, cappuccino, mocha, affogato, with endless refills. Reality was less forgiving. So, I made more coffee the old-fashioned way to fight off sleep.

Back on the balcony, I spotted a family on the sidewalk, barely dressed against the bitter cold. A luxury Audi stopped nearby- four people inside, laughing, eating, drinking. Not much clothing on them either. Indigence and opulence– two sides of the same, exposed coin.

A girl stepped out, pizza in hand, unaffected by the biting wind. She strolled past the children. One boy stared at her pizza, eyes probably heavy with hunger. She paused– maybe she'd share. Her phone rang. The moment shattered. She walked away.

The boy looked at his empty bowl again, as if hoping food would appear. I wished for a "Google Bowl" for him– type anything, and the bowl fills. But could he even write?

His parents gathered wood scraps from a spot I thought was just a garbage dump. Once a children's park, now a wasteland. Convenient for us to toss trash from our balconies.

The fog thickened. The cold cut deeper, or maybe it was the sight of that boy, winds biting through his tiny frame. His older sister carried him, then set him down to help their mother. The bowl slipped from his hands, ringing like a temple bell. He moved to chase it.

As he walked that bit from me, he vanished in the mist, just like his bowl. Then his sibling, and then the whole family, all of them disappeared into that fog.

His laugh echoed faintly, though, swallowed by the fog. The moon faded. Silence settled. I gave up on work, buried myself in my warm, lavish quilt, covered with a sea-blue Bombay dyeing cloth. In my dreams that night, I remembered him chasing his bowl into a giant and monstrous foggy maw, The Great Indian Google Bowl, the one he needed most.

All of a sudden, the moon, which now looked like a bowl, stirred that memory as the old man and I continued sharing our silence.

Through the rhythmic screeching of a train's slowing wheels that just arrived on the platform, a sandpiper's cry cut through– harsh and shrill. Was it truly that discordant, or was it my mother's long-gone voice in my head, reminding me that a sandpiper's (Titehari in Hindi) call was a bad omen? I wasn't sure. But it did bring me closer to the usual railway platform chatter. I was more alive.

The very next moment, I found myself staring at the old man's wrinkles.

What if I dropped a water droplet over his bald crown, I thought. Which wrinkled route would it take to reach his chin? Would it tickle? How about an ant? His face, as a matter of fact, could serve the purpose of a labyrinth for an ant, and scientists could probably use it to test intelligence in its species, if they succeeded in reaching his chin. But how do you tell an ant that its goal is to reach a chin? Sugar, of course!

Chapter -7

When Destiny Was at Play

The Nagercoil Express moved through darkness, its passengers distant, their destinations unknown to me. My destination was not a place, but a memory: Hapur Junction's silent platform where time seemed to blur away. Though I was there as an operative on a mission, on that quiet night, I was a boy again, sitting on a bench beside a silent old man, grappling with the echoes of a life I thought were now behind me. That recollection felt sharper than the berth beneath me, more powerful than the scent of steel and antiseptic all around.

BULANDSHAHR→ HAPUR → LUCKNOW
(DAY 1, NAUCHANDI EXPRESS)

The train whistled hard, but it wasn't the Nauchandi Express that would take me to Lucknow the next morning.

Instinctively, I looked to my right to check whether my train had arrived too. Under those iconic tin shades that scream

"Indian Railways," a half-lit LED billboard blinked, the carved number '5' shouting its presence from a distance. Platform number five. But no sign of our train.

The same engine on platform one whistled again, signalling its departure towards Delhi.

"Come back fast! It's almost time!" a middle-aged woman shrieked from twenty feet away.

A man's voice, laced with annoyance, called back, "I'm coming, I'm coming." He waved dismissively from a food stall fifteen feet west. Every living thing, from the trees to the organisms near the Mariana Trench, must have heard her. That's how loud he was! The kicker? I'd seen them standing right next to each other since time immemorial, until just moments ago, the proud man went to provide for the family with some snacks.

"Why didn't she just tell him when they were close enough to spit on each other?" I wondered.

I scrutinized her with my usual judgmental gaze, trying to find a sign of her being mentally retarded, even by a cent, as the most logical explanation for the act of her totally avoidable, scratching and comical shouting. She anxiously studied the movement of the train at platform number one, half-confused. Well, it was not all her fault; and no, she was not out of her mind. She just happened to shout like how middle-aged women should, watching their trains leave, while their husbands are away for their beloved Chai. Just one small catch? It wasn't her train. Wrong train, right drama.

"Coming from Meerut, via Hapur, Shahjahanpur, and Muradabad, and traveling to Lucknow, departure of train number 14512, Nauchandi Express, is delayed by one hour and twenty minutes. We regret the inconvenience caused," the omnipresent railway station lady announced.

The 'superior' man returned, frowning. "Still want me to hurry?" he snapped, throwing a water bottle into the lap of his 'could-have-been-retarded' wife, while she sat on this cemented bench not too far from me. The woman was a bit hurt– her expression crumpled, making it clear. "Why are you angry at me? I didn't make the train late," she defended herself with rustic innocence, cracking the bottle's seal.

So, precisely, I was coming from Bulandshahr, a small city about 70 KM from Delhi, on the Nauchandi Link Express. Two bogies– one tier 3 AC, one sleeper class– attached to a local passenger train, leaving Bulandshahr around Six PM, detaching at Hapur around 7:45 PM. Then, re-attachment to the Nauchandi Express (Saharanpur to Allahabad) around 9:15 PM. I was in sleeper class, waiting for a train, which was now delayed by eighty minutes. as announced by our dear omni-present railway station lady. Mrs Gupta was in her proud air-conditioned coach. It was already 9:18 PM, and any hope of "Railways Standard Time" aligning with "Indian Standard Time" was lost. It took me a moment to fully absorb the frustration.

I'd wanted to ask the 'could-have-been-retarded' woman to keep it down when she pierced my ears, but her 'superior' husband's way of doing it stopped me ... .not because of my morality or ethics. It's just that I found it familiar. I sighed. This felt like home. My neighborhood in Bulandshahr overflowed with such 'superior' husbands like him– a brotherhood of belittlers, united in their contempt beyond caste, creed, and age. A sense of unity in their superiority. I looked again at the 'could-have-been-retarded' woman. Her pain was now seemingly gone, and she was okay in about ten seconds after the bottle landed in her lap. The husband went for a smoke towards the other side of the platform. She stared at him watching him go, and then loosely gazed towards platform number one, wiping the water droplets off her lips with the side of her fore-arm. Sadness doesn't last long for Indian middle-class women. Another minute, and she'd found a new companion, another woman whose husband was off smoking, or spitting out his red spit, or just taking care of the itch below his balls. Watching them chat, I wondered: would I also become a "superiorman" someday?

Knowing I had time, I walked towards platform five. The old man was still sitting there in silence, patiently. Platform four (where my compartment was) and five were adjoined. I found another empty bench.

Being an observer is hard. A gift, a highly misunderstood skill! You could read, write, sing, and then read again. You could stare at people and things and people again, even dogs, and form opinions about them. It sickened me to see their constant need for validation of their own happiness. Urgh...! You could also pass silent judgments on those who deserved to be abused, and kick their asses from a distance– a completely non-violent act towards justice, yet showering the joy of vengeance in your colon. Well, I could even stare at a totally blank, pure polar white wall and write stories about it. The point is people like me could be alright with being alone. If there comes a day when you cannot move out or the entire world comes under a lockdown, I might turn out to be the lone happiest soul. And for this reason or the other, I longed for this lone time on a crowded platform. And here was this dusty, scratched, kind of ugly, but not-broken and more importantly, an empty bench.... to reward me this much needed time with my own sweet self.

Ah, the feeling when my butt hit the bench!

My gaze fell on a familiar carving etched into the painted cement. "Waiting for 8 hours now." The frustration of some artist had been immortalized here, scratched into the bench for all weary travelers to see: "8 ghanta se pratiksha mai!". But wait– the '5' had been scratched over, reshaped into an awkward '8.'

Someone else, another weary traveler, must have faced the wrath of Indian Railways for longer and decided to correct the record– amending history rather than create their own mark. A silent camaraderie between strangers bound by shared misery.

And that's when it clicked. I had sat here before. I faintly remembered laughing at this very thing, some five or six years ago, maybe more.

That's the thing about Indian Railways. You don't just pass through stations; you return to them. Over years, and over lifetimes. The infrastructure is built to last, and so is the graffiti. People come and go, but their stories stay, etched into benches, scrawled on walls, waiting for the next passenger to add their versions.

Anyway, my exhaustion seeped into the bench, like it had found a way to be drained from me, and down into the earth. The infinite capacity of mother earth!

It was grounding, even comforting. Sensations coursed through my bloodstream, like a gentle tide washing over me. I plugged in Kishore Kumar on my earphones, a soundtrack for this moment, and let myself settle into its rhythm.

All set.

Then….! Darn it. All set for hell.

Remember those days when you weren't a kid anymore, but not adult enough to resist temptation either? That golden, reckless stage where every small rebellion felt like a declaration of freedom.

It's a fine autumn afternoon. Parents gone. The house is too quiet, like it's daring you to do something wrong. There it is– the bottle in your father's cabinet, amber and glowing like forbidden treasure, the kind reserved for "special guests." You've walked past it a hundred times, pretending not to care.

Today, you don't.

You open it. The smell hits like distilled rebellion. You pour just enough to feel clever, swirl it like you've seen men do in movies. "Just one sip," you whisper, as if moderation could erase the crime.

You raise it to your lips, heart pounding with the thrill of your own audacity. It burns, then warms. A taste of adulthood– smoky, bitter, and secretly disappointing. But you smile anyway, proud of your private, foolish victory.

And then… Ding-dong! The doorbell.

All set for hell.

Parents back early– and with guests. Aunty wants to "see the new flooring." You freeze, glass in hand, bottle half-corked, heart hammering like it's about to confess. You shove the evidence under a cushion, pretending you've always sat with your back all straight.

That exact feeling– the thrill of a private rebellion followed by the cold panic of being caught– is what returned to me as I found myself again among my fellow travellers. I'd been judging them from a distance, marinating in my own superiority. But guilt, I realized, doesn't just follow sin. Sometimes it follows arrogance– that quiet, stomach-dropping realization that you're not better, just better when hidden.

And just like that, destiny sent my lesson, wrapped neatly in human form.

I was genuinely surprised I'd managed to avoid the blessed gathering of my sleeper-class companions for this long– especially when the train was running an hour and twenty minutes late.

How had they not yet turned their collective frustration into a public spectacle? And how had I, of all people, been allowed this quiet sitting alone, pretending to be some sixty-year-old philosopher lost in thought? Yeah, right. Not for long.

Two of those country lovers stood right before me– close enough to invade my oxygen supply– brimming with the confidence that only half-baked wisdom and full-baked tobacco can provide.

My first instinct was obvious: raise the volume of Kishore Kumar and vanish into "Zindagi Ek Safar Hai Suhana." But two things stopped me–

First, Kishore's songs are too dignified to compete with men who believe patriotism and pan masala are synonyms.

Second, their enthusiasm wasn't confined to words– it came with choreography. Squats, elbows, and the sort of energetic body language that makes you pray for sudden deafness.

"You know, in Europe, people value their time; all trains, buses– they're never late," said the one who recently came back from his honeymoon, while pulling at his shirt to reveal an unfortunate flash of his orange underwear and a blood-red vest, as he clasped his shirt between his chin and the chest, and the pants suspended above the knees in his classic squat posture that he carried to not let the pants fall further below.

"Yeah, but it's not Europe mere bhai (my brother), so it's okay," the other tapped his shoulder which almost made Mr Red Vest lose his pants.

Disgusted yet hypnotized, I looked away. But these men had gravitational pull– the kind of stupidity that demands attention. Assholes. Assholes and funny faces, everywhere! Maybe all of them deserved to be late, I decreed, partially forgetting I was also one of them.

And then, like divine comic timing, the drunkard appeared on the platform. Seriously! Where the hell were these people all this while? His presence into our circle, though, did manage to distract them from cursing the Indian railways. All their sacred remarks were now shifted to the poor dipsomaniac who struggled to stand straight, while urinating on the rail tracks. "This fella is good for nothing," said one. The other one nodded with a slight 'yes,' and after a brief act of spitting a parabolic stream of red-spit on the other side of the platform, he voiced, "See, no one would even care if he just jumps, shits his pants, or falls right here on the tracks and gets run over by a train, you imagine."

Mr Red Vest smirked, "You know if he died like this in Japan, the railway company would hunt down his living family members and charge their asses with a few thousand dollars a bill."

Naturally, I thought he was bluffing; making the shit up and probably using his Europe-trip as a cover for its validity. But then I checked my phone. Damn it– he was right. Mr Red Vest suddenly gained an iota of my respect for sharing this weird fact. Obviously, what else would you learn from those cheap websites? I prompted myself in my defense for not knowing the same.

"Huh, at least one less reason to die!" the other chuckled.

This time, however, the drunkard seemed to have reckoned that he was the topic of their conversation, he hastily moved towards the fantastic two. His little fella was saying 'Hi' to everyone through his open fly; the guy was seriously doomed. He coughed and maybe tried to hold it inside of him, but couldn't, and after coming very close to them….,"ooaagghhh," he threw up. The fantastic two barely managed a clear distance from the puke. So did I; it sniffed horribly.

"Youuor talking 'bout me…," while spewing another jet stream, "huh.., then talks to me…you…" and the rest of his words got lost in the loud sound of the train's whistle, coming from towards my left at platform number five.

As the train slowed down, my eyes began searching– through the open window panes of each passing coach, one after the other, as if I were trying to spot someone. Someone of my own. Someone I longed for.

Without thinking, my gaze moved too swiftly from coach to coach, and soon enough, a dull ache settled just above my eyebrows. The strain wasn't new; neither was this urgency. I had done this before. Right here.

This bench.

The same bench I had just sunk into a while ago, the one with its scratched complaints about "8 hours of waiting," the one where laughter once slipped so easily from me– that bench had been a witness to this exact search, years ago.

That day too, my gaze had darted along the moving coaches, desperate yet stubbornly hopeful. And that day, someone had actually appeared.

I felt an urge, almost primal, to run after the train, just like I did back then. Back when the air wasn't this cold, or maybe it was, but I didn't notice because there was warmth waiting for me.

But it wasn't just déjà-vu. It was a rollercoaster of déjà-vu–the anticipation, the aching scan of windows, the breathlessness. Cold sweat trickled down my spine.

The railway clock, unapologetically indifferent, stood in front of me, the same as always. Yet, I checked my wristwatch again, knowing too well that both would agree. Still, something inside me wanted to be sure.

What was real? This frantic search? Anxiety? Or the memory pressing against it like fog on the glass?

When the train finally stopped, the world seemed to stumble into slow motion. My breathing faltered– I felt as though I was waiting for someone, like a soldier on a death-bed for his family. A few passengers disembarked. My eyes kept hunting, fueled by equal parts hope and despair. The glandular cocktail inside me did its job. Adrenaline. Dopamine. Yet, it all felt... misplaced.

I stood on the same old platform, but I wasn't standing the same way anymore. I was hollowed out. My vision roamed, unsure whether it sought someone out there, or just someone within me.

And just like the last time– except so unlike it– I turned back. Only this time, I stumbled. A careless hit against a luggage cart. My head met its metal handles, and after a few moments of recovery, I was thrown back into the present– to the chatter, the calls for chai, the couples, the lone travelers, the crying child.

They were all there, these fellow passengers to Lucknow, just like they were years ago.

Maybe it was me who was missing all this while.

The air felt naked against my skin, colder than it should be. Not the cold that makes you shiver, but the kind that crawls under your clothes, like the quiet realization of something lost. And suddenly there was stillness in the air, as if the wind had changed its mind.

Absent-minded, nursing the bump on my head, I lowered myself to the base of a truss column, observing everyone. The fantastic two, the drunkard, even the fantastic four– everyone exactly where they were supposed to be.

But they felt different. Or maybe I did.

My anxious search for Ira was over. She was here six years ago, but today, it was just me and these fellow travelers.

I saw them now– not just with my eyes, but with something else. Love, care, and respect. For them. For all of them. For this strange tribe gathered on the platform. I didn't know why. Or maybe I did but couldn't pin-point.

The fear of losing something had vanished, as if the wound I was unknowingly hiding had finally surfaced; not to torment, but to heal.

A calmness settled over me, like I had finally caught up to the train I missed.

Maybe today, I belonged with them. The universe - playing, as it always does.

I could do nothing but accept what life had placed before me.

Chapter – 8

That Day

The Nagercoil Express hummed with the steady energy of early evening. Around me, the sleeper coach was a picture of settled routines. Families were unpacking their steel tiffin boxes, the scent of tamarind and curry leaves mingling with the metallic air of the train. A group of college students was laughing loudly over a card game, while vendors patrolled the aisle with calls of "Kaapi, Kaapi..." and packets of crunchy murukku. The sun had long set, leaving the window as a dark, rushing mirror reflecting the life inside. The train began to slow, the change in tempo, a subtle shift in the carriage's rhythm. A brightly lit signboard announced our arrival: Dharmapuri Junction.

I glanced up from my own thoughts, my eyes drawn to the platform outside. Everything was different from the North, the language on the signboards, the scent of jasmine flowers worn by women, the humid air that clung to the skin. Yet, as my gaze drifted up, I saw it. A large, round, unapologetically old-fashioned station clock, its black hands ticking with the same indifferent patience as the one at Hapur. The sight struck me like a physical blow. A different place, a different time, but the same feeling of being trapped in a loop, of watching time move while feeling stuck. The world outside my window dissolved, and the memory of Hapur Junction, no longer a gentle drift but a tidal wave, crashed over me...

BULANDSHAHR→ HAPUR → LUCKNOW

(DAY 1, NAUCHANDI EXPRESS)

This station clock.

A perfect circle- what an odd shape to attach so many feelings to. Yet, somehow, we do. It's everywhere, not just on paper or in geometry books, but right here, in our lives, in the air. People say life is a circle, maybe because it keeps dragging us to places we have already been, like an old record refusing to skip the scratched part. Or maybe because everything is just a pattern. The weather. The days. The nights. Crops and harvests. This life. Perhaps, the death itself.

And for people, the ones who quietly follow duties and routines without too many questions, all are unwavering followers of this very circle. Build. Repeat. Standardize. We call it 'process' , 'order' and 'normal'. But what is it, really? Just a circle dressed in uniforms. And when we finally get bored of this new 'normal,' we desperately start looking for a new circle. Sometimes it's comforting, sometimes cruel. Yet, we stay on the ride.

It struck me like never before, sitting there against that old truss-column, staring at the big round station clock. It wasn't just keeping time; it was mocking me, turning and turning like it always did, like it did the last time I sat here all those years ago. That day too, it caught my eye, forcing me to sit still and notice. Today, it was doing the same, pushing me into remembrance, as if the universe itself had set the hands of that clock to repeat a scene I had almost forgotten but never fully left.

I sat there, watching it, knowing the truth, knowing the present, that I should be out there, among my fellow passengers, anywhere but here, the fantastic two, the drunkard, the chooran goli kid, the whole lot or whatever, just not here. Not with the truth. Not with reality. But I couldn't move, trapped somewhere between a memory and the present. The longer I sat, the clearer it became. It wasn't just clocks that went in circles; it was me too. My thoughts. My days. My life.

There were days when I would feel unhappy and depressed and, unsurprisingly, I would keep feeling the same for the whole day or sometimes for a few days until, just like that, those feelings would decide to leave my home, in the same way they had entered– quite uninvited. In those days, I would find one negative thought leading to another negative thought, leading to another negative thought, and so on, until, just like that, the sun would come peeking through grey clouds, and joy would return-through a kind word, a silly joke, a good cup of tea, or the warmth of a familiar tap on the shoulder. And that day, I would feel happy. That day, I would talk to Shiva, or Adrien, or my college roommate and only friend at Lucknow, Benjamin, or eat something delicious or read something interesting or smile at a stranger at the bus-stand or do something meaningful or share a laugh or just feel the chest pumping up with each breath. Happiness would find ways to grow bigger, only to fade again. Around and around. My last six years, nothing but these circles.

Were we all just moving from one circle to another-sad to happy, happy to restless, restless to numb, numb to longing, longing back to angry, followed by sad? Was life nothing but a sequence of loops, one thought feeding the next, one feeling slipping into another?

And yet, what dictated the shift? What unseen force decided when one circle would break and another would begin?

I exhaled sharply, pressing my fingers to the center of my forehead. A dull ache pulsed there– a reminder. My fingertips brushed over a tiny, defiant bump, the work of that damn luggage cart handle. I let out a half-smirk at my stupidity for knocking into it. And then curses flew naturally off my mouth to the coolie who had left it there, as I rubbed the bump again.

With my hazy vision, a dull throbbing at the top of my forehead, and an unrelenting flood of thoughts pressing down on me-through it all, I hear–

"Hey! I'm here."

A voice.

Her voice.

It comes like a current, sweeping away everything in its path. I don't move, don't even breathe. A sudden stillness overtakes me, one that isn't just external, but something deeper-like the world itself has paused to listen.

I look up, and there she is. Waving at me.

From exactly the third window left to the front door of coach, S4.

A strange, sharp relief spreads through me. The weight of the station, the exhaustion of wandering, the unsettling questions-everything dissolves. The moment I heard her voice, I was already gone-past the present, past reason, past everything real.

Her train hasn't even stopped yet. It's still in motion, rolling in steadily, yet here I stand, frozen at the base of the truss column.

And then, as if from a different world, I glance toward the fantastic two.

I don't know why. But my eyes find them, and theirs find me. A fleeting second, and yet, something unspoken transfers between myself and the fantastic two. Their expressions-something in them tugs at me. Not a demand, not an order, just a quiet invitation. A presence. A reminder.

"Hey, come, join us! You must." Their eyes called for me.

I flinch. My body doesn't move, but inside, I feel the disturbance ripple through me.

"No." I fight them back.

Her voice comes again–"I'm here, TJ!" and I turn back so fast. Too fast. Like I'm afraid if I give the fantastic two a second longer, they might pull me back into something I don't want to face.

Yet... even as I turn away from them, I can still feel them. Their presence lingers, something solid, something real. Unlike this. Unlike what I'm choosing.

And then, it happens.

For the first time, I feel it– the pull.

Not just toward her, but away from the present.

It had never been a choice before. It was out of the question to even think of going to them, and not accompanying her.

But their crying eyes wouldn't shut up, and kept filling my head with this horrible calling to join them. Why the hell would I join thosc irritating comrades from some stupid tribe? Still, I can feel the gravity of it all. Platform Four– where the fantastic two, the drunkard, and my fellow travelers stand, waiting. The present. Reality.

And Platform Five– where she waits.

Where memory lives.

"This isn't a choice."

It never has been.

Yet, something inside me knows the truth. Knows that she isn't real, that this is just another moment of slipping, another moment of ignoring the present, another moment of longing for what can't be brought back.

But knowing doesn't mean stopping.

I hear her again. I see her again.

And just like that, I'm already gone. As a prisoner of lies, I choose her.

"Fuck psychology. Fuck you idiots. I'm going to her," I exhale, the words falling from my lips like a declaration, like a spell breaking.

A strange weakness settles in my chest, but at least the battle is over.

No more dilemma.

No reason to turn back.

And just like that, I was there.

The truss column, the station, the present– they dissolved. The weight of 'now' lifted as the 'past' swallowed me whole, and I gave in, willingly, helplessly.

Her train finally came to a halt.

"Wait, I'm coming," she shouted with a subtle smile on her face, standing at the front door of coach S4. It was just the right kind of smile, the one that comes just before laughter and just after a little twinkle. My world slowed. Even the giant station clock, with its relentless ticking, seemed to hesitate between seconds.

Through the crowded exit, I caught glimpses of her– moving with the flow, yet slightly apart from it. A theatre troupe was ahead of her, buzzing with energy, their costumes shimmering under the platform lights. Maybe it was their destination stop; their enthusiasm could tell. Glittering shoes, tall cityscape backdrops in their arms, latex jackets, makeup-smudged cheeks, voices rising in chaotic melody. And amidst them all– HER.

She walked toward me, lost, yet certain. My own certainty vanished.

I forgot everything. My thoughts, my carefully constructed cool demeanor, my practiced ease. All undone the moment she stood two feet away.

This was it.

This was every word I had ever wanted to say. Every song I had ever longed to sing. Every place I had ever wished to see.

It was all here. She was here.

Time and distance could never weaken this gravity, this force that bound me to her. The highest form of belonging. A meditation so deep that it witnesses the marriage of my mind and the soul.

Right there, near the seventh pole of platform number five, my entire existence converged.

Words she actually spoke. Words left unspoken.

She extended her hand.

A simple gesture, yet my entire being trembled.

"You with me, wearing a black gown, holding my hand, on a spring night. The moon slipping behind the clouds. I see your eyes-God, they're beautiful. I want to say a million things, but silence is what we share. Holding your hand… just wandering, together… toward the farthest place I can imagine… with you… holding your hand. That's it. That's everything."

That's what I had told her when she first asked me about my idea of a perfect date. We were twenty-one. Almost kids. Just figuring out life. Figuring out ourselves.

And now, here I was– living it, about to hold her hand, relive her touch.

My heart pounded as I reached for her hand, but only after rubbing my palm against the back of my jacket first, kick of an old nervous habit, wanting it to be perfect.

But just before I could touch her–

KaBoom!

The train's siren split through the air. The same hideous sound, approaching the station from my left.

She vanished.

The moment shattered like glass, leaving nothing but silence in its place.

I wasn't standing with her anymore. I wasn't holding her hand.

I was sitting at the base of the same truss column. The luggage cart's handles are still digging into my back. The rough metal is still cold under my fingertips.

Reality. The same cursed, venomous reality.

The memory had swallowed me whole, and now, it had spit me back out.

The memories from my last train journey with Ira, in the same train, about the same time. Memories from the times when you're one with someone. When the universe deciphers it for you, you're in love.

Love, the kind I once knew; and the kind that doesn't come easy when life has stripped you bare, when it has ripped both your parents away, one after the other, until you're an orphan to the world but a stranger to yourself. And when you can no longer tell who you really are, or were, or are left with!

It had been what– five, six years? The exact number didn't matter. The only thing that mattered was that I had just lost her again.

Just like I had lost everyone.

And yet, my mind rebelled. What if?

What if the train hadn't been delayed that day, too.

If it hadn't been… maybe she would have missed it. Maybe everything would have been different. Maybe I wouldn't be here, staring at the same rusted metal, haunted by the same memories, asking the same impossible question: could she still be here?

Chapter – 9

When the Universe Interfered

The Nagercoil Express carved its way deeper into the southern night. The rhythmic clatter of the wheels had become a meditative hum, a sound that seemed to pull memories from the very marrow of my bones. I was still sitting by the window, my reflection a pale outline against the rushing darkness. I felt a profound sense of dislocation, not just physically, but existentially. I was a man who had stopped existing in his own life, only to be pushed into a new one he didn't understand. The feeling reminded me so strongly of a story I once heard, a story about a man who had to lose everything to find himself. The memory of my PhD professor, the legendary Dr. Elrond, and his final, unforgettable lecture rose from the depths, as vivid and immediate as if I were sitting in that university hall again...

BULANDSHAHR→ HAPUR → LUCKNOW
(DAY 1, NAUCHANDI EXPRESS)

If it's about the feeling, it surely isn't your day. But if it is about the feeling, it surely is. It depends on which part of the feeling you want to live.

And just like that, I was back– sitting right there at the base of the truss column, staring at nothing, feeling everything.

My mind was exhausted from this relentless loop– the past…. the present. How long had I been fighting this same battle? Clinging to memories, rejecting the now. I knew what was real. And yet, I longed for what was not.

And it was then that another voice from another time surfaced, unbidden. A voice from my second year of doctorate studies. A voice that spoke with a melody so distinct that it was impossible to forget.

"If it's about a feeling, it surely isn't your day. But if it is about the feeling, it surely is. Depends which part of the feeling you want to live. The key is to just acknowledge wherever you are and whatever you feel."

I closed my eyes. Professor Dr. Walter J. Elrond.

He had once said these words in his final lecture. That lecture. The one I had never forgotten, though I hadn't truly understood it– until now.

And just like that, his story began to unfold in my mind once again.

Professor Dr. Walter J. Elrond, born and raised in Ireland, had settled in Norway but traveled to India every year to teach a course on Value Education at our institute. India had been his great discovery years ago, though perhaps it was the institute that had been lucky to discover him. A renowned orologist– a scholar of mountains– he was entangled in the vastness of science, the mysticism of philosophy, and the towering presence of nature.

His voice carried an old-world charm, his words flowing like a melody, like the kind of song you knew you'd never hear again. He was more than a professor; he was a legend. We didn't just admire him– we revered him. My long-time roommate, Benjamin, and I often recorded his lectures, playing them back in our hostel room late into the night, debating them with a passion that blurred the lines between science and philosophy. Those debates would stretch past midnight, and we would lose track of when we had stopped talking science and when philosophy had taken over.

It was the second year of my doctorate when rumors swirled that this session would be his last. These whispers had echoed for years– eight years, to be exact– yet somehow, his two-year contract kept getting renewed. This time, however, the rumors were true.

"So, today," he had said in that final lecture, his eyes gleaming with the lessons of time, "let me tell you all a story."

And just like that, he began…

"Summers in aestivation, winters in hibernation. Time kept slipping away. Losing hands, losing hopes. Everything in the world looked sullen. He once told me he believed in magic– perhaps he was waiting for that to happen, though he did nothing to summon it.

Days, nights, weeks, months, seasons– he was off, but that one fine day, he woke up gasping for air. Nobody had seen him like this in thirty months. He was fighting for breath, as though someone had smothered him in his sleep, pressing a pillow against his face, suffocating him. He ran. Out of nowhere, into oblivion. Chasing his own breath, as if it were escaping him. As if breathing had ceased to be an involuntary act."

My roommate leaned toward me. "What the hell is he talking about?" he whispered.

It felt like a play unfolding before us, and we were on the edge of our seats, waiting for what was to come. Professor Elrond paused for a breath, and so did we.

"But why? Why did he suddenly become conscious of living? What had pulled him back?

He wasn't a man who sought enlightenment, nor had he been awakened by the strains of an Indian raga at dawn. And yet, that morning, the dewdrops on the flowers of that sublime hill stared at him in curiosity, reflecting his urgency as if they, too, needed answers.

His name was John. And John was a musician.

Or, rather, he had been."

The professor suddenly straightened, his tone shifting into something more deliberate, more professorial, as if to make us understand something.

"If we consider the pronoun 'He' as the subject, then grammar dictates we say 'is'– because John is alive. But if we consider 'musician' as the subject, then the past tense applies. Because John no longer played music. The musician in him had died.

But thirty months ago, he was a musician. His flute and guitar had been his companions."

We followed his every word. Not a single breath stirred in the hall.

John had spent his evenings performing. Every night, he returned home with a single plucked flower for his beloved wife, his guitar slung over his shoulder, his flute settled in his hand.

After four years of their passionate love, their relationship came out of the veil with a beautiful wedding on that hilltop, beneath the open sky, at night, under the light of stars and moon at the horizon. This was the same place where they had made love a thousand times, forgetting everything else in the world but themselves. They both worshipped just being there and sleeping in each other's arms, in the sun, under the trees, at night and under the various colored skies, with the warmth as if they were closer to God.

Samantha.

It was her name.

She had been his everything. A sharp, beautiful, and tall girl with brown eyes deep as the earth itself, black hair, and golden skin. Her skin tone was the color you see in reflection of the first ray of sunlight, when it falls on the fresh mountain snow. Her beauty went beyond all words. If the world had given him the power to declare a masterpiece of nature, it would have been her.

Professor Elrond paused, a quiet smile curving his lips as if he, too, could see her.

"They weren't just making love," he continued. "They were living it. Exploring and layering it with seasons and time, weaving it into the very air they breathed."

And in those first years, they had been untouchable. They had moved together like tides and moons, inseparable. It was Samantha's idea to explore what their love meant for each other. Her heart pounded with a wild hope. She wanted more than fleeting moments of passion. She yearned to explore the intricate dance of their souls, not just in stolen kisses and whispered promises, but in the mundane rhythm of their shared life. Sometimes, it was like they went to sleep under a heavy blanket in winters, and woke up to the morning of cuddly spring.

She planted saplings on the hills while John created music. The villagers' community didn't know much of the world anyway. Nature and art, each growing in their own way.

She wished to see those saplings grow into big trees and bear fruits. For her, the hill and John was her whole world. She used to tell stories of the nature God from various parts of the world all the time, like how people worshiped nature in the past, and how they were afraid of it in the early days. These were her topics of concern. Unlike John, she loved the sound of thunderstorms and used to laugh, matching the intensity of the clouds at such occasions. She was of the idea that she was born for nature.

"Will we ever marry, John?" She asked, "We've been together for over two years now; shouldn't we plan something for our future?"

"Sam! I love you because I do. I just do. I don't want any of us loving each other as a responsibility. What if this responsibility changes into a burden? I think we're good this way. And by the way, we're already married, it's just that we haven't been wedded. That doesn't make a difference. Does it?" John replied persuasively.

This was the first and the last time that they ever discussed their future– wedding and all. Only this short conversation!

But then, one night, John returned home with a blue jasmine in his hand, his heart full, and his mood that of a happy toddler.

Samantha was a toddler too!

"Maybe this was the reason they happened to be together." We all chuckled with the professor as he continued carrying us.

And that night, with all the reckless certainty of love, he had said to her:

"I'm tired of loving you with my so-called definition of being careless. I want to take your responsibility, like a father does. I want my mind to be occupied with you, my schatzi. Oh love, marry me."

The words fell like a thunderbolt, shattering the stillness. Samantha froze. Then she wept– a cry so fierce it could have bent the trees. She clung to him, her lips on his face, his hair, his eyelids. Not even a single millimeter of his head was left unkissed. John too drank in all her tears. And that night, beneath the stars, outside the house they had built with their own hands, they melted into each other.

A night unlike any other.

A wedding unlike any other.

A love story unlike any other, just as Samantha had imagined.

When John searched for Samantha on the porch a month after their wedding, he suddenly heard her voice drifting from the woods. He followed the sound, his heart quickening. Samantha was perched at the edge of the hill by the fencing, reaching for a cat stuck in a tree. A strong mountain girl, she knew her way around these hills– but John panicked and ran toward her, his voice breaking against the wind.

"Wait! Samantha... stop... don't– Samantha!"

She couldn't hear him. The mountain winds swallowed his cries. Two nights of rain had weakened the fence– Samantha had asked John to fix it, but like any lazy fool, he had done only the bare minimum, just enough to keep her off his back. He never told her the repair was only for show.

As he drew close enough for his voice to reach her, she turned, their eyes meeting. With one hand gripping the fence for balance and the other outstretched toward the cat, she smiled– an unspoken reassurance that she was fine, that she would be back in a moment, that they would return home together for dinner.

Then came the snap.

"Chrrr...thukk..."

The fence gave way, and with it, something inside John tore apart. Time froze. Tears slipped down his face, his breath stifled. He felt his body go cold, his limbs seizing in horror.

But then, as if waking from a nightmare, he lurched forward. She might still be there, clinging to something, hanging on like in movies. He believed in magic– he had told her that once. Peering down, he saw nothing. No sign of her. He scrambled toward the valley, calling her name, searching every tree, every shadow, even places where his common sense refused to take him, the places where she couldn't possibly be. In small holes, behind bushes, as if she were a lost key.

And in a way, she was.

She was the key to his happiness, to his melodies, to his very life. And now, she was gone, locking away every door she had once opened.

For a month, he searched. Without food, without sleep, without sanity– he searched. But Samantha was never found.

When he finally returned home, he shut himself away. Days blurred into nights. No one knew what he ate, what he thought, or if he thought at all. Thirty months passed. Perhaps even he did not know how he survived.

"Do you hear it, John?" she had once asked him.

"What?"

"Shh... listen. The song of nature."

She had whispered it to him the night before she vanished. "The rustling leaves, the owls, the insects... Close your eyes. Listen to all of them at once. This… melody."

"Yeah," John had replied, gazing at the northern lights. He hadn't really been listening. Not then.

She had been different, attuned to nature in a way no one else was. She had always said she was born for it. And in the end, she became part of it. Maybe she had simply returned to where she belonged.

Thirty months later, John awoke. With all his body parts functioning normally, he ran into the woods, and nobody knew where. This was no less than magic for him. His belief in magic worked.

The weather was a little cool that day. The wind made the leaves fly like a bird with it. The sun was coming out of the horizon. Half of the sky was reddish yellow. He could see the sky lying there in his bed and the chirping of the birds as well. A few families had also settled there in those thirty-odd months. He could hear the voices of children's morning cries.

And then he heard it. The song. The one Samantha had tried to show him. The wind, the birds, the silence itself.

"Yes," he murmured. "I hear it," lying in his bed.

Then, he ran.

As fast as he could.

Through the woods, up the hill– to where they had met, where they had loved, and where they had promised each other forever. He ran until he reached the place where she had disappeared.

The saplings she had planted were no longer small. They had grown into trees, stretching toward the sky. Her dream had taken root, living on in the earth, in the air, in the melody she had left behind.

Tears streaming down his face, John looked up. Sobbing. Smiling. Crying. He shouted into the wind, "Yes, Samantha! I hear it now!"

A pause. Then, with a voice that trembled with both sorrow and joy, he whispered, "I hear your song."

The entire lecture hall sat in stunned silence, eyes glistening, breaths held. Not a single clap. No questions. Just stillness.

Then, after three unbearable minutes, Professor Elrond-the man who had just spun this tale-removed his glasses, cleaned them, put them back on, and smiled.

"But do you know why I chose to share this story today? In my last lecture."

The students looked at him, searching for an answer.

He exhaled slowly. "Because I want you all to understand that… LIFE GOES ON."

A hushed murmur moved through the hall, like wind stirring a still pond. But then, as if caught in an unseen moment, silence reclaimed the room. They hung on his every syllable.

"And because," he continued, pausing, "…I want you all to know… that I am John. Walter John Elrond."

A gasp. A sharp inhale from dozens of throats.

And then, just like that, we never heard of Professor Elrond live again.

I remember how I felt that day in the lecture hall, but the understanding was academic, distant. Now, sitting on this train, hurtling toward a danger I couldn't comprehend, the story felt different. It felt like my own. I finally felt what it meant to be "un-Johned." Just yesterday, on the train platform at Hapur, a simple tap on my shoulder from Ganesh had jolted me out of the phantom of my past, forcing me back into the present. It was a moment of reconstitution, a quiet rebirth.

My friend Benjamin and I had often spoken about Professor Elrond's story, but I only truly understood it now, in the hum of these steel wheels. It wasn't just about grief; it was about what he created the moment he chose to live again. For the first time, sitting here on the Nagercoil Express, I felt truly connected to John. I finally understood why Professor Elrond had shared his tale. It wasn't just a story; it was a roadmap.

Chapter – 10

Becoming Someone Else

I went to roam across all three compartments– S10, S11, and the AC coach B1– to find and report anything unusual my eyes saw. Negative. Nothing. The faces were a sea of weary travelers, none betraying any hidden agenda. Salem was the next major station. I pulled out my phone and sent a quick, encrypted text to Trishulin sir: Any update on your ETA? All quiet here.

His response came back almost instantly. "Yes, one of the teams should be. We're delayed. Just keep an eye out for interesting boardings from Salem."

I texted back with a simple acknowledgment and slipped the phone into my pocket. With nothing more to do for now, I came back to my side-lower berth in S11 and settled in. The quiet hum of the train was beginning to lull me into a false sense of security– only time would tell. I leaned my head against the cool glass of the window, my reflection a pale outline against the rushing darkness. The memory of Professor Elrond's story, of a man named John who had to lose everything to find himself, still lingered. It was a story about being "un-Johned"– about shedding a skin of grief to feel the world again. Yesterday, a simple tap on the shoulder from a stranger had been the catalyst. Now, on this new train, I was remembering that moment of transformation, the quiet, seismic shift that had occurred on that platform in Hapur...

BULANDSHAHR→ HAPUR → LUCKNOW
(DAY 1, NAUCHANDI EXPRESS)

A tap on my shoulder. And here I was, right beside one of those fantastic fours.

John– before his transformation. John– after his transformation. Just a moment separated the two. And I wondered: was it that tap on my shoulder that did the same for me? And with that thought came a revelation– perhaps John was never the point at all. Perhaps even John himself was merely a placeholder for something deeper, something more fundamental. Beneath his journey lay something far greater: the moment he became truly conscious of the world around him, the moment he became one with it, the moment he became consciousness itself.

In all this retrospection, as I recollected Professor Elrond's last lecture again, every word he had spoken echoed through my mind– not merely as sentences but as reflections of time itself. It brought back memories. It sparked inspiration. But more than anything, it captured something I had never been able to grasp before-the essence of feeling within a moment.

Perhaps such moments appear in all our lives at different points, scattered across a lifetime. But we find them only when we find them. Those fine moments.

When Professor Elrond shared his last lecture with us, we had all felt lucky, even proud, believing he had chosen our institute, our batchmates, to share the Thing. Maybe we had been wrong all along. Maybe he hadn't done it for us. Maybe that day wasn't about us at all. Maybe he had simply needed to speak it aloud, for himself.

That day, he had told a story about a moment long past, a hilltop in Ireland, a love lost to the wind. But now, I understood something deeper. I had not just heard about transformation in a particular moment, on a particular day, on that Irish hill; I had witnessed it, right in front of me, as the professor spelled it out for us in his last lecture. The rest was history.

And now, here I was, standing at the edge of something I could not yet name, with a tap on my shoulder pulling me from the depths of my own mind.

My moment! While I sat at the base of the same truss column, swallowing the crisp, cold air into my mouth.

"Hey buddy, what's the score?" Ganesh asked with a tap on my shoulder. "Bhai, score kya hua?"

"Huh!?" Confused, I could only gesture with my head, tilting it back and forth in that familiar, unsure expression.

"The score!" he said, pointing toward my phone. "How many wickets?"

I had absolutely no clue. My phone was playing a cricket match between India and New Zealand, apparently the final of some T20 series. The only good part about it was that no one would've thought I was crazy when I zoned out or blankly stared into nothingness, thinking about John and my life in between. To them, I must have looked like a nerdy cricket fan, lost in the drama of the sport.

I hated cricket.

"Ahh… five down. Thirty-two more needed off twenty-five balls."

"Still five! Damn," muttered Ganesh, one of the fantastic fours, lightly slapping his thigh before walking off, thanklessly, the way most Indian strangers do when they meet fellow strangers of the same gender. The thump of his palm on his thigh was the last distinct sound I processed before everything began to fade into the usual. Within a moment, the platform returned to its default setting, the same old mundane chatter, the tea and food vendors shouting over each other, the light, cold breeze whispering through, and that awful stench of piss… and with it, the shittier stench of shit.

The drunkard had rejoined the remaining fantastic two, and from the looks of their gestures, they'd become some version of friends in the meantime. Last I remembered, the drunkard had charged at them like a furious bull, as though ready to grab them by their necks and either kick them off the platform or fling them onto the tracks.

My brain, just then, projected a slideshow of pictorial memories from the past twenty minutes, though only in disjointed fragments, from my reverie-with-open-eyes state. Twenty long minutes where I must've stared at those strangers while the live match played on my phone like a prop in a background scene.

I recalled the drunkard, weeping softly; Mr. Red-Under helping him sit up, while the other offered him water; a janitor cleaning up his puke; a baby suddenly appearing out of nowhere and sprinting toward the tracks– almost falling– only to be snatched back just in time by some fatso hero who reacted instinctively; and a coolie hauling around luggage for Mr. Fatso, who barked out instructions like a military sergeant.

And that cart– damn it! The same cart that had rammed into me and gifted me the bump on my head. "This asshole," I muttered, glancing at the coolie as if discovering the culprit in a murder mystery. As if on cue, my fingers moved up to check the bump. It was nearly gone.

But what was more surprising was seeing that trio– the fantastic two and the drunkard– together, not yelling or abusing. Just three men who, moments ago, seemed ready to kill each other, now sharing space like old acquaintances.

Undoubtedly, an interesting takeaway from just a short while.

Now that I had better control over looking at things objectively, I wondered, were those annoyingly avoidable yet oddly captivating fantastic fours and the drunkard the only interesting subjects in my vicinity? Or was I destined to meet them? I wouldn't know.

The moment had finally come to bid adieu to Hapur Junction. The Nauchandi Express stood arrogantly on platform number five, its engine already fired up. It stood there shamelessly, without the slightest hint of apology for being late. That kind of audacity, I wished I had it in my life.

As I walked towards my coach, a strange rush of feeling ran through my bones, as if I was about to miss something. Not something dramatic. Just… something. This rush couldn't be filed under good or bad, it was simply made of memories. The train let out a proud whistle, its tone almost empathetic, "Don't worry, my child. It's alright."

I reached my compartment and stood by the gate, not even bothering to check on my beloved reserved seat. I watched everything– the benches, the bridge, the people standing, chatting, laughing, sliding away behind me. To my greatest surprise, the old man was still sitting at the same half-broken bench. No one beside him. I thought he was waiting for this train only.

Wow! We may live so close to one another, yet are galaxies apart. He never let me know that he waited for no train, even when we talked about their delays.

That glowing LED hoarding with the number 5 stood out like a marker, reminding me that this was the place I had made memories, the kind that would stick. Every now and then, I tried to look ahead, scanning the train's forward direction, but my heart kept pulling me back, to what I was leaving behind.

Just then, the train sirened again, as if affirming something. And right at that moment, another tap on my right shoulder.

I looked back, startled. It was the same one from the fantastic fours again, Ganesh.

"India is already defeated, brother. Such a waste," he said, leaning casually over the washbasin by the compartment gate, cupping water into his mouth.

I was still trying to register whether he'd really tapped me or not when– pssshhh!– he spat out his paan (the infamous betel leaf–areca nut combo) into the night air. With a light hand gesture, he motioned me to shift aside so he could stand at the edge of the doorway.

"The first spit can sometimes choke the sink," he said, flashing a clingy-cheerful smile. "So, as a responsible citizen of India, I always spit beneath the open sky."

And just like that, he officially became the biggest idiot I had ever met.

Then came another mouthful of water, a swift gargle, and this time he spat it out in the sink, clearly confident that it wouldn't clog now.

"See, that's why we never watch these sucky cricket matches," he added, throwing a glance at my phone, still in my right hand, while my left clung to the iron bar for support.

He didn't even wait for a response.

"We're going to have dinner. Care to join?"

"Ugh…" I searched for words for three whole seconds. "Yeah, sure," I replied, because my brain couldn't seem to locate a 'no'.

"I'm Ganesh, by the way. My friends call me Gannu," he said, introducing himself in slightly broken English while subtly adjusting his underwear, presumably in pursuit of dinner-time comfort. And for reasons only God might understand, I found myself making a fleeting attempt to catch a glimpse, trying to guess what colour he was sporting down there, recalling his friend Mr. Red-Under.

The same red traces of paan flashed across his wide smile when he turned back to guide the way, like a twisted garnish on his oddly warm hospitality.

Just as we were about to move, another man appeared behind him, shirt untucked, hair windswept, and with the same sacred conviction in his eyes. He reached the washbasin, took a sip of water, and with dramatic timing, let his first spit fly straight into the open air, just like Ganesh. The second gargle, of course, was directed into the basin. Order had been restored. Tradition upheld.

I stared at them both, these unofficial keepers of oral hygiene and skyward-spitting rituals. Was this… some universal knowledge passed down in secret? A hidden curriculum of etiquette? Did their parents sit them down at some point in life and go, "Beta, this is how we become responsible citizens of India"?

Looks like I'd missed a lot in life by not eating paan masala.

Had he introduced himself or invited me for a meal just a couple of hours ago, there's no way I would've even considered replying. I literally hated people like him, for no other reason than just being themselves. But by some god's grace, and maybe his good luck, I didn't find him worth hating anymore. In fact, if I'm being completely honest with myself, just now, when he flashed that slightly brown smile behind his lips, something unusual happened. An authenticity shimmered over his face. And I had just… seen God in him.

Yes– God. Just like Benjamin had once described, seeing God in people.

My roommate and friend, Benjamin, a South Indian Christian, born to a South Indian Brahmin father and a Christian mother, would be proud to hear this coming from me. He was a wonderful guy: calm, composed, always cheerful. He worked at a chartered accountant firm in Lucknow. We did our graduation together. I studied chemistry; he studied commerce. After graduation, our paths diverged, but we stayed together.

During one of our many spiritual tête-à-têtes on religion, on God, on Christianity, and Hinduism– my intention, shamelessly, was always to make him accept defeat. I once asked him if he'd ever seen his God.

He went quiet for a few moments. I didn't interrupt, of course. I just waited there, smiling smugly, as temples, churches, and mosques flickered across the screen of my unsettled mind.

Then he finally said, "Yes, I have. I've seen God."

He continued, with the soft presence of someone channeling something beyond himself:

"Every day, while going to the office, I see an old man fixing bicycles with such utter dedication. No regrets on his face. I've never found him sitting in sorrow when there's no customer around. Every time I pass by his shop, my head bows down– like yours does in a temple, or mine in a church.

Once, we exchanged smiles. It surprised him, I think. Since then, I still see him daily, but have never got the chance to say hi again. Still, sometimes… he gives me goosebumps. I see God in him."

He paused only for a second, then carried on with an unwavering calm:

"But not just him. I see God in the one-armed fruit vendor I always buy bananas from. In the old woman who sells coconuts and seasonal vegetables– always with that vivid, unshakable smile. In the night-duty security guard of our colony, whom you once found studying late at night when we returned home at 1 a.m., and again at occasional **6 a.m.**s when we go out for a run.

I've seen God in all of them– filling me with grace, with reverence. They inspire me to live more, to do more. And they give me a feeling… a special feeling that hasn't yet found its name, its adjective, or any popular identity, at least not to my knowledge."

His words had landed like poetry wrapped in everyday realism. His face didn't change; his eyes just stayed gently moist, sincere.

And then, with a small, quirky smile, he added, "Which God, by the way, are you talking about?"

At my core, I was completely captivated by his monologue. But I still remember how my naïve self and dabbling soul had argued with him anyway.

But not today, Benjamin. Today, I feel you. My heart whispered this softly, as I looked at Ganesh, remembering his brown, yet oddly pious smile.

Chapter – 11

Fellow Travelers

I slid the window open a crack, letting in a gust of humid night air, fragrant with the scent of damp earth and distant woodsmoke. The Nagercoil Express maintained its steady, rocking momentum, a different beast entirely from the frantic energy of the Nauchandi. Here, the evening had settled into a quiet domesticity. A few more berths down, a woman was tying jasmine flowers into her daughter's hair, the sweet perfume momentarily overpowering the train's metallic tang. They were getting ready for their stop, Salem, which was still more than an hour away. The excitement of meeting her cousins for the holidays, right after the exams! Outside, the dark silhouettes of what might have been mango groves or banana plantations slipped by under a sliver of moon.

It was this quiet order, this peaceful unfolding of a hundred small lives, that felt so alien. I'd forget, probably every ten minutes, that I was there on a mission, not as a traveller. To stay a ghost. To observe. But the quiet domesticity of this journey felt so profoundly different from the one that had ended just that morning. The faces on this train were passengers, retreating into their own private worlds. The faces on that train… they had been characters in a rolling drama. Unwittingly, they had been the first players in this new, terrifying chapter of my life. My mind drifted, pulled by the insistent memory of the men who had shared my space, my food, and a sliver of their souls with me. The 'Fantastic Four', as I had silently dubbed them. It all started with Ganesh's ridiculously cheerful, paan-stained smile…

BULANDSHAHR→ HAPUR → LUCKNOW

(DAY 1, NAUCHANDI EXPRESS)

…"I'm Ganesh, by the way. My friends call me Gannu," he had said, introducing himself in slightly broken English while subtly adjusting his underwear. For reasons only God might understand, I found myself making a fleeting attempt to catch a glimpse, trying to guess what colour he was sporting down there, recalling his friend Mr. Red-under.

His introduction was the perfect end to the day. He spontaneously declared that we were friends already, and I could call him Gannu. He looked at me with a twinkle in his eye, as if saying, "Now it's your turn!" Less than ten seconds had passed before his desperate vermilion teeth peeped out again, waiting eagerly for my reply.

Not that I didn't want to speak. I was just beginning to regain some momentum, coming back into the present, shaking off the sluggish, daydreaming state I'd been floating in. Add to that the background score of the train's relentless whistling, and people blocking the corridor with their asses, I just wasn't in the mood.

"Just a moment, brother," said a dry voice, belonging to a middle-aged someone– early forties, maybe– as he tried to fix his luggage on the side-upper berth, commanding us to halt mid-passage. His ugly belly bubbled out of his pants with every up-and-down motion. How long would his Gujarati-floral-print shirt hold that beast in, anyway?

This little sojourn gave Mr Gannu three full opportunities to flash that horrible grin of his.

"My name is Tarun Jayadevan," I finally muttered, mostly out of sheer compulsion, before he could beam at me one more time. I had already started developing a strong hatred for his smile, but then this tiny voice inside me piped up, "Hey, don't be so grumpy!"

Still annoyed to the core, just as I was about to yell, "Hey asshole, shut-the-fuck-up your grin already, would you?", my lips betrayed me with a peaceful, "My name is Tarun Jayadevan."

"Harish," came another voice. A second middle-aged man, slightly rounder than the first, passed a bag forward to be placed under the side-lower berth in the next cabin. Okay, at least now we had a name to go with the Gujarati floral-print shirt. Harish was clearly the fitter one between the two; hence, he took on the athletic responsibility of fixing both their bags. We even got a good peek at the valley between his butt cheeks as he crouched over, grinding down to stash the luggage under the berth. A performance worthy of a standing ovation, had we not been standing already.

"Very well! So, you're a South Indian, then!" Ganesh exclaimed, his excitement launching a misty spray of saliva directly onto Harish's floral shirt. The irony of that shirt, barely holding on to his overflowing stomach, worn by someone with a thoroughly flowerless face, was just too much. He had to be one of those local Baniyas from Hapur. Honestly, I would've preferred someone just vomited on him instead, for all the nuisance he had been so far.

But of course, why would he give us an inch of space to pass? That would break his sacred momentum.

"Sorry, brother, very, very sorry," Ganesh apologised, his voice sincere and slightly shrill.

In return, he received only an eye glare. No "It's okay." No "Hmm." Not even a dismissive wave. Just a plain, expressionless, soul-crushing glare. Over time, I had found this glare to be indigenous, exclusively native, to moderately educated, medium-build, middle-aged North Indian men, especially those hailing from towns orbiting Tier-1 or metro cities. When such men travelled, it was always sleeper class. This glare meant only one thing: I am definitely not okay with this shit, but I won't say a word.

I knew these men. They couldn't say 'It's okay'– their ego wouldn't allow that kind of forgiveness. But neither could they erupt into abuse, because they feared the brawl it might start. A public fight was a humiliation their fragile masculinity couldn't survive. Hence, the glare: a non-verbal middle path between rage and submission. Efficient, emotionless, and pointed.

Not that Ganesh was some intimidating figure either. He wasn't so well-built or fierce-looking that he could frighten a moderately educated, medium-build, middle-aged North Indian man.

It's just that this man, a middle-aged North Indian man living in a town near Tier-1 or metro cities, was already carrying the deadweight of so much frustration. Family. EMI. Back pain. Bosses. Vendors. Politics. Inflation. Cricket losses. Road rage. This heart. Diabetes. Hair loss stopped bothering him anymore, three years ago already. And now, keeping up with this just-turned-rich neighbour living in the metros, in his second home, a 3-BHK mortgaged apartment, who would come home every Diwali, flaunting his gadgets like prized medals.

And under all that, being perpetually pissed off at everything, he'd lost touch with the very legitimacy of his own anger. Forgotten his own strength. And thus, the pinnacle of that strength, ahead of any possible fight, would simply be that particular glare.

Now, if he'd been just a little less educated, or a little more Gurgaon-urban, his instinctive reaction would've involved the choicest mother-sister expletives, probably followed by a few shoves and punches from both parties. A full-on desi showdown.

Gladly, that didn't happen.

"So, you didn't tell– are you a South Indian? How come you were coming from Bulandshahr?" Ganesh continued.

"No… no, it's my native place. My father was in the Army, a Subedar. Back in the mid-nineties, he was posted at Wellington, a cantonment town in the Nilgiris district of Tamil Nadu. My mother was expecting me then. One of his seniors there, Colonel T. Jayadevan, was very dear to him, for his discipline, honesty, and that charismatic personality my father used to recall. He didn't know the Colonel's first name, so instead of naming me just 'T', he called me 'Tarun' and borrowed the surname - hoping I'd grow up to inherit some of his qualities."

"Woah, brother, so there's really a story you've got behind your name," Ganesh replied, eyes widening with awe. "Hope you lived up to your father's expectations, then!" he added with a flattering laugh. "Anyways, come…let me introduce you to my friends here."

Chapter – 12

The Difficulty of Knowing

The call of a bathroom break pulled me from my thoughts, a mental retreat back to the moon and to Ira. I made my way towards the lavatories at the end of the coach, the motion of the train steady under my feet. A short, orderly queue of two people stood waiting, their faces patient in the dim blue light of the corridor. A man emerged, nodded politely to the next person in line, and moved past. It was all so… civilised.

The simple, quiet courtesy of the scene struck me with an unexpected force, a stark contrast that instantly transported me back to the chaotic battleground of the Nauchandi Express lavatories just the night before. That memory, sharp and visceral, emerged without warning…

BULANDSHAHR→ HAPUR → LUCKNOW

(DAY 1, NAUCHANDI EXPRESS)

While the group continued their chatter, my bladder demanded a break from the moonlit sightseeing and the many memories of Ira.

Hurriedly, Ganesh stood up to follow. "Wait, I'm coming too," he said, flashing those dreaded maroon-stained teeth. I still hated it.

We walked towards the lavatories. All were occupied. Three minutes passed. No signs of life from inside.

How the hell could people shit day in, day out, morning till night, even at this hour? Why eat so much if you're going to shit it all out? Eat, shit. Eat, shit. These weren't people. They were pigs. I was really anxious, holding it inside.

I remembered my brief stint at an NCC camp (National Cadet Corps, the youth wing of the Indian Armed Forces) in early college days, courtesy of my father's stubborn insistence. One day, a fellow cadet raised his little finger to ask for a bathroom break. The instructor, an army man, denied it. "This is a test of your manhood," he'd barked. Apparently, the longer one could hold it, the more manly he was.

I never stepped foot on those parade grounds again. But somehow, that one ridiculous declaration stuck. Every time I had to really hold it in, like then, that belief came crawling back, and I'd start doubting my reproductive viability.

And so began the quiet war, between my pelvic muscles and an unverified definition of manhood.

Another two minutes passed. Finally, one of the doors creaked open. My analogy was bang-on, it wasn't a man. It was something closer to a male buffalo.

He emerged slowly, going through the motions of unhooking and re-hooking his pants, a process that barely tamed the rebellion of his stomach. His belly jiggled, a brief, silent protest as it tried its best to reach the floor. With all this glory on display, he brushed past me, his side belly grazing my bum.

No wonder Indian trains are always late, every seat's carrying the weight of two, slowing the whole journey.

I knew Ganesh was waiting too, probably just as desperate. But screw courtesy. I bolted. Didn't ask. Didn't look back.

Maybe I'd put my manhood to the test some other day.

Right now, I let that warm P-P stream flow through the toilet hole and onto the tracks, with all the satisfaction of defying both social grace and NCC masculinity myths.

When I came back, Ganesh was not there. He had probably gone into the other loo, I figured, so I stood by the compartment door, waiting for him. Amroha Junction had just passed, and now the train was running at full speed. Cold gusts of wind, a light head, no thoughts– none good, none bad– just peace. Nothing could compare to what I was feeling in that moment: joie de vivre after emptying the long-withheld bladder.

I looked up at the sky. The moon looked familiar. It brought back feelings I remembered vividly. With no clouds around to rob it of its right to spread this calming coolness across the world, the ineffable kingdom of moonlight seemed to have a story to tell.

A story from the mountains. A story from the place seekers go, hoping to find what they seek. A story from the Himalayas. And from the time when the future only mattered until next weekend. A story from when we were both nineteen, me and Ira.

Looking back, I can't say with certainty what it was I sought beneath those clear night skies, amid Himalayan peaks. But maybe fate was seeking me!

I sat down on the snow while the world slept. The clouds came for a moment, like companions. Darkness ruled. No human voices. No man-made sound. I could hear the rush of my bloodstream, and the soft, intermittent drip of dew falling from pointed pine leaves onto the snow nearby.

I wondered about the colour of this darkness that surrounded me. It wasn't black. Maybe grey. Maybe blue. Maybe violet, or red towards the east. Or a mixture of all, I couldn't tell.

Then the clouds drifted away. That fine line of luminous dark, where the sky met the jagged mountain peaks, appeared again.

By the eleventh beat of my heart, it was moonlight's kingdom once more, the very same I had just witnessed from inside the Nauchandi Express on its way to Lucknow.

Snow-covered peaks. Herb-mixed cold breeze. Unspoken sounds. That nature-composed smile on my face. There was so much I could have taken away from that night.

But all I took with me was the look in her eyes, locked into mine. This feeling at nineteen! With Ira.

She was nature. My mountain.

Maybe what they said was true, maybe wishes were heard in the lap of the mysterious Parvati Valley. Maybe seekers did find what they were looking for.

And maybe that's why I saw her. Up close. Right there. Ira.

I wasn't the first to speak of the mountains' beauty. I won't be the last either. But there I was– some 13,000 feet closer to the Sun– when a gust of warmth passed through me, when I heard her voice for the first time.

"Hey, can I sit here too?" she asked.

As if the weight of the world had suddenly pressed on my chest and lifted the next moment, my breath stopped. A small nod was all I could manage.

Though it felt like a lifetime, we sat there for maybe fifteen minutes. Once, her shoulder brushed mine. Twice, a few strands of her hair floated into my face, all thanks to the Indian deity Pawan Deva, the God of Wind. No words. Just two silhouettes sharing a plain stare into the darkness.

"Okay, so… thanks," she stood up. "I felt suffocated. I have this problem… umm… anyway, it's okay now. I'll go back to my tent. Thank you!" She said it all in one breath.

Numb, I only blinked. I doubt she even saw that.

I was living my once-upon-a-time moment. Racing heartbeats. Heavy breaths. Trembling limbs. That cold-hot-cold feeling surging through me, that odd mix of panic and magic, reassured me it was all real. Ah, those teenage feelings.

Within moments, it slowed again. This was the time I should've said something.

Standing straight, she squeezed her shoulders, half-expecting a word from me. I didn't speak. I couldn't.

Time felt like it was slipping. Like I was running alongside a train, just feet away, seconds from missing it. A fancied train to the pious land of once-upon-a-time.

"Ooh…kay," she sighed once more, softly, and turned to leave.

I watched her go. Then finally, gathering everything I had, "Hey!" I called out.

She turned back.

"Good night," I said.

She waved. Maybe she smiled too.

And I watched her until my eyes could follow no more, until the tent swallowed her silhouette whole.

A story from the mountains, where the moon shone just as bright as this very night.

"Why are you making this a scene, brother?" Ganesh's voice cut through the quiet, stirring me from the folds of Ira. Ira Acharya. Ira– like the Goddess, ever watchful, with eyes that saw more than most.

"What's the matter, Ganesh?" I turned back and moved towards him.

Another man, probably late in his thirties, stood in the passage connecting the two compartments, one foot already in the air-conditioned coach, Ganesh remaining on the sleeper side.

Without budging, the man snapped, "It's because of people like you that people like us have to suffer." His face twisted further with disdain. "Why can't you just use the lavatories in your own compartment?"

To my relief, I could tell this was going to be nothing more than a dog-bark fight.

This wasn't just an argument about toilets. It never was. It was the eternal standoff: Us versus Them. I'd seen it before. We had all witnessed it. Religion, caste, gender, designation, category, there was always some new metric of imagined superiority. Even the Second World War hadn't been spared that disease.

Ganesh glanced at me and subtly signalled me to stay back. "I'm really sorry, sir, if it caused you any inconvenience," he said, voice calm, face composed.

But instead of cooling down, the man only grew louder, like an engine that can't idle, feeding on its own fumes.

Clearly, he didn't want peace. He'd already gotten an apology, what else did he need? And then I saw it. He wasn't listening. He hadn't heard a word Ganesh said. That's what anger does, it deafens, it blinds, it consumes you.

His toddler daughter, who'd been standing beside him the entire time, tugged at his fingers, quietly urging him back to their seats.

Just then, the other lavatory door opened, on the sleeper-coach side.

A teenager stepped out, half-asleep. He looked at us briefly, washed his hands, adjusted his hair, carefully shaping the strand above his right ear, and then walked off. Into the air-conditioned coach.

We all watched it quietly. The toddler looked at the man. The man looked at Ganesh. Ganesh looked at me. And I looked at the man.

All in a single second.

Without meaning to, I let out a half-laugh. The man shot me one of those classic indigenous glares.

The toddler tugged at his fingers again. He looked at her. And in about five seconds, he disappeared into his dungeon.

Both of us had just witnessed a giant man being dwarfed by the open heart of a little child.

"His daughter needed to use the loo," Ganesh said, turning towards me, anticipating the outburst I hadn't yet started.

"You know how kids are, right? So when I came out and walked towards our coach, it ticked him off. It's fine."

I was stunned, not just by his calm, but by his clarity.

What would I have done if I were in his place?

He stood at the door, extending his left hand into the rushing cold wind.

Droplets of air-mist slid across his palm, all the way to his fingertips– until they vanished into the night.

"You know," he started, looking out into the dark, "my father used to ask me this question as a kid, 'Who are we?'"

"'Brahmin,' I'd always say. My grandfather was particular about such things."

"Hearing me say that, my father would scrunch up his face– he hated it."

Ganesh paused. "Now I know why." He sighed.

Then he turned slightly, his tone sharpening, not bitter, just real.

"What we just saw here… on the surface, sure, it looks like the man was tired, annoyed, whatever. But if you look deeper– it's Us vs. Them. As if we're two different species. Segregated by the resources we hold, governed by something as silly as money.

Fighting for survival, without realising, if we fought together, we'd all survive better."

I didn't have to reply.

Strangely enough, my brain had just processed the same thought, only in different words.

"When I decided to become a theatre artist," Ganesh began, "my biggest motivation was my father. I chose not to carry an identity defined by beliefs my soul couldn't accept. Not that I disliked anything about my roots, in fact, I'm proud of them. I just wanted to understand them."

"I read the Vedas, the Ramayana, the Mahabharata… all the great epics. Met gurus, wept at their feet. And ten years later, I finally learned the one thing my father was trying to teach me."

"What?" I asked, leaning in.

He didn't answer right away. Instead, he tore open a pan masala sachet, stuffed it into his mouth, chewed slowly, then turned his head and let out the first red stream from his lips. Only then did he speak:

"That there's just one: in everything. Us, them, it… all running on the same energy."

He pointed towards the lavatories and chuckled. "Damn, we even shit the same!"

I didn't respond. This wasn't a new idea. I had heard it from many babas, saints, self-declared philosophers.

"And," he continued, spitting again, "you can't get it by logic. You get it through love. Through devotion." He looked at me. "You just… get it, when the time comes."

And then there was silence again. A full couple of minutes. Just the hum of the rails and the cold wind brushing past us.

"So, you're a theatre artist!" I exclaimed, trying to shift the conversation, gesturing with my hands as we started walking back to our seats.

"Any doubts?" he shot back instantly, grinning, pulling me into the play, making me a sport in his scene.

As we walked, a thought quietly drifted through my mind:

Maybe knowing was never enough. Maybe understanding was what really mattered. And maybe… the words of wisdom haven't changed over the years at all, it's just that their meanings unfold differently for each of us, in our own time, in our own way.

Returning to my own berth after the bathroom break on the Nagercoil Express, the contrast was jarring. The quiet, the order, the unspoken respect for shared space, it was a different world. Ganesh's words echoed in my mind. "You just get it, when the time comes." On that chaotic journey, I had started to get it. I had seen past the dirt and the noise to the shared humanity beneath. Now, on this silent, tense journey south, I had to do it again. I had to see past the mission, past the threat, and truly see the people I was trying to protect. Understanding, I was beginning to realise, wasn't just tough; it was the entire point.

Chapter – 13

Oneness

The train continued its relentless push south. It was past 10 p.m. already, and Salem was still the next stop. The train was delayed. Once again, I had walked the length of my assigned coaches– S10, S11, and the AC coach B1– my senses sharp and focused. It was already my fifth visit since the start of the journey. But everything was quiet. Too quiet. Just like countless other Indian train journeys. Families were settled down; a group of young college boys were playing a board game, their laughter muted. In B1, the silence was even more noticeable, the gentle snores of a few passengers the only sound breaking the hum of the air-conditioning. This calm, this veneer of normalcy, somehow felt more unnerving than open conflict, especially after Jayadevan Sir's half-cryptic message. Why did he say he and the rest of the gang were delayed?

Moreover, this quiet was a stark contrast to the passionate, chaotic debates that had defined my previous journey just the previous night. It was unbecoming of me to find disquiet in quiet.

Returning to my berth in S11, I watched a family across the aisle share their food. There was a silent dignity in the way the mother served her husband and children, a simple act of care that felt profound in the dim light of the coach. The scene pulled me back, triggering the memory of another meal shared among strangers, a meal that had spiralled into a fierce debate about the very soul of the nation. I remembered Sahoo's fiery passion, Verma's cool pragmatism, and the unexpected wisdom of a man we had all dismissed. The memory rushed back, vibrant and clear…

BULANDSHAHR→ HAPUR → LUCKNOW
(DAY 1, NAUCHANDI EXPRESS)

…I took a cursory look around as Ganesh and I walked back to our seats and noticed that the old man still just couldn't let go of the lovebirds having their own time. How in the seven heavens could a man keep such an unyielding face for so long?

One of the gentlemen who had boarded the train from Hapur Junction seemed to be a self-proclaimed, half-baked young life consultant. I'd been hearing his nasal voice non-stop, blabbering over the phone ever since and dishing out tired old adages to some poor soul at the other end. One of many comic tragedies you would find unfolding on Indian Railways.

The other guy, a veterinarian, had already established himself as the beloved "uncle-next-door" of the entire coach. Every basti, mohalla, or colony has one of his kind, the type who knows every household's dog by name; to whom your mother would always ask the whereabouts of the vegetable vendor whom she had just heard shouting "Sabji le lo" from inside the house; who fondly reminds all aunties when the milkman is on strike, and warns everyone to fill water tanks before the power cut hits. The kind who insists on helping the postman, even though the postman knows every address by heart, and gets mocked as a village idiot by the local gossip gang for being an "over-doer". And the one who, even after knowing that people called him names, would still be the first to help your guests navigate the shortest way to your house.

I already had a soft spot for such people, the rare breed who manage to keep the balance of the world intact with their inconvenient kindness. I could see God in him, the same way my roommate, Benjamin, used to say.

It still amazes me how that fellow, Benjamin, could see God in everyone. "We're all made of the same mitti– the God mitti– then how can we be different?" he would say. "We all have just one identity."

Once, in the first year of college in Lucknow, he had asked me to stop by the roadside near a dusty old bus stand. A municipality water-supply pipe was leaking there, sending out a playful arc of sparkling water that had already gathered a curious crowd of stray dogs, thirsty crows, and the occasional paan-chewing rickshawalah rinsing his hands.

"You see that water flowing from the pipe?" Benjamin said, his voice turning firm, eyes fixed on the leak like it was a holy sight. "It's the same water that flows into the fountain of the Shiv temple down that lane, the one where I bow before the idol every Monday, and also into the water tap behind the church I attend on Sundays."

He was a Lucknow localite. Born into a house where religion came in twos, his father a staunch Catholic, his mother a devout Hindu, Benjamin had grown up flipping between a crucifix and a kalash, chanting shlokas in the morning and singing hymns by evening. Naturally, questions came early. And when his conscience outgrew the narrow lanes of inherited belief his parents had drafted for him, he began carving his own path.

"My mother and father always insisted on the sacredness of their waters. Temple jal for Maa, holy water in a silver bowl for Dad. Sometimes, I used to visit both places one after the other, half out of love, half to keep them both off my back. Then one day, I went on my usual rounds and found no water at either place. Not even a drop. Some municipal repair work had choked the supply, I was told."

"I was eleven or twelve, I think. Curious, I followed the trail of the pipeline. And that's when I realised, both temple and church drew their holy waters from the exact same source. Same pipe, same origin, same end. It only became 'ours' and 'theirs' once it entered those holy gates."

He paused there, his eyes softening, the wind carrying a strange calmness around us.

"In that moment," he continued, "I knew. Water– untainted, indifferent, and giving– that was the real God."

And then, right there by the roadside, as motorbikes honked and vendors shouted over chai and cigarette smoke, Benjamin gently bowed his head. Not to any idol, not to any altar, but to the very gush of leaking water that sparkled under the late afternoon sun.

The bow encompassed both gods at once.

Back then, I didn't understand him. Not even a shred.

We were already reaching our seats; still, Shukla instructed us to join him, calling us with quick, jerky hand gestures.

"You check the data," Sahoo was saying, his voice animated. "Half of India's population, half, depends on agriculture, directly or indirectly. And yet, their contribution to the GDP stays stuck at less than one-fifth. You want bigger proof of disparity than that?"

His words fell heavy. Verma, lounging near the window, seemed unbothered, like someone waiting for his chai to cool.

Ganesh and I looked at Shukla, seeking context.

"Verma says poverty in India is self-inflicted," Shukla muttered under his breath, face blank. "He thinks people are poor because they don't want to work. Sahoo… well, he takes that stuff personally. Comes from a background like that himself."

"Exactly what I'm saying," Verma jumped back in, spitting a red streak of paan masala through the grilled window. "Why do they cling to agriculture? We have schools, colleges… why not just study and do something better?"

"Because not everyone is born with a silver spoon like you," Sahoo shot back. "And not everyone gets to be the white tiger in a slum like your father. Try pulling water from a dry well and then talk."

Verma scoffed, brushing imaginary dust off his sleeve. "Then stop complaining. Stay where you are and keep crying over fate. Curse the government, light another candle, whatever suits."

"Ah, now you sound like the perfect logical engineering graduate," Sahoo deadpanned, a faint smirk hiding behind a tight jaw.

"So why don't you bless me with your IAS logic then?" Verma said with a mock tilt of his head, flashing the kind of thin smile you'd find carved on a knife.

Sahoo inhaled deeply, long and hard, like someone drinking in silence instead of firing back. And just like that, the argument ended.

And then came Mr Vajpai ji, in his weird, tipsy stance, his gaze flicking back and forth between the two, absolutely clueless, like someone who woke up in the middle of a jungle after sleeping in his cosy bed the night before.

Sahoo was about to say something when Mr Vajpai ji gently held his hand and raised a finger, asking for permission to speak.

"If I may," he began, almost in a whisper, "I believe the root of this whole mess started decades ago, around the time of the Green Revolution."

Groaning slightly, he shifted from his half-slouched pose into a more upright sitting position, adjusting the shawl draped lazily over his shoulder like a late-winter priest.

"Before the 1970s," he continued, voice slow and scratchy, "India's farm produce was modest. But then came the Green Revolution, bumper crops, overflowing godowns. Still, nothing changed for the small farmer. You know why? Because the key to that success was High Yield Variety seeds, HYVs. Great for productivity, yes, but they demanded high capital. Fertilisers, irrigation, machinery… you name it."

We all leaned in slightly, surprised by the unexpected gravitas of the drunkard from a few hours ago.

"Small farmers," he went on, "had no choice but to borrow. Loans from sahukars, microfinance guys, even moneylenders who smelled interest from a mile away. One harvest, two harvests… the debt just kept mounting. They managed their do waqt ki roti, but the dream of a better life? Always just out of reach. And those who somehow escaped the debt trap–well, they didn't know what came next. No roadmap. No guidance. Blame it on the lack of education, perhaps."

He paused, catching his breath, then coughed, wet and long. All of us exchanged glances; no one said a word.

"And," he resumed in a softer tone, his eyes now glassy and his voice even more drained, "during the Green Revolution, the whole focus was on crop yield, and rightly so. People were starving. But when the granaries filled up, the attention shifted to the environmental impact, chemicals, groundwater depletion, soil erosion. That too, perhaps, needed looking into."

He paused again, this time staring somewhere into the blur of the night outside.

"But what never truly entered the conversation," he added, "was the socio-economic impact. No one asked how the small farmer fared. Sure, temporary band-aids were applied, loan waivers, subsidies, election-season sympathy, but over time, these remedies haven't really changed much, have they?"

Just then, another violent coughing fit took over. He fumbled for his steel water bottle and sipped. We all waited, half-expecting more gems to spill from his mouth. But instead, he lay back against the seat, head rolling to one side, and within seconds, the man was snoring like a bullock cart over gravel.

All we could do was share glances of pure astonishment.

"What the hell did he drink?" Shukla blurted out, half-laughing.

"I swear I didn't understand a dime," Ganesh added, giggling. "Please don't make him talk again, or I'll end up scratching my scalp bald!"

"So, you're preparing for the IAS?" I asked Sahoo. "By the way, what do you all do, professionally? Never really got a chance to ask."

"Yes, I'm preparing for the civil services. Verma runs his father's company. Shukla is a bank PO. And Ganesh… well, he's a theatre artist," Sahoo replied, deliberately stressing the word "father's" while shooting Verma a side-eye, making sure we all got the point, that the company wasn't exactly self-made.

"And I… am an associate professor at the Allahabad Agriculture Institute," Vajpai ji announced out of nowhere, suddenly springing up from his nap like a jack-in-the-box. The words had barely left his lips before he collapsed back into the seat, snoring again, as if the burst of academia had drained all remaining battery.

"Seriously, what stuff is this guy high on?" Shukla muttered, shaking his head.

I looked at them, perplexed, a little hesitant, and finally said what had been quietly gnawing at me for a while. "Sorry, guys… I'm just a bit confused. Don't take it the wrong way, but you all are so educated, aware: I mean, IAS, a company owner, bank PO, professor… And yet, you spit paan, litter on the floor like it's nothing. Why?"

The four of them looked at one another and broke into a knowing smile. And then, almost in unison, as if rehearsed: "Because, damn, we are rebels!"

"Bhai, chewing paan and masala is an old habit," Ganesh chimed in with a chuckle. "A gift from our ancestors, and from this mitti. This isn't going anywhere anytime soon."

"And the littering?" I asked, raising an eyebrow.

"Haha! That… was just a one-time thing. A social experiment," Ganesh explained, with a half-guilty, half-theatrical shrug. "An idea I had for a new show I'm working on. Wanted to observe who, if anyone, would actually stop us. How they'd react. You've seen it yourself, we've been on this train for hours now, and not a single person has stepped up. Not one."

He paused, and looked at me with a gentle smirk.

"Not even you did."

I exhaled, shaking my head slowly, my face caught somewhere between confusion and reluctant amusement.

"Really tough for me to understand all this," I sighed, more to myself than anyone else.

"True… but you did judge us, didn't you?" Ganesh pointed out immediately, his voice soft, smile still kind, eyes steady. "It's easier anyway," he added, almost like a gentle jab.

Shukla chuckled. "But I only agreed with Ganesh because sometimes… it just feels good doing so!"

"Doing what? Becoming a nuisance and damaging public property?" I quipped back, a trace of sarcasm escaping with my words.

"Nope," Shukla replied, his face suddenly a notch more serious. "It's like… putting a hammer to this corrupted system. Since I can't cause any real damage, my conscience won't let me, but these cheap acts, these little rebellions - They let me vent. They make me feel like I've shouted back at something that's been shouting at me for years."

There was a heaviness in his words now, a kind of pressure that made his voice sound like it was straining between his teeth. Apparently, he had lost an officer-rank job at the Railways, as Ganesh told me later, due to some bureaucratic blunder, the one he never stopped thinking about. And now he was stuck with the role of a Bank Probationary Officer, which didn't exactly thrill his soul.

"That's why I keep telling you all, just shift to Europe while you still can," Verma interjected casually, as if offering vacation plans.

"And that'll solve everything, will it?" Sahoo fired back.

"No. But maybe it'll solve something for you. Why try to fix the whole world? Just fix your own life."

"Okay… okay… okay," Ganesh suddenly rose, waving his hand like a referee calling time on a heated match. "Maybe someone has to fix the world… or maybe no one has to..."

He turned, walking a few steps down the aisle, stretching his arms with the ease of a man who had just ended a street play.

"…but we've got the whole night to figure that out, haven't we?"

The train rumbled gently underneath us. A baby cried somewhere down the coach. And a chaiwala's distant voice rang faintly through the corridor.

We were rebels, fools, thinkers, and drifters, all packed into one moving iron shell. And the night was still young.

There came a moment when all four of them were in my direct sight, and something passed through me, like a drop of truth, caught only in the blink of an eye. Maybe… maybe they were all the same. As if they were placed there, together, by some design of fate for a common goal. The emotions were different, yes, but the core, it felt singular. Anger in one. Kindness in the other. Passion in the third. And a certain careless detachment in the fourth.

For the first time in my life, I could clearly differentiate the feelings on the outside from the person on the inside, the inside that felt the same in everyone.

"We're all the same," Benjamin's words rang in my ears. I felt them floating, winding through the feelings of the day, moving and rearranging something within me. Creating sensations, sharp, vivid. And in that vividness, every cell of my body seemed to align to a single pulse.

How could this be? Us all, being the same?

Was this a mystery to be untangled by science? Or something to be soaked in slowly, like philosophy, never solved, only surrendered to?

"Sometimes, you can only feel it through love," a voice filtered through my thoughts.

It was that life consultant from Hapur Junction again, still at it over the phone, still dissecting emotions as if they were code. "Just love… and nothing else!" he concluded with the finality of a man who'd solved everything in a line.

I glanced out of the window. A half-lit factory blurred past. The air smelled of iron and smoke. Inside, the Fantastic Fours were tidying up, sheets, pillows, slippers, getting ready for the night's surrender to sleep.

And somewhere between their beds, and my thoughts, and the hum of the train, a part of me curled into stillness, questioning, if we're all the same, then who was I?

The memory dissolved back into the present moment on the Nagercoil Express. The train felt different now, less like a container of anonymous threats and more like a vessel carrying countless stories, countless struggles. Sahoo's idealism, Verma's pragmatism, Shukla's simmering rebellion, and Ganesh's profound kindness, they weren't just characters anymore. They were frameworks for understanding the world I was now sworn to protect.

The question, how can we all be just one?– wasn't just a philosophical musing anymore. It was a strategic imperative. Maybe, to defeat whoever was behind those explosions, I had to understand what fueled them to choose that path, their anger, their motivations… and just maybe, their lives too.

That first journey hadn't just been a ride; it was the start of my true discovery.

Chapter – 14

Who Was I?

The train moved through the deep south of India with a gentle, rhythmic thump, a hypnotic mantra in the dark. The conversations of the night before, the memory of Sahoo's passion and Verma's cynicism, still echoed in my mind. The final question from that journey– if we're all the same, then who was I?– had lingered. It felt more urgent now, here in the quiet of this sleeper coach, on a mission that had been thrust upon me because of a life I never knew my parents lived.

Staring at my own faint reflection in the window, a pale outline against the rushing black, the question returned, sharp and insistent. For years, I had built a persona, a shield. Average Bittu. The boy in the middle. But that identity had been shattered. Stripped of the story I told myself, who was left? The memory wasn't just a memory anymore; it was an interrogation. I closed my eyes, and the story of the question began to unfold.

BULANDSHAHR→ HAPUR → LUCKNOW (DAY 1, NAUCHANDI EXPRESS)

…Looking at all the fantastic fours in my direct sight, a strange sense of peace settled in, staring out at the darkness rushing backwards outside the Nauchandi Express. What's my identity?

What's my identity? I asked myself, reflecting on this journey, my entire life in a single breath.

Average Bittu.

That's what all my friends called me. Average Bittu. Not in a mean or mocking way– just one of those nicknames that stick with your close ones. From the earliest days, it followed me around like a second skin. I even embraced it. Whenever I'd call my childhood gang– Shiva, Chandu, and Adrien– from the Lucknow institute's landline, I'd say, "AB this side," as if that abbreviation somehow gave weight to the nickname.

I was a single child, born in Bulandshahr. The toddler years were a blur of moves– Delhi, Chandigarh, Shimla, the landmarks of a government job trail. Then came Kolkata when I was nine or ten, and finally, the most golden stretch– my teenage years– spent in Pantnagar, Uttarakhand.

That place... those days… they shimmer in memory like a sun-drenched photograph.

I stayed in Pantnagar till I turned eighteen, the official age of consent, or as the government calls it, adulthood. Then, like a tossed coin, my parents moved back to Kolkata, while I ended up in Lucknow for higher education. Why Lucknow?

Because my father was supposed to be transferred there. But life had other plans-he was recalled to Kolkata.

And me? I stayed on. Tired of shifting like furniture with every new transfer order, I decided to anchor myself. So, Lucknow stuck.

Thanks to my father's transferable job, I grew up everywhere, and yet, somehow, belonged nowhere. Or maybe... I belonged everywhere. I'm still unsure if there's any difference between the two.

But it all started from a local stationery shop in Pantnagar. I went to buy a notebook once. It came in three types– small, medium, and large– both in size and in the number of pages. "Which one?" the shopkeeper asked. "Uh… average– the medium one."

The next day, it was a pen. "Three rupees, five, or ten?" "The five one," I said, almost automatically.

It became a pattern. Anything I went to buy, I'd always pick the one priced in the middle. Strangely, I never noticed it myself. But Shiva– an A-hole of a friend if there ever was one– spotted it long before I did.

We were at a sports shop once, looking for a tennis ball. I was still scanning the aisle when he turned to the shopkeeper with a wicked grin. "He's a middle guy, uncle. If you've got three options, just hand him the one that costs in the middle!"

The shopkeeper laughed. I wished for the floor to open and swallow me. But the bastard was right. That was me. That is me. And yes, I still bought the one that costs the middle.

Maybe it was my way of hiding. We couldn't afford the expensive stuff. And buying the cheapest, one-well, that felt like announcing my poverty with a megaphone. So I always settled for the middle, the safe zone. It didn't matter whether the middle option worked better than the cheapest one. I just needed to blend in. Not be noticed. Not be judged. That's how I learned to be invisible.

On some days, I told people my father was an Army officer, not just a Subedar. On others, my mother became a "working woman," even though she wasn't. And on a particularly fine day, we magically owned three houses and a big estate back in Bulandshahr.

None of my friends ever knew. Then again, none of them ever cared. They were real ones. I wasn't.

Not that my life was some tragic, grey-tinted melodrama. Life gave me happiness– plenty of it. Almost every day. Buckets full. But everything always felt… predictable. Cliché. So painfully similar.

I cannot say we were the poorest of the poor. Nor can I say I had a particularly comfortable life.

I didn't have a multimedia phone, but I did have a phone. Branded clothes were a luxury, but my clothes were always clean. I had friends– not sure if they were the best ones– but I wasn't ever alone. No sworn enemies either.

I was never angry at my destiny. Never raged against society. Never cursed the government. I had no ideological standoffs with anyone, no grand beliefs to defend. I followed no idol. I believed in no ideal. I didn't have a favorite dish. Or a favorite place.

It never really mattered if I liked someone. And it didn't matter much if I didn't.

Not that I was sad– not really. And maybe I wasn't particularly confident, or especially happy either. But I did sleep better as a child. That much I remember.

And then, one day– just like that– I heard it over the phone: My mother had died.

The fever got serious, they said.

She was in Kolkata. I was in Lucknow. And I can't even remember our last conversation. There was no clear memory. Just a void.

She died on a Sunday. By Tuesday, my father was back on duty.

Only her ashes made it to our hometown.

I think I blamed him. Or maybe he wasn't to blame at all. Maybe... if only she had been admitted to a better hospital. What if? But what if she was in a good hospital already?

After she died, I fought with my father. And after that... we just sort of went quiet.

Maybe I owed him an apology. Or maybe I didn't. Maybe I could have been the one to break the ice.

Then I met Ira. And suddenly, many things started to matter.

We met in college. She studied History. I studied Chemistry. We both got average marks– But there was a difference: she loved the arts. I... never loved science. I was just, well, average.

Somewhere deep down, I knew I had wronged my father. I had wronged my mother. My friends. My family. This entire life.

And yet– amid all that guilt-there was love too. Love for Ira. A strange warmth that coexisted with shame. I still owe it to my father, maybe.

Three years later, I returned to Bulandshahr for the first time since my mother passed. I wanted to talk to him. Shout at him. Fight with him. Hug him.

Tell him how I used to fake his introduction-calling him an "officer" to impress my friends, when all he ever was… was honest.

Tell him how much I'd missed him all these years. How I was sorry. So, so sorry.

I could've said it the day he left for Kolkata. But even then, I judged him. Thought it was too much travel for just a Subedar. The apology could wait, I told myself.

It didn't come. And I became a fugitive– Only to become a prisoner of my own guilt.

Forever.

He never returned. Only his uniform did.

And then– just like that– Ira was gone too.

We were on this same train.

She boarded from Saharanpur. I boarded at Hapur. And we both were off to Lucknow.

My father dropped me at the station first, before he left in his army jeep. "Take care. I'll catch my train from Delhi. Hopefully, I'll come visit you in Lucknow on my way back." Those were his last words.

I remember feeling happy at that moment. As if nothing was left to hide. As if all the burdens I carried… had quietly lifted.

All laughing and talking, Ira and I stood by the gate of Coach S4. The same Nauchandi Express. Moradabad Junction was approaching already.

And the next ten minutes… they still feel like a dream. Like they never happened. Like they never should have.

The train was about to stop. It had slowed just enough for me to get down. I stepped off– smiling, waving to Ira– signaling that I'd be right back. She loved tea. I wanted Parle-G.

I paid the vendor. Two tea cups in both hands. Parle-G stuffed in my left pocket. Right pocket swollen– phone and wallet packed tight. I never kept them in the back pocket. Not at Indian railway stations. "As if my ass had turned sides from back to front"– a last laugh still echoing in my head from that night.

And then… I saw him, my father. Or maybe I thought I saw him– as others kept telling me later.

Wasn't he supposed to be in Delhi by now?

There he was– walking fast, in the opposite direction of the moving train. Phone to his ear. Eyes scanning the coaches like he was searching for someone.

I followed. Tried to match his pace. Even tried to outpace him. But he was too fast. I still couldn't see his face clearly-yet something in me knew. It was him.

Then, hardly a minute later-a sudden burst of sparks. A loud screeching sound.

I looked back immediately. Everyone nearby did.

The train had started moving– It didn't even complete its scheduled stop.

And then, another sound-sharp and metallic, like a blacksmith slamming his hammer against an anvil attached to a loudspeaker.

A sudden flash-scintillation on the platform. People began rushing, fast, in every direction. Before I could make sense of it, there was a flicker of fire near the wheels of a coach– probably the one next to ours.

I was still a few coaches behind. The train was already picking up speed. And now that I could see clearly– the fire was right below the door where Ira had been standing.

But she wasn't there.

One more sound. Louder. Sharper. Then– a full-blown stampede.

I tried climbing back onto the train, but others were pushing to get off. The speed of the train increased.

A few more seconds– and then someone leapt off the moving train, crashing into me.

I fell. Hard. My thighs screamed in pain. My forehead slammed into the platform.

Lying on my stomach, I watched the train disappear.

The sparks– they kept growing brighter. The train– faster.

I managed to glance back, half-conscious-half-hopeful.

Maybe my father would come and pick me up.

But nobody came.

The train was gone.

Looking back, I still ask myself- could I really not have caught that train?

What if I were just a little stronger, not this average– maybe I could've moved faster, reached her in time.

What if I had just a bit more courage? Did I try hard enough? Did I even try?

Had my conscience sensed danger? Did some part of me know not to get on? Or did I just give up too soon?

Could I have done more? Did I not love Ira enough?

But… she was all I had.

Wasn't she?

The train was gone, out of sight.

I stood up. The chaos around me had begun to recede, at least to the eye.

I didn't know what to do. Still dazed, I began to run towards the end of the platform, as if I could still catch it. As if running would somehow undo it.

But all I found was darkness hugging the railway tracks.

My fingers were sticky– with spilled tea and sugar, a result of the chaos.

Snapping back a little, I searched my pockets.

Right one-empty. Left-just crushed biscuit crumbs.

Numb. Emotions blurred. I couldn't even name what I was feeling.

I turned back-searched for my phone, my wallet. Wandered aimlessly for half an hour.

Nothing.

Eventually, I sat beside the tea vendor. So many thoughts. So many memories.

Ira. My mother. My father. Friends from every city I'd ever called home.

I glanced around the station-still hoping, somehow, to see my father.

But now I wasn't even sure if the man I saw… was really him.

How could he have been here? He should've been on his way to Kolkata.

But if he was here– if that was truly him– I would have told him how sorry I was. I would have told him I loved him.

And as my voice cracked within, as my hands trembled in the memory of her fingers-I whispered aloud, to no one, to the world, "I wish I could've told you this while you were here, Ma… I love you. So much."

Feelings, memories, thoughts… so many of them. I spent the night at the station, the same place.

It felt like a bad dream when I woke up early the next morning, as if it had never happened. I wish it never had. But probably, I was at the receiving end of God's fury. It was all true.

Travelling without a ticket till Hapur Junction, and borrowing rides from there without a penny on me, I reached my hometown, Bulandshahr.

Bought a new SIM card. Bought a new phone. And dialed Ira's number.

Eight digits. I typed eight digits. Despite my best efforts– I could not recollect her phone number.

How could this be possible? A number I could recite in my sleep– I just couldn't remember it.

I started dialing random numbers, relying on memory and instinct. No voice of Ira returned.

I even got this new SIM card ported to my original number, thinking maybe, just maybe, she'd call me back.

And I waited. I knew she was never on social media, but still, I searched for her everywhere.

How could it be so difficult to find someone in this connected world? I waited for her call, with a plan to leave for Lucknow the next evening, to look for her in college.

Nobody called the entire day.

The next morning, the phone rang. All excited– "it must be her!" I ran to it. But life, I think, had worse to offer.

"Son, this is T. Jayadevan."

I heard the man's voice for the first time, even though I had known of him and heard about him since forever.

"There was an accident here. The Jeep's brakes failed. Your father…they all fell off the Howrah Bridge. I'm sorry."

No other phone call came the entire day. Yet again.

The next morning, a box came– with my father's belongings. His uniform. Some badges. Some papers. Bank statements.

The man who delivered it promised everything that was needed for my care.

The bank statements showed he had saved some good money. Definitely no less than being rich.

But how did it matter? He was gone. Just like my mother.

How did it matter if he didn't use that money for my mother's care when she needed it the most?

I cursed him. Again. Cursed him for letting my mother go so early. Cursed him for letting himself go as well.

Loss. What do people know of loss? What do they know of love? What was the purpose of their existence? My existence? Am I even needed here?

It felt as if the entire world had fallen away-nothing made sense. Where should I go now? What should I do?

I never recollected Ira's number, nor did I ever hear back from her.

After mother, it was Ira's magic that brought light into this life. And now, even that is gone too.

I think I became tough. Harsher. Stopped believing in anyone, anything.

With best friends-I started using sarcasm, jokes, as defense. And strangers? They were all just sons of bitches who should've died the day they were born.

It was a fucked-up world-the system, the government, this society.

I never felt love again like I did for Ira. Still kind of searched for her in every face I saw.

Searched for her to save me from this slow, relentless despair.

Years passed. And I waited.

Was I waiting for her? Or just for the pain to subside?

Was I still the average one-the middling-as Shiva would say?

But I was definitely not the T. Jayadevan I was supposed to become. Or… was I?

This entire life whipped by me in an instant as I kept staring at the darkness outside the moving train.

To my surprise, all these memories drifted by like white clouds on an autumn afternoon.

I felt nothing. No gloom. No sorrow. No happiness. Just a profound blankness.

There was no happiness either.

Could I have changed anything? Stopped any of it? Done something more?

What was I becoming?

My eyes opened. The train was still moving, the world outside still dark. This journey, unlike the last, was not about uncovering the past. It was about facing the future. The story of 'Average Bittu' was over. He had been a construct, a shield built from fear and loss. The man who was left, Tarun or T. Jayadevan, was still a stranger to himself. But he was ready to find out who he was, not by looking back, but by moving forward.

As the train's horn blared, signalling our approach to Salem Junction, the spell of the past finally broke. A few passengers began to stir, rustling through their bags. The girl with the white jasmine flowers in her hair, now slightly wilted, was already awake, her mother helping her with a suitcase. The present, with all its immediate tension, returned. I checked my phone. No new texts from Trishulin sir. My heart pounded in my chest a little faster. I tried calling him, but the call went straight to voicemail. The station approached. Lights streaked past the window. As the train slowed, my eyes scanned the platform, searching for any anomaly, any face that seemed out of place. A family got down. A young couple came onboard. My eyes couldn't discern anything. What and who was I even looking for?

Just as a tight knot of anxiety formed in my stomach, my phone chimed. A text. "I'll keep you posted when the team is aboard. Nothing to worry." It was from Trishulin Sir. A wave of reassurance washed over me. I took a deep breath, the tension easing slightly. This was the job now. Waiting. Watching. I got up and began to walk the length of my three assigned coaches again, my gaze sweeping over each passenger, my mind alert. The journey into the unknown continued.

PART B:
JOURNEY TO CONSEQUENCE

Chapter – 15

The Alchemist's Apprentice

While I was hurtling south on Nagercoil express into the darkness, and sinking into the ghosts of my past, the rest of the team remained at IISc, caught in a different kind of storm. The mystery of the energy signature from the lab test had become their immediate focus. Adrien and Ishan refused to leave Kai's side, their reasons deeply personal and woven into the fabric of the crisis. Ishan, as Kai's doctor and friend, felt a profound duty of care, his empathy chaining him to the bedside of a patient whose suffering was beyond any medical textbook.

Adrien's motivation was even more acute; it was his art, his beautiful, mesmerizing insects, that had become the vector for this plague. He was consumed by a guilt so profound it was a physical weight, and he could not bring himself to leave the person his creation had so grievously harmed.

Chandu, ever the pragmatist, established his own command center in the hospital's server room. He had nowhere else to go. Just that morning, before the reunion, he had walked out of his high-paying job at the AI startup. He was tired of building algorithms that predicted consumer behaviour, of using his intellect to convince people to buy things they didn't need. It felt hollow, meaningless. He had packed his life into two bags and was about to head home to face the inevitable prospect of joining his family's business when Adrien's call had come.

Now, faced with a real-world crisis-an alien, a plague, a nano-threat– he felt a surge of purpose he hadn't felt in years. For him, Kai wasn't just a patient; he was the most complex data set he had ever encountered, a problem that mattered. He argued that leaving Kai unmonitored was a catastrophic intelligence failure and immediately began integrating the hospital's diagnostic equipment with his own systems, determined to find a pattern in the chaos.

It was this separation of concerns that allowed Shiva, his mind alight with a new hypothesis, to return to the lab with Trishulin.

"It doesn't make sense, sir," Shiva said, pointing at the data on the holographic display. "The energy signatures your team detected this afternoon, the one with your tachyonic fingerprint, it's sharp, inert, only with a sprinkle of, say, life-like signatures, on top of it. But the signals from Adrien's insect and that of the Kai's skin are exactly the same, purely biological. I can definitely confirm they are two distinct events that happened at the same location."

Trishulin stared at the two distinct wave patterns, his expression hardening. "Then what was it?"

"The test detonation," Shiva theorized, his thoughts racing. "It was a pure nano-reaction as you know of it, a Substrate, a Reagent, and a Catalyst. But the signature is different from the Moradabad files. The decay is longer, more consistent. It's almost as if… something has materially altered the way these chemicals interact, more like how gases react. What if they've modified it? Unlike solids before, what if they have changed the physical states of these chemicals? Turned it into an aerosol, or a gas which is more consistent in giving such signals? That would change the reaction dynamics entirely, allowing for dispersal over a much wider area with terrifying efficiency."

As Shiva spoke, Trishulin felt a cold dread creep into his heart. His son. His son was a student here, a brilliant but troubled young man studying aerosol dynamics. He had dismissed the thought as a father's paranoia, but now… the coincidence was too precise, too cruel.

"I need to see my son," Trishulin said abruptly, his voice strained.

He found Kiran in his hostel room, and the meeting was tense. There was a distance in his son's eyes, a guardedness that hadn't been there before. He talked to his father while standing at the door, before Trishulin was interrupted by a call in less than five minutes. While Trishulin talked, Kiran stayed at the door for five, four, three, two, one– five long seconds before he shut the door. His father being away, almost always, was an unresolved conflict between the two. Trishulin didn't knock back. And no further talks occurred. He returned to the lab, his instincts screaming, and made a quiet call, requesting discreet surveillance on his own son and everyone he met in the last two days. He asked Adrien, with his unassuming, artistic air, and being his son's idol, to go and find a way to his room, and gather if his illusionist senses communicated something irregular inside.

When Adrien walked past Kiran's room, making sure he was noticed, Kiran ran to him, all loving adoration, to tell him how big a fan he was. Adrien, with his easy charm, invited himself into the room. Kiran, star-struck, couldn't refuse. Just as they went in, Adrien's sharp eyes caught a flicker of movement. Two other students were hastily stuffing a small, shielded canister inside a seemingly hollow Cajon (a box-shaped percussion instrument). The students, dressed older than they were, exchanged artificial smiles.

"Prepping for tomorrow's show," one of them said, a little too quickly.

"Oh, I love Cajon. Can I play?" Adrien asked, already picking up the box, making his request meaningless.

"No, no… it needs… a repair," the other student said, snatching it back.

"Careful!" Kiran shouted, almost instinctively. Realizing his mistake, he quickly added, "We just got done repairing it." For Adrien, the over-the-top concern for a simple wooden box was as clear as a confession.

Before anyone could react, Adrien knocked thrice on Kiran's door from the inside-a pre-arranged signal. The surveillance team moved in. The students were apprehended, and the truth, when it came, was a dagger to Trishulin's heart. His son, embittered by a lifetime of feeling second place to his father's duty to his country, had fallen in with a radical group. They called themselves The Alchemists, an anti-establishment cell that preyed on disillusioned intellectuals, channeling their talent, in the name of cleansing, towards acts of terror.

It was Kiran who had cracked the code to aerosolize the Catalyst. It was Kiran who had conducted the test detonation in the lab. And it was Kiran who, in a highly emotional, tear-filled confrontation with his father, finally confessed the full extent of their plan.

"It wasn't just about feeling neglected, father," Kiran wept, the years of resentment pouring out of him. "It was about what you were neglecting us for. 'The nation,' 'duty,' 'the motherland.' Those were the words I grew up hearing, the reasons for every missed birthday, every school event you weren't at. To me, India wasn't a country; it was my rival. It was the other entity you loved more than your own family. And don't you dare say you did it happily! I saw you. I saw the look in your eyes when you had to leave. You were unhappy too. You were a prisoner of this same false construct you served. You sacrificed your own happiness, our happiness, for an idea– for lines on a map."

"The Alchemists…they found me online. They didn't talk about terror. They talked about my papers on aerosol dynamics. They praised my mind. They listened. And then they showed me their philosophy– that nationalism itself is the disease. That governments and borders are the cause of all suffering, all inequality. For them, it's not terrorism; it's a rebellion against a flawed system. They didn't see my anger at you as a weakness; they saw it as a righteous awakening. They gave my pain a purpose. They made me believe that my bitterness wasn't just a personal failing, but a correct response to a sick world that had hurt us both. They made me feel… seen."

"It was never about IISc," he sobbed. "This was just a proof of concept. The real experiment… the first large– scale test of the new Catalyst… it's tonight. On the Nagercoil Express."

Trishulin's blood ran cold. He looked at the clock. It was 10:05 PM. I was already on that train, alone, a solitary observer sent to watch a storm I had no idea was about to break.

"Get everyone," Trishulin roared into his comms, his voice breaking with the agony of a father and the fury of a commander. "We have to get to that train. Now!"

"You can't stop it now from happening, father. PLEASE don't go there and save yourself, for us" Kiran cried. "The entire system is designed such that it can't be stopped by any possible external force." A message chimed on the phones of Trishulin's staff, a taunt from The Alchemist: "We will blast the Nagarcoil Express tonight, and you won't be able to do anything."

"Chandu, trace that," Trishulin commanded.

"Already on it, sir," Chandu replied, his voice calm amidst the chaos, his fingers a blur across his console. "It's routed live through a decentralized, encrypted network. Blockchain-based. Virtually untraceable… but they left a breadcrumb. A single, repeating data packet embedded in the transmission. It's timestamped near a minor station. Ambaturai Junction, just before the Dindigul Junction. Madurai is right after Dindigul. Whoever sent that message is at Ambaturai now." It was a declaration of failure aimed at the government's intelligence apparatus.

"What do you mean it can't be stopped?" Adrien asked Kiran, his voice sharp.

Hesitantly, Kiran explained. The train was supposed to be delayed by the time it reached Salem. And after that, even if it slowed down below a certain speed during the course of its entire journey, the canister would strike open and release the catalyst. The aerosolized Catalyst was inside a similar, larger canister. It could only be stopped by opening it with a special key and following a series of diffusing steps he wasn't aware of. He didn't know where the Substrate and the Reagent were, only that coaches S10, S11, and B1 were involved, an information Trishulin's team already had, and the key was with a person they regarded as 'The Alchemist.'

'The Alchemist?' All questioned with their looks in utter surprise.

"Is there a way to get on the train, if we can't stop it?" Adrien asked again.

"I only know that the train will be slowed immediately after the Madurai junction for some final supplies. But it will not be stopped."

"It must. My gut feeling says, this person on the message was the Alchemist himself. And if he's at Ambaturai now, the train will take its unscheduled stop there or he might get on board from Dindigul. But the train will definitely stop at one of these two places." Chandu decreed with sheer confidence while staring at the train's map route.

Trishulin's first unit at Salem had just missed the train by an agonizing minute. Their last chance was a probable stop at Ambaturai that Chandu had just identified. It was a desperate scramble.

"Show it to me," Adrien said, snatching the decoy Cajon from one of the students and pulling out the shielded canister. Kiran produced a strange, circular key. Adrien opened it, only to find not wires, but a complex, multi-layered puzzle. He studied it for a moment, his magician's mind seeing not an obstacle, but a sequence, a performance.

"The instructions… they're a logic puzzle," Adrien said, a flicker of cold confidence in his eyes. Chandu scanned the device with a high resolution camera, feeding the images into his AI. "He's right," Chandu confirmed. "The mechanism follows a recursive algorithm. It's designed to trap you in a logic loop. One wrong move and it locks itself permanently. Most likely I can map the sequence, but Adrien, you're the one who has to execute it."

Adrien looked at Trishulin. "If you can get us on that train, we can disarm it."

While the world was exploding in Bengaluru, I, oblivious, had just finished my dinner on the Nagercoil Express. The train had passed through Salem. I had scanned my assigned coaches, found no unusual suspects, no immediate threats. The quiet hum of the train was beginning to lull me into a false sense of security. I was preparing to settle in, maybe even get some sleep. I had no idea the real storm was just getting started.

Chapter – 16

When the Universe Takes the Wheel

The reassurance from Trishulin Sir's text message did little to alleviate the tension coiled in my gut, but it provided a thin layer of security. For now, completely unaware of the threat that loomed, there was nothing to do but wait. I leaned my head against the cool metal of the train wall, the vibrations a familiar comfort. In this unwilled stillness, it was easy to think about fate, about the unseen forces that pull our lives in directions we never anticipate. One small decision, one chance encounter, one delayed train, and the entire course of a life could change. It felt like that on the Nauchandi Express the previous day.

After nearly missing the train at Bulandshahr, the long, strange wait at Hapur which introduced me to Ganesh and his crew, to Shukla who had even planned it that we met, that I indeed met Trishulin Sir too, and found the truth about my parents, about Ira… the whole journey itself had become a rolling crucible of debate and revelation. My mind drifted back to the conversations we shared inside that sleeper coach, where a simple question from Ganesh had set us on a course I never could have predicted…

BULANDSHAHR→ HAPUR → LUCKNOW
(DAY 1, NAUCHANDI EXPRESS)

…"By the way, TJ bhai, what's your story?" Ganesh asked suddenly, breaking the silence after my deep introspectory questions on finding my identity. "What do you do? Strange, how we never asked till now."

It felt like I had forgotten to care about my own existence.

"Uhh… I'm a research scientist," I replied, almost surprised at my own voice. "At the Indian Institute of Toxicology Research here in Lucknow. I work in the area of nanomaterial toxicology. And on the side, I'm trying to develop green synthesis processes for nanomaterials."

Ganesh let out a long breath. "Well then, it's better we didn't ask before!" he said, grinning.

"So you're a scientist!" he repeated, mock-dramatic. "Glad I held my curiosity back."

"My childhood friends, or maybe my mother…they influenced me a lot," I added. "Honestly, I couldn't think of anything else."

"So… this nano thing, are you working on some groundbreaking experiment? Will you win a Padma Shri someday?" Shukla chimed in, tapping my shoulder.

"I think the work is novel," I said. "But I'm not sure if I'm any good. My friends are, though. Maybe they'll get it someday."

"Seriously, becoming scientists? Does our generation even do that anymore?" Verma shook his head.

"What made you choose it?" Sahoo asked. "Were you always some passionate science nerd-dreaming of this nano stuff?"

"Obviously!" Shukla interrupted before I could respond. "Otherwise, even I would've been a scientist by now."

"There wasn't even a shred of interest," I said with a half-smile. "Maybe I was a little intrigued. But passionate? No, not really."

"India definitely needs more scientists to grow," Sahoo nodded, suddenly serious.

"Yeah, the only scientist I know is Dr. APJ Abdul Kalam," Verma offered.

"The only scientist I know is Dexter," Ganesh laughed. And then, without warning, broke into song:

"ye hai dexter,

Dexter ki la-bo-tory,

Jaha ye baccha,

Sabse hoshiyar,

Par D-D iske experiments,

Karti hai kharab,

Aur phir gam aur gusse ka- sama chha jata hai….. Dexter ke lab mai……"

("In Dexter's laboratory

Lives the smartest boy you've ever seen

But Dee Dee blows his experiments to smithereens!

There is gloom and doom

While things go boom

In Dexter's lab!")

We all burst into laughter.

For a moment, it felt like I was back with my childhood friends.

"No, come on now, seriously..." Sahoo leaned forward, resting his arms on his knees. "What do you think it would take for people to choose science-especially those from the lower strata of society?"

"I wouldn't know, man," I shrugged. "Maybe some awareness, some confidence, patience, hardwork... that they can make it here. I don't know."

"Hmm..." Verma hummed, a thoughtful sound. "I get that awareness and hard work matter. But maybe people need something to trigger that belief. To activate that confidence in themselves– to do something different. Break that loop Vajpai ji mentioned earlier."

There was something about the way he said it. Not preachy. Just real. He was getting into his zone, the way people do when they speak from lived experience.

Starting as a peon in a soap factory to owning that same factory twenty years later, Verma's father had charted his own course to success. And he hadn't just built wealth– he'd passed on his values too. You could hear it in Verma's voice. The confidence. The fire.

But Sahoo wasn't letting the optimism slide unchallenged.

"It's deeper than that, Verma," he said, his tone softer now, but edged with concern. "There are places in this country where even the idea of 'confidence' doesn't exist. At the bottom of the pyramid, there's no room for dreaming. You're a different breed, bhai. You're an entrepreneur. A successful one. That's rare."

He paused, scanning our faces.

"I've seen it growing up," he went on. "The rich keep getting richer. You look at India's GDP data– it'll show phenomenal growth over the last two decades. But what that graph won't show you is the polarization of wealth."

There was an imperceptible change in the air. A hush fell over us, like before. I feared if it would break into another Sahoo-Verma one-on-one. Even a couple of passengers in the adjacent cabin seemed to pause their own conversations, subtly drawn to ours.

Including one I'd started noticing more than I admitted– my favorite co-passenger. The veterinarian.

"And building confidence? My foot." Sahoo almost snapped, leaning forward again. "Maybe it works for two, three, even ten people– but we're talking lakhs here. Lakhs of people. You think they can eat confidence for dinner?"

The cabin went quiet again. He wasn't shouting, but the conviction in his voice sliced through the usual train noise.

"All these babas, these gurus– what do you think they've been trying to do for years with their jnana? Build confidence, right?" He looked around, as if expecting an answer. "How successful have they really been?"

No one responded. To my surprise, not even Verma.

"I think," Sahoo said, slowing down now, "the answer lies in something more fundamental. You need an ecosystem. One that nurtures these thoughts, this belief, from early on. Maybe… just maybe, TJ had that invisible ecosystem around him when he was growing up."

His words lingered.

I didn't say anything. Maybe because I wasn't sure if I agreed, or because I wasn't sure if I didn't.

Sahoo leaned back this time, his voice softer, but steadier.

"You see, I believe this– true synchronization across all sections of society isn't just idealism. It's a prerequisite. Not just for India to function properly, but for the world, in this era of globalization."

He glanced toward the window, as if seeing through it.

"History's a bystander," he continued. "Any time systems clash, societies adjust. But adjustment's not always kind. Sometimes it's cruel. That's just nature, right? Even tectonic plates shift. And when they do, the surface feels it– as earthquakes."

The analogy was stark. But fitting.

"What will producers sell if consumers don't have the money to buy?" he asked, looking at no one and everyone.

"So yeah… inclusive growth– it's not charity. Not some noble act. It's a necessity. An eventuality. Because if we don't pull everyone along, society will adjust itself. In one way or another. It's just a matter of time."

"Ahh, similar to what we saw about that delicate balance and the circle of life in the movie The Lion King, right?" The veterinarian chimed in with a child's keenness, breaking the silence after about five seconds that felt longer than it was.

Maybe none of us were learned or brave enough to comment on Sahoo's monologue. He was good.

Everyone chuckled at what our great Indian uncle said, a collective moment of lightness, and turned back to Sahoo for his verdict.

"Yeah, kind of," Sahoo nodded, much to my surprise. I had braced for another wave of philosophical deep-diving– but he kept it simple this time.

A quiet calm followed. The new visitor, Mr. Vet, had retreated to his berth. Only the emergency lights glowed now, bathing the compartment in moon-blue, almost dreamlike hue.

I turned toward the window.

And like a reflex, my mind began tracing the evening– starting from Bulandshahr, then the chaos at Hapur Junction, to now, and everything in between. The faces, the voices, the thoughts.

Somewhere between this smoke, the stories, and this silence, something had shifted.

This journey… had already changed me.

Bit by bit, I was becoming more accepting– of people, of stories, of pain. Maybe I had forgiven the world a little. Or maybe, it was the other way round.

Maybe my parents had, too.

Or maybe it was just that I had begun to forgive myself. Time really is a strange healer. It had already been five years.

But it felt so much more peaceful today.

Peacefully exhausted, I let out a long, noisy, shamelessly loud yawn, stretching out in my seat like it was home.

And just then–

"I have an idea," said Sahoo, jolting us from our half-sleeps.

His voice had a new energy to it. For the first time in this whole journey, I found myself more eager than the rest to hear what he was about to say. His energy didn't just stir the group– it charged something inside me.

"Let's go to the general (non-reserved) compartment, just for an experience," Sahoo suggested, his eyes scanning our group, lit with a mischievous hope.

Verma and Shukla were already shaking their heads before the idea had even fully landed.

"Anyway," Sahoo pressed on, locking eyes with Verma, "if it weren't for people like us, Richie Rich types like you wouldn't have even stepped into a sleeper coach, right? Now that you've already touched commoner territory, what's a little deeper dive into the general class?"

There was a glint in his eye that made it hard to say no.

"Yes, count me in," I said, without waiting for anyone else.

"Sure, fine by me," Verma relented, smiling. "And Ganesh, you?"

"Yeah, what will I do here by myself? I'll come," Ganesh said, stretching. "Maybe I'll find some inspiration there for my shows."

"Great. I'll stay here to keep an eye on our luggage," Shukla announced dutifully as we all turned to look at him.

"Lazy ass," Ganesh muttered under his breath, then leaned closer to whisper, "Keep an eye on Vajpai Ji too."

But Shukla was already out cold, head tilted back, mouth slightly open, snoring softly with the grace of a man who had made peace with the world a long time ago.

We quietly gathered ourselves, slipping on sandals, adjusting shawls and sweaters. The train wobbled gently beneath us, a rhythmic lull that had become familiar. Each step echoed both excitement and uncertainty as we moved towards the gates.

None of us said it out loud, but we all felt it– this was no longer just about curiosity. It was something else. Something unspoken.

Like a ritual.

A pilgrimage.

A walk into a different kind of India.

And maybe, into a different part of ourselves.

"So, general compartments aren't connected to reserved coaches from inside. We'll have to board them from outside," Sahoo announced, brimming with energy, as we all stood at the gate.

"Now you want us to crawl over the top of the train to get there?" Verma snapped, clearly both frustrated and a little scared– his newly wed wife waiting for him back home flashing across his face. "Did you sneak a sip from Vajpai Ji's secret stash or what?"

"Relax, shithead. We'll get down at the next station and switch coaches there," Sahoo replied with a wide grin.

Verma masked his embarrassment behind a half-smile as the rest of us burst into laughter.

"Awesome! Next stop is Moradabad. The train halts there for ten minutes– we'll have plenty of time to switch bogeys," Sahoo said, giving a motivational clap like a coach prepping his team before the final innings.

My heartbeat skipped. Moradabad.

The name struck like a gong in my chest. Memories from that night came charging-sharp, swift, like arrows splitting through bone. My breath shortened. Feet froze. The body felt compelled to move forward, but the soul screamed to recoil, to crawl under my seat and disappear. Why are there always two paths? Why can't life just be… mechanical? A sequence of inputs and outputs, without these cruel forks?

Blinking. Heavy blood surging.

Then came Ganesh's hand on my shoulder.

"Shall we?" he asked, wearing the same freshness that morning carried. Like the moment cool water touches your burning soles on a June afternoon, or when a twisting hunger is suddenly relieved with the first sweet bite-his touch, his presence, brought a quiet flood of calm.

Although it was slowing, the train hadn't stopped yet. And all four of us– Sahoo, Ganesh, Verma, and I– stood anxiously near the lavatories to step off. Dhadak… dhadak… dhadak… dhadak… The wheels drummed their endless rhythm, as if the train had no intention of halting.

What if it doesn't stop at Moradabad? I wondered.

But no. It would. It had to.

"So," Sahoo nudged, "how's the trip been for you so far, TJ? Liking our little gang?"

"Yeah, except for you, it's perfect," Verma grinned, pulling Sahoo's earlobe.

Everyone chuckled.

"No, seriously," I said, "you all are… an extraordinary bunch."

"Urgh! I could just fall off the train and die now. Thank you, God, thank you!" Ganesh exclaimed dramatically, full actor-mode engaged.

"Why thank God now?" Verma locked onto the phrase, eyes narrowing. He had that habit of catching a word, twisting it into an argument. Now it seemed God had landed under his radar.

"Okay, thank you, Devil," Ganesh replied, still in character.

"No, really," Verma pushed. "Why do people need to bring God into everything?"

"And why shouldn't they?" Sahoo countered calmly.

"Because– first, it makes you weak. And second, it gives you permission to pretend you're not weak at all," Verma fired back. "Something good? Thank God. Something bad? His will. Fail? Your command, O Lord. Win? Not me– It's Him."

He matched his words with big, exaggerated gestures– clearly warming up for a full-blown debate.

"So, you don't believe in God?" Sahoo asked, his tone smug, as if posing the question from a moral high ground.

"I do," Verma replied calmly, "but I prefer to believe in Man more."

"And who do you think created that Man?" Sahoo shot back, drawing out the 'A' mockingly, like a schoolboy.

"A man's father and mother," Ganesh jumped in before Verma could respond, "on their honeymoon, just like your parents created you two geniuses. Should I explain the process too?" He raised his eyebrows, feigning seriousness. "C'mon now, you two…"

And just like that, all tension melted in our laughter. His timing– perfect as always. There was something unexplainably comforting about Ganesh's humor. He didn't just tell jokes–

he rescued people from their own spirals with it.

I took another deep breath.

Moradabad Junction. The signboard appeared in the distance, its white letters glowing under the yellow station lights. And strangely– this time– it didn't claw at my chest like it used to. No tightness. No noise inside. Just… relief.

Not joy, not fear. Just peace.

"Okayyy, boys... time to go...!" Sahoo rubbed his hands together like someone about to light a bonfire, excitement bouncing off his skin. Dopamine had clearly taken charge of his bloodstream.

And me?

Well, I thought I was hiding it. But I wasn't. Not really.

The moment I jumped off the slowly moving train, an unneeded display of excitement was out in the open. I was ready.

Ready for whatever this journey, this universe, had in store for me next.

My eyes snapped open. The memory of the journey to Moradabad and the debate about God, so vivid and consuming, dissolved, leaving the quiet hum of the Nagercoil Express in its wake. That night, the universe had steered my boat, pushing me towards a revelation about myself and the people around me. But tonight was different. Tonight, The Alchemist was trying to steer this boat, and the destination was a catastrophe. My brief sense of peace evaporated, replaced by the cold, hard reality of the mission. The universe wasn't always a gentle guide; sometimes, it was a battleground. And I was on the front lines of it.

Chapter – 17

The Thaw

The memory of Moradabad Junction, of standing on that precipice between my past and an unknown future, lingered like the faint scent of diesel in the air. That decision, to follow Sahoo into the chaos of the general compartment, had felt like a pilgrimage. It was a descent into a different kind of India, raw and unfiltered. Now, on this sterile, mission-led journey, the memory of that descent felt more important than ever. It was in that crowded, struggling space that the abstract debates of our sleeper coach dissolved into the harsh reality of one man's life, a reality that had chipped away at the ice that had encased my heart for years. The memory of Bhartu, and the story he shared, returned with the force of a crashing wave…

BULANDSHAHR→ HAPUR → LUCKNOW
(DAY 2, NAUCHANDI EXPRESS)

…The train eased gently into stillness at Moradabad station.

The others climbed down after me. I stood tall on the platform, wearing the subtle pride of having been the first to disembark, as if that gave me some strange seniority. The clock read 12:35 AM. It was a cold night, still and hushed. The platform was mostly deserted– just a handful of sleepy passengers and the occasional chaiwala whispering through the mist.

"I think we might find the general compartment emptier than usual," Sahoo speculated, scanning the empty stretch of concrete around us. "Bad luck, Verma! You won't get the real 'general class' feel of sitting with four people in a space made for one," he added with his trademark mischief.

But as we neared the compartment, fate– or irony-stepped in. It was packed to the brim. Not just packed, but swollen. The kind of crowd that makes even air feel like a luxury. People hanging by the doors, half-asleep but wholly determined. It looked like half of India had squeezed into that one coach, and the other half was waiting to join.

"Woah," Verma exclaimed, panic in his voice. "Guess my good luck's of no use tonight. Let's just go back. This looks like an ant colony. How do these people even breathe in here?"

"Not happening, brother," Sahoo replied, grinning with the confidence of someone about to storm a castle. "See, the trick is to just get past the first three people. Once you cross them,

'God' will take care of the rest." He deliberately stressed God, like a little nudge at Verma's earlier argument.

Surprisingly, Verma didn't resist. Not a word. Not even a grumble. Just a quiet "Okay." This was not like him.

I watched his face, looking for signs– maybe irritation, maybe sarcasm– but saw neither. He wasn't excited. That much I could tell. Maybe, just maybe, after that small debate earlier, he felt a need to prove that it was man– and not God– who decides his fate.

And this was going to be his battlefield.

One after another, we clambered in.

The space which– just a moment ago had looked absolutely incapable of fitting a single shoe– somehow kept accommodating our entire bodies as we shuffled deeper. It was like some twisted magic trick: squeeze, squirm, and slide in sideways. After making it through three cabins, we decided to "camp"– which basically meant standing still without toppling over.

Hardly a minute had passed and I was regretting my choice already. "Coming to experience," I said under my breath more to myself than the group, "was the shittiest and most wasteful idea ever."

Physical exhaustion. No place to even lean. Sweat from strangers. Strange smells. Strange people. And far too many. It was sensory overload, the kind that made you want to shut down your mind and disconnect from your body. There was nothing "to experience." And if someone calls this misery an experience, then what is survival?

Even Sahoo– the mighty instigator asshole-looked irritated now, his face halfway into remorse but not fully ready to admit it. My romanticism of "living the real India" had clearly expired. I shoved my earphones in and blasted heavy metal. Meditation by destruction.

Ganesh, though, was the only one still observing– his eyes darting from one person to another like he was preparing for his next monologue. But even that didn't last. Within minutes, all four of us had retreated into our beloved phones, with one and only one intention of keeping the mind busy, willingly swallowed in the virtual universe that didn't smell like stale socks.

At that moment, I envied Shukla with my whole heart.

We exchanged a look. No words, no gestures. Just that silent language of shared pain and collective misjudgement. We all knew it, we all felt it. And we all blamed Sahoo with one synchronized stare.

"What's the next stop, bro?" I finally asked, trying not to sound too desperate.

"Rampur," Sahoo answered like a human railway timetable. "Fifteen-twenty minutes maybe. But the train only stops there for two. We'll have to move quickly." He caught on immediately to my intent.

Sahoo was that guy. The one in every train journey who always knew exactly how long it would take to reach anywhere. The unofficial IRCTC mascot. People would ask him about the arrival time at their destination even if they'd already checked it four times on their own.

Ganesh whispered how Sahoo had used his skills to get a girl's number during his last journey. I raised an eyebrow, impressed, about to congratulate him when Ganesh added with perfect timing, "Of course, his railway and bus bulletin knowledge helped us– the girl and myself-drop a station early and still reach Lucknow in time."

Ganesh smirked, nudging Sahoo with a wink. "But Arpita was really impressed with your knowledge, bro."

We smirked together. A little antipathy. A little pride. Pure camaraderie.

"Stupid girls fall for stupid men," Sahoo remarked, annoyed.

Straightening his collar like a proud hustler, Ganesh turned to Sahoo. "Hey– did you know that Arpita came to see me off at the station?"

Like a cat unable to catch its prey, scratching the wall in frustration, Sahoo flushed red. One could be all–knowledgeable, a smartass, a politician, even an IAS officer– but when it comes to matters of the heart, every man is but a man.

"Be that as it may," Ganesh muttered, shaking his head, "I'll fly if I have to, but I can't stay here anymore."

Just then, catching the stillness in my body and the jumbled look on my face, a middle-aged man-likely a daily-wage worker-looked over kindly and asked, "Sab theek, babuji?"

"Yeah… just tired, wondering if we'd get a seat here," I replied, almost instinctively.

"Ahh, don't worry, babuji," he nodded, pointing at six people crushed into the same cabin, "this group's getting down at Rampur. Just five-ten more minutes. But you stick close-grab the seat when they move."

We all glanced at each other.

"Don't worry about us, Uncle Joe," Ganesh said under his breath, and another telepathic understanding passed between the four of us. "We all want to get down at Rampur too," I added in my head. We'll run for it as soon as the train halts.

Verma, surprisingly quiet so far, seemed engrossed in his own world.

"What's up?" I asked, lifting my eyebrows.

He looked up, voice heavy. "See… that's why I said it– Man created man. Because if God had done it, he wouldn't leave some of his children rotting in a shithole while showering the others with all the riches in the world."

We were quiet. Moved. All three of us. Instantly.

His words suddenly made me confront my own sense of victimhood– I too had succumbed to the feeling of us vs. them. Maybe I wasn't any different. Maybe nobody is. The superior always tries to cow the inferior. And this time, I was the superior one.

The realization hit like a gentle punch-silent, clean. As if a layer of fog lifted and I could finally see myself. Full. Flawed. Humans. Humility followed quietly.

At that very moment, standing there didn't feel as painful as it had been since we entered this compartment. I turned back to glance at Verma.

"Let's stay!" Ganesh exclaimed suddenly.

"Yes, let's stay… one more stop. Shall we?" he added, a new resolve in his voice.

A silent, well-timed nod passed through the group. Agreement, without debate. Maybe even peace.

I looked around. Everyone was welcome here the same way no one was. It must have been the only place where passengers remembered their purpose with purity-just one goal: reaching their destination. Strip away comfort, class, even identity. AC coach, sleeper, general– what did it matter? Just reach. Just reach.

How wonderful it would be if we could carry that same mindset wherever we were-hold tight to why we were there in the first place.

"Very well," the middle-aged man said softly when we finally got seats at Rampur Junction. There was something in his eyes– a quiet satisfaction, maybe even pride, like he had helped a few more travelers cross their little battle.

Rampur faded behind us. The train picked up speed almost instantly, the rhythmic sway of motion settling back into our bodies.

Drowsy and sore, the thought of retreating to our own berth came back. "Just one more station," I sighed, drawing in a deep breath.

"So, where are you going, brother?" Ganesh asked the man who had convinced us to stay.

"Shahjahanpur," he replied simply.

I turned toward Sahoo, expecting his hum– Google Maps answer.

"Next to next," he mumbled, gesturing with half-raised fingers and half– closed eyes.

"You work there, or it's your home?" Ganesh asked gently, trying to get acquainted with him.

"Leave it, babuji," the man replied hesitantly. "Just consider this train my home."

"No, no, brother, it's alright. We have all the time," Ganesh said again, insistently, but with warmth.

I was dead tired. I didn't want to hear another word. I pretended to be attentive, nodding slowly, but I was already halfway into sleep.

"I came from my village, searching for a home… for my kids, my wife, my family," he began.

I didn't want him to. I just wanted to rest. Maybe I was okay if he kept speaking– just as long as no one nudged me, no one woke me up. Not that anyone could wake me if I chose to sleep. But no one wants to be that guy– the guy who sleeps through a poor man's life story.

"A home where water doesn't flood our floors in the middle of the night during monsoons…"

My eyes snapped open.

I was wide awake. His words hit like a cold splash across the face.

"A home where there's a little warmth for our trembling bodies during the winters. A home where we can take a short nap after two sips of water on a summer day, safe from the sun that melts your spine. A home my kids can call their own– where they know they have a place to sleep, every night. Clean water. Food. Twice a day, every day. If not school, at least some dignified work. Not the kind where they rummage through filth looking for scraps of metal to sell for pennies-pennies that can't even feed one stomach. A home… a place where we're not looked down upon just for being born lower than others." He swallowed air for a moment's breath.

"We boarded this train from my village near Allahabad. Well, everyone in the village from my caste was going to Delhi; we also followed. My son caught a fever on the way. High. Scary. We got off here– Hapur Junction. I ran to the hospital. My wife waited at the platform with our daughter."

"I'll be back soon. We'll catch a train in the evening," I told her before I ran.

"It took him ten days to get discharged. All the money I had saved for travel– to last until we found work– was gone. We decided to stay a week. Just enough to save some more. I found work the next day at a nearby construction site. My wife joined. We ate once a day to stretch every rupee. My kids sold knickknacks at the station. After fifteen days, we were ready to leave. But the site manager refused to pay for the last three days unless we finished the month. We had to stay. Then the weather changed. Skies turned. Winds blew colder. One thing led to another… days became weeks. It has been six months now. And under the stairs at the Hapur station– beneath the bridge– that's my home."

He smiled when he said it. A smile trying its best to hold back the tears his eyes were fighting hard not to drop.

I immediately remembered– a woman and two kids sitting there, preparing something near the bridge at Hapur Junction, when I was walking by. My emotions swelled to a point I couldn't contain– but no words came. Not from me. Not from anyone. Only silence.

He hesitated briefly, drawing in a breath that seemed to scrape against the inside of his chest. Then he went on:

"It all feels like a story now. Just a small change in plans… and our whole lives went for a toss. There's nothing left for us in the village anymore. And Delhi– it feels too far off now. Maybe I dreamt too big. A home. Maybe this is the best I was meant to get. I don't even know anymore whether I should feel happy or sad for what I have today. Whether it's too little, or just enough, or– anything at all. But every single day… when a crowd forms by the tracks… and people point at something lying there– with a shocked face, or a sad one– my heart stops. And I think, maybe … maybe that's my son. Maybe he slipped beneath the wheels while selling water from a moving train."

"I fear a lot, babuji. Every day, I fear a lot– for my kids. For my family."

His eyes brimmed. And then the tears came– quiet, unashamed.

We sat there listening, numb. Utterly numb.

The thrill I had expected from exploration– that so-called desire to "experience"– came to a full stop. I didn't feel like speaking. Even looking around– at any face– felt like standing in front of God Himself. Guilty of something. Something I couldn't name.

He had seen so much, lived so much, that even hope had withered under the weight of endurance. This wasn't about needing a motivational quote. This wasn't about man creating things, or chasing dreams, or defying God, as Verma had insisted.

This was life. Unfair. Exhausting. And entirely indifferent to his family.

What struck me the hardest was that his wasn't the only story. I remembered seeing it clearly– more families on the other side of the tracks at Hapur. I'd passed them all. I'd seen them.

But this– this was the first time I felt them.

I looked at everyone.

Ganesh, as always, wore the strongest face-neutral, unreadable. Verma kept his gaze fixed outside the window. Sahoo's face was burning, wrinkled with worry.

"Today, I'm going to Shahjehanpur to meet some 'Sethji' from Delhi," the man continued. "He owns a garments manufacturing factory in the capital. I've heard he helps people like me, in whatever way he can. I just hope God finally hears my prayers today. One of his workers said I could meet him at 2:00 PM in his office."

"This anxiety wouldn't let me sleep," he added with a sigh, "so I decided to travel tonight itself."

"So… what will you do there the whole day?" Ganesh asked, probably just to have something to say– clearing the tickle in his throat.

"I'll just roam around," he said. "See what kind of people come to his place. How he treats them when he meets them on the road. Don't know. Will see."

I was astonished again– not just as a fellow human, but as a tactician– at the clarity of his judgment, and the simplicity with which he shared it. There was something authentic in his lens: watching, observing, letting a person reveal themselves in the in-between spaces.

"Oh, and you were saying something about getting down at the next station?" he reminded us after a brief silence, this time with a half-smile-as if to say, enough about me.

"Bareilly is arriving."

Contrary to my expectations, none of us said much after that. Only Ganesh spoke-wishing him luck and pulling him into a hug as he rose to leave. He exchanged names as we moved to leave. Bhartu– it was his name.

Verma couldn't meet his eyes– I noticed that. He was the first to move toward the exit.

I looked the man in the eye and passed him a humorless smile, nodding. He returned the gesture– mirroring me exactly. Then Sahoo. Then Ganesh.

We all followed Verma in that same silent order.

The platform was sparse. Few passengers stood scattered under the pale light. Across the tracks, I spotted a small bonfire glowing in the dark. A group of people huddled around it, shivering in the cold. A boy– maybe nine or ten– was tending to the fire, gently adding wood logs with care.

I watched his innocence shining through the night in the dim-light of fire that fell on his face.

It was 1:45 AM. I checked the time and wondered, Would he have a school to go to tomorrow morning?

And just like that, all my coldness– the one I'd boarded with at Bulandshahr, the one that had crept in through that general compartment– vanished.

"I'm sorry, Papa... Mumma."

Looking up at two stars shining bright in the northern sky, I folded my hands in a silent pranam and closed my eyes. I remembered all those moments in my life when I should've apologized to the people I loved– and hadn't. So I passed my thoughts to them, letting the universe carry my voice where it needed to go.

It felt lighter-my chest, my breath, my being.

As if someone released me from the prisons I had built within, one by one. And as the locks came undone, moments of elation followed-quiet, peaceful elation-like I was weightless. A feather. I could feel the currents on my skin, the air brushing past me, the breath going in… and even the exhales.

As we reached our sleeper compartment, I stopped for a moment at the door– one foot on the train, the other still on the platform. I looked back. And for a few seconds, I saw God in everything– the empty platform, the vendors, the sweeper with his broom, the child warming his hands near the bonfire, the foggy night sky, the cold, the wind… even in the man who had shouted at Ganesh for using the AC lavatory.

I felt alive.

"Verma?" Sahoo called out from behind.

Verma didn't turn. His voice was low but clear. "God didn't create any shithole," he said. "Just like he didn't create palaces or kingdoms… He only created man."

And at that moment, we heard nothing else.

Just silence.

The memory was so powerful it was almost a tangible force in the coach. The quiet dignity of Bhartu, a man who had lost almost everything but his fear for his children, was a world apart from the ideological fanaticism of The Alchemist. One man was trying to hold his family together in a world that was unravelling ; the other was trying to tear the world apart because of his own broken ideas as we would later learn. That journey into the general compartment had melted something frozen inside me, forcing me to see the individual faces in the crowd. Now, hurtling toward a new crisis, I knew that was the only way forward. I had to see the humanity The Alchemist was trying to erase.

Chapter – 18

The Father's Gambit

While I was lost in the ghosts of my past, hurtling south on the Nagercoil Express, a different kind of storm was brewing in Bengaluru.

"Get everyone," Trishulin roared into his comms, his voice a raw mix of a commander's fury and a father's agony. "We have to get to that train. Now!"

The confession from his son, Kiran, had shattered him. The Alchemists. The aerosolized Catalyst. And at its center, his own child, twisted by a pain Trishulin had seen but never truly understood.

As the team scrambled, mobilized by the sheer force of his command, the first report came in from the ground team at Salem. It was a crushing blow. They had missed the train by less than a minute. The Alchemist was on his way, and they were pursuing a phantom.

Trishulin stood frozen amidst the controlled chaos, the secure comms unit in his hand feeling impossibly heavy. The protocol was clear: report and hand over suspects immediately to the interrogation team at Bengaluru command, and be gone in the wind, on ground. That meant handing over Kiran, letting the system absorb him. But what would a father do? A terrifying new logic seized him. Kiran was broken, but he was also their only source. The intel about the train slowing near Madurai was their only lifeline, a detail coaxed out not by an interrogator, but by a father. If he handed Kiran over now, his son would disappear into the machinery of the state, becoming another sterile file in a long investigation. Any further information, any last-minute insight that could be the key, would be lost to procedure. It was a fair logic, a commander's gambit. But it wasn't pure. Underneath it was the desperate, selfish hope of a father trying to shield his son.

His mind reeled. He even wondered if this was part of The Alchemist's master plan. First the taunting message, now this. Was he being played? Was Kiran's capture intentional, a strategic move to cripple him, a commander, with sentimentality? Was any of the information real? He wouldn't know until they followed the lead. For a paralyzing moment, he considered the unthinkable: keeping his son's confession a secret, using his paternal connection as a strategic asset to save the mission, even if it meant betraying every rule he had ever lived by. He was, after all, just a man. A father, facing an impossible choice.

His secure phone buzzed. He glanced at the screen. TJ Calling. My name. He let it ring, the sound an accusation he couldn't bear to answer. He couldn't speak to the son of the man he had failed, not now, not while he was contemplating a failure of his own. The ringing stopped. A moment later, a text message appeared.

Any update on your ETA? All quiet here.

My words. Simple. Trusting. The text glowed on the screen, and in that moment, it wasn't just a message. It was a mirror. He saw my name, T. Jayadevan, and the memory was no longer a ghost, but a sacred debt. He remembered my father, his unwavering belief in the integrity of the man he served, a faith so profound he had named his own son after him. That faith was now on a train, hurtling towards a catastrophe, relying on Trishulin to be the man my father believed him to be. The weight of it, the simple, profound trust stretching across generations, brought him back from the brink.

With a shaking breath, he opened the channel to his Bengaluru command. His duty, paid for with a piece of his soul.

"The Alchemist is playing with us," Trishulin said, his voice now cold, the father again subsumed by the commander. "That taunting message has to be a diversion, a way to make us focus on a single point of failure while he slips through our grasp. Let's prepare for the worst. But anyhow, we have to be on that train. Let's see if Kiran has more to offer. Take him to the command."

Adrien and Shiva met his gaze as the words hung in the air.

"The train will be slowed immediately after the Madurai junction," Adrien repeated, recalling Kiran's confession. "For final supplies. But it will not be stopped."

Chandu's fingers were a blur across his console. "Kiran's intel is our best bet, but it's too vague. The Dindigul-Madurai patch is over 60 kilometers long. And if we add the variables at Ambaturai and God-knows-what-comes-right-after-Madurai, then we're talking of a minimum of a hundred-plus kilometers. We can't guarantee where or when it will slow."

"And that's why, we need to be airborne. Now," Trishulin said, his voice more confident than ever, a father's grief shrouded by a soldier's duty.

A military helicopter was already prepped from the Bengaluru Command. Trishulin, Shiva, Adrien, and Chandu, along with a small tactical team, were rushed to a secure helipad. As the rotors began to beat the air, Trishulin's gaze fell on Adrien.

"You're sure about this?" Trishulin asked, his voice nearly lost in the noise. "Once we're on that train, there's no turning back."

Adrien met his eyes, his face pale but resolute. He held up the decoy canister from Kiran's room. "The lock is a performance. I understand its mechanism. I can bypass it."

The plan was desperate, a thread of hope woven from Kiran's partial intel, Chandu's knack for reading and connecting data, and Adrien's unique genius. Chandu would monitor the train's speed in real-time. The moment it dipped below a critical threshold, the helicopter would descend, allowing the team to rappel down onto the moving train-a manoeuvre so perilous it verged on suicidal. My presence on the train was now a crucial, if unwitting, component of their plan. I was their inside man, unknowingly thrust into such a perilous situation, kept calm by a lie so that I would be ready when the storm broke.

As the helicopter lifted into the night sky, banking sharply to the south, the team was a tableau of focused tension. Here, chasing a train through the darkness, were three of the five Pantnagar friends, their lives inextricably intertwined. And there, on that same train, was the fourth, sitting clueless and alone, engrossed in his own thoughts, unaware that the heavens themselves were giving chase. And the fifth remained with Kai, fighting another battle that was just too much for anyone to fathom.

Chapter – 19

On Love

Trishulin Sir's false reassurance had worked. The immediate anxiety had receded, leaving behind a quiet space that my memories, persistent and unending, rushed to fill. The train rumbled on, a steady, soothing rhythm in the darkness. Outside, the landscape was a blur of black, a perfect canvas for the mind to paint its pictures. The memory of Bhartu's quiet dignity had stirred something deep within me, a sense of shared humanity that had been frozen for years. And with that thaw, came the flood of other feelings, other faces. Most of all, the memory of Ira. I remembered our last journey on the very same Nauchandi Express, a journey that had been filled with a quiet, unspoken magic, a feeling so potent it seemed to freeze time itself…

BULANDSHAHR→ HAPUR → LUCKNOW
(DAY 2, NAUCHANDI EXPRESS)

…Even after returning to our reserved seats, Bhartu's words still echoed in my ears. I could feel the warmth in his voice-the same warmth with which he'd asked us to wait till the next station, promising we'd get seats. Bhartu. His mother called him that. A gentle variation to his original name, Bharat, as he had told Ganesh in a single, breathless line.

"India, that is Bharat…" Sahoo murmured, recalling maybe an Article of the Indian Constitution, his voice careful not to disturb the night. "India," he sighed again, tracing an imaginary map into the air with his index finger, eyes fixed blankly above. "There are just so many of them… millions of Bhartus…. scattered across India," he whispered-softly, carrying the weight of a profound thinker in his voice.

"You're right, Sahoo," Verma spoke, his tone calm but heavy. "Those man-created-man theories, all that motivational management talk… none of it exists in the frame of reference these people live with. They don't even have the luxury to feel demotivated to work on a Monday."

He shook his head slowly. "For people like Bhartu, life is just what it is. He was ready to work. Work hard-far harder than most ever do. He had intent, he had grit. But for what? What were all his efforts worth in the end?"

Verma paused. His eyes held a melancholy we hadn't seen in him yet. "I wanted to help him. Give him some money… maybe even offer him a job. But how many Bhartus are there? Dozens? Hundreds? Thousands? What could I possibly do? I'm no Bill Gates."

We didn't respond. We couldn't.

Half-awake, Vajpai Ji and Shukla now stared at us with questioning eyes, as if they'd caught only the ending and were searching for context-or maybe for an answer that didn't exist.

The train had left Bareilly Junction.

Ganesh, breaking the silence, started narrating the story-our story-with Bhartu. Slowly, calmly, like a bedtime tale no one asked for, but everyone needed.

Vajpai Ji sat up. Whether he was sober, still high, or lost in-between, I couldn't tell. He looked at Verma and gently grabbed his elbow, gesturing to him to sit down beside him.

"You have all the reasons to be frustrated, young man," Vajpai Ji said, his voice unusually calm, almost fatherly.

"See… they are amazingly simple people with simple lives. Yes, they need help, they need support. Life has always been unfair to them-education, knowledge, food... and convenience, forget that word altogether." He paused for a slow sip of water. We listened, our attention gripped not by his tone, but by the unexpected clarity behind it.

"But," he continued, wiping his lips, "you don't need to carry it all. Just do your bit-whatever that looks like to you. Life goes on, anyway. Whether you do something or nothing at all."

Maybe this drunkard did have some wisdom in him. It caught us all off guard.

With a yawn that could've rolled across the floor like a tumbling ball, Vajpai Ji lay down again and drifted off, as effortlessly as he'd spoken. His words-perhaps not comforting, but strangely grounding–left a soft quiet in our cabin.

The train sliced through the thin fog, slowly picking up speed once more. And we all sat still, gazing out the window at nothing in particular, as if that nothingness was suddenly full of meaning.

Peeping out through the windowpanes, I nodded off. Sahoo woke me up, asking if I wanted some tea. I wasn't one of those ferocious tea lovers who could sip in their sleep, but I did love tea.

"Ahh, yes, for sure."

"Cool! We're about to reach Shahjehanpur."

The name triggered a wave of thoughts about Bhartu. I wondered where he would go, how he would spend the night, and if his wait outside Sethji's office would bear fruit. As the train reached the platform, caught in the hustle of waking from a nap and still partially asleep, I was about to jump off– and only then realized I hadn't worn my shoes.

And this, standing there by the gate without shoes, took me to a place I never wanted to come out of.

"Ahh, it hurts. I think something pricked– maybe grit or something."

"Ohh, let me see! It's my fault, I shouldn't have made you come out barefoot," Ira cried, jumping off the train and crouching instantly at my feet.

"It's alright, don't worry. Let me get the tea first."

With a broad smile, I ran toward the vendor, still feeling the warmth of her touch lingering on my right foot.

I'd have faced swords for her, yet she worried about that small grit.

The thought slowed the whole world to a crawl. Even the hard stone of the railway platform suddenly felt soft. Nothing sounded discordant anymore. A TTE glanced at me for what felt like five seconds. I do have tickets, you sucker, I wanted to shout, throwing them in his face. But he had walked away before I could even reach my pocket.

My heart pounded. I tried to hold my breath beneath that gummy smile, thinking it might calm the palpitations so she wouldn't hear them. What's wrong? Why is everyone staring at my right foot, as if they all wanted to steal Ira's touch off me? I wondered, as we walked back toward the train with teacups in our hands.

Her lips… they defied the very idea of beauty. I loved the way they came closer and fell apart in perfect rhythm to let her voice out– sounding like the melody of ages when she spoke. She lifted the cup, tilted it gently toward those lips, and took the first sip.

"TJ! TJ, brother!" Sahoo's voice pulled me out of this priceless memory with Ira, from a journey that felt like it belonged to another lifetime. It was just the one before I lost her, forever. Still staring at my feet, I stood frozen right beside our compartment door.

"Hey, you came without your shoes! Don't worry–I'll get it for you."

"No, no, it's okay. Coming!" I shook my head, stretching my eyelids with my fingertips to force the drowsiness out.

"It sucks," I said, reacting to the first sip of tea with a wince. My face wrinkled with clear disgust. "It always tastes the worst," I added, referring to my previous attempt at having tea with Ira. Even her presence hadn't improved that godawful brew.

"Worry not, my friend. I know how to make this a delicacy. Let me reach my bag first," Sahoo said, already digging into his backpack. The way he shook his head and twisted his lips signaled he had a trick up his sleeve.

Just then, a young gentleman walked over and tapped the veterinarian uncle who was asleep on the lower side berth adjacent to ours. His voice was proud, needlessly firm.

"Uncle, these two kids up here– are they with you?" he asked, pointing to the upper berth where two adolescents were sleeping.

"We have a reservation here. Move yourself and your family to your actual seats." He directed again before Mr. Vet could respond.

The old man stirred in his seat and answered with utter kindness, "No worries, son. Please go ahead and call the TTE. Both myself and the kids have taken these seats with the consent of Indian Railways. Just don't wake them up yet– they're sick."

The young man, undeterred, muttered, "Okay, if you want it that way," with even more rudeness, and walked off toward the exit gate in search of the TTE.

Both Sahoo and I looked at each other– surprised. We knew those kids had been there from the very start of the journey. We also knew he wasn't traveling with them.

Curious, I turned to him. "Uncle, why did you say that? The kids aren't with you."

"Yes, son! That guy himself has entered the wrong compartment, I'm sure" uncle said with a twinkle in his eye. "These kids and I are exactly where we're supposed to be. And mind you, this is a special coach– meant specifically for passengers from the remote towns of Khurja and Bulandshahr.

It is unlikely that someone would get a reservation here from this station. I'm just giving him a little lesson– on being aware," he added convivially, "and more importantly, on how to speak to his elders."

Sahoo and I burst into soft laughter, stunned by the old man's presence of mind and gentle cunning. The kind that doesn't seek revenge, just a quiet course correction.

Barely twenty seconds later, the gentleman returned-red-faced and sheepish, probably having just confirmed over a phone call with his fellow travellers that he was, indeed, in the wrong coach. Without meeting anyone's gaze, he picked up his bag that anger had made him leave it there, and he slipped out. I caught the glint in the old man's eyes– the shimmer of wisdom– and a smile so wide it could've been a full moon. He leaned back onto his pillow with the satisfaction of a teacher who had given just the right pop quiz.

"Here, try this," Sahoo nudged me, distracting me from the scene as he emptied a tiny pouch of powder into my cup.

"What's that?" I asked, already intrigued by the subtle aroma that lifted from the cup.

"My mother's secret tea masala, brother," he said, voice softer now, as if the word mother carried its own echo. His expression changed-tender, nostalgic, a trace of pride.

The tea now tasted different-warmer, fuller. Maybe it was the clove or the cinnamon or the hint of cardamom, but every drop was delicious. This wasn't just tea; it was a feeling, a memory, a story passed down in generations.

I sipped slowly, caught in a trail of thought. How everyone, no matter where they come from, carries that one thing-something so unmistakably, unforgettably theirs from their mother. A taste. A smell. A stitch on a torn kurta. A lullaby.

What was mine?

I tried to recall-tried to identify one thing that stood out. But nothing came. It was strange. Everything from her felt… fine. Not ordinary, just… even. Even-tempered, ever-available. Not special in a dramatic way.

Or maybe… everything she touched was special? Or maybe I was blind this whole time to even notice what it was.

I never said it out loud, but I loved her. I loved how she made me feel about this life. When I hid behind lies, tangled in guilt and self-blame, she never demanded explanations. She just brought me back with her love-soft, wordless, forgiving. "It's okay," she would say, without even asking what wasn't.

No judgements. Just love and care. Oh, mother! My mother!

The train picked up speed again, carving through the darkness like a memory in flight. I checked the time– 3:05 AM. Everyone was asleep. The quiet felt sacred.

For the first time in the entire journey, everything stilled, even all my fantastic fours-except the wheels beneath us and the occasional, soft whimper of a newborn. The baby's cry wasn't troubling– it was rhythmic, almost musical. Curiously, there was no sound from her mother. No hushes. No lullabies. Just the tiny, steady cry of need, maybe.

A part of me wanted to stay awake-dive into this silence, dissolve into the darkness beyond the window, and let my soul drift, untethered, into that infinite world out there. Another part of me– just as strong-longed to close my eyes and dive inward, hoping to find the beginnings of some answers. About myself. About life. About Ira. About my parents. About how everything that once felt solid could just-disappear.

For years, those questions had stayed like shadows in the corners-always present but never loud. But this journey– this slow, raw, endlessly human journey– had handed them voices. Clear. Bold. Unignorable. They weren't whispering anymore. They were talking clearly and honestly.

And just as I began to consider listening deeper, sleep– the quiet goddess of surrender– began her gentle approach, calling me back to my last journey with Ira, on this same train. I stopped resisting.

- - - - -

"The weather seems to have changed here. Feels like it might rain," Ira said, listening to the rumble of distant clouds. We sat facing each other on the side lower berth, our legs stretched out, toes touching. With half-shut, sleep-deprived eyes, I looked out too. Just a couple of hours ago, the moon had shone brightly in the sky. Now, it has vanished. The cycle of change spares nothing– not even something as divine as the moon.

A louder roar of thunder followed a jagged streak of lightning that cut through the sky, and I saw it– her smile. Tremulous, uncertain, yet shining.

I remembered her fear of storms. She'd told me stories- how she'd hurry home when clouds gathered, whispering little prayers for the rain to wait until she was safely inside. Thunder, to her, was something to escape.

But that day… that day was different.

That day, she danced with the thunder. Her smile matched the lightning. The higher the curve of her lips, the fiercer the sky responded. When the train stopped at the next station, she even stepped out to breathe in the storm. Arms outstretched, she welcomed it. Under that vast, blackish-blue sky, she looked invincible.

That day, she wasn't afraid. That day, she was stronger.

"Tell her. Tell her how you feel about her," whispered the angel on my right shoulder, voice sly but sincere.

I turned away from him, smiling lazily. I wasn't ready. Or maybe I just didn't want to risk losing the moment.

If that freedom wasn't love, then love had no other name. I saw her– rain falling softly now, but she didn't mind. I heard her heart, beating in rhythm with mine. And somehow, I heard it too in the fruit vendor behind us adjusting bananas on his cart. I heard it in the silent man under his umbrella, watching another train disappear into the mist. I heard it in the clink of the tea vendor's glasses as he wiped them quickly to fill them again. I heard it in every passerby as she walked beside me on that platform.

I felt their hearts. I felt their lives. And at that moment, all of me was here. Those few minutes– we were a world unto ourselves. I could have lived forever inside that fragment of time.

Walking, at the far end of the platform, we even let our footprints sink into the wet mud. I knew the rain would erase them soon. What if we never had a moment like this again? The thought stirred an unease within me. What if life pulled us apart, like it so often does-quietly, mercilessly?

But then, her smile drew me back-wordless, yet comforting. As if saying, don't worry, we'll remember we were here.

Walking back to the train, she fidgeted with a small shell that had lodged in her sandal. I laughed. She asked me to sing. She always did. Said she liked it when I sang– even though I wasn't any good.

Still, I sang. She smiled, and tried to match her voice with mine.

And in that moment, we were connected.

She was there. I was there. And maybe that was all that mattered.

I came closer and held her-one arm around her waist, her hand tucked gently into mine– and we danced to the magic. Hidden, peeping through the corners of bluish clouds while it still drizzled, the moon brought the spotlight. Wind helped bring the stars' sparkles too. I was for her, and she was for me, and– this world, those breezes, the trees, the shrubs, the whole nature– it was all ours.

Tap on tap, round and round. She laughed. She chuckled. She hushed. She leaned in and cuddled.

"Phew, not again! Where do you get lost time and again?" She nudged me, waking me up. I dreamt again. But maybe we danced. Yes, we did. I felt her, or maybe she did too, I could never know. But there, just the thought of it, thought of holding her close, was like that ocean breeze after dusk, the chill of the mountains before dawn, the fragrant whisper of flowers from the valley, that chirping from the forest, that silent, vacuum-like stillness from the wooden plank by the lake. It felt like even the drifting clouds touched us too, here on the ground, before moving on, back into the sky.

And I gathered it all, all of nature– every bit of it– and poured it into a single cup. Then sipped it slowly, with every touch of hers, every glance that caught her face.

And in that moment, I let our souls fly– free and wide– dancing to the eternal music of life, in all the ways it has ever known to exist.

Chapter – 20

What Remains

A few hundred kilometers north of me, under the sodium glow of the Bengaluru Command Center, the blades of a military helicopter began to beat the air, lifting a team of desperate men into the night. Inside the vibrating cabin, Trishulin sir stared out at the receding lights of the city, his mind a raging storm. The memory of his son's tear-streaked face, the weight of his fatherly duty warring with his duty to the nation, was a fresh, raw wound. Beside him, Chandu's face was illuminated by the glow of his console, his eyes glued to the train's distant, steady progress. "Speed is constant for a while at eighty– four kilometers per hour, sir. They're a long way ahead." Adrien sat with the decoy canister on his lap, his eyes closed, his fingers tracing the intricate patterns of the lock in his mind, preparing for a performance with no room for error. Shiva, hunched over a tablet, reviewed the molecular structure of the aerosolized Catalyst, searching for a weakness, a flaw, anything.

Somewhere on the dark highways between Salem and Erode, another part of the chase was unfolding. Headlights cut through the black as the ground team that had missed the train pushed their vehicles to the limit, a frantic, earthbound pursuit guided only by the ghost of the train on Chandu's map. The entire mission was balanced on the knife– edge of Kiran's fractured intel and Chandu's timestamp finding-that the train would slow, somewhere in the vast, dark stretch of land between Dindigul and Madurai.

And on that train, in coach S11, I, the unwitting inside man, was blissfully unaware of the heavens and earth giving chase. The false reassurance of Trishulin Sir's text had been a powerful sedative. My body, lulled by the gentle rocking of the carriage, was relaxed. My mind, finally quiet after the emotional tempest of the last twenty-four hours, had drifted into that soft, liminal space between wakefulness and sleep. It was a space where memories lived, not as ghosts, but as gentle companions. The memory of Ira, of our last journey together, rose not with the sharp pain of loss, but with the sweet, aching nostalgia of love itself– a love I once had, a love I thought I understood, a love that was about to be redefined in the quiet hum of the wheels…

BULANDSHAHR→ HAPUR → LUCKNOW
(DAY 2, NAUCHANDI EXPRESS)

…"Yeah, I…, that's what I'll do. That's… I'll do," Vajpai Ji muttered suddenly in his sleep, pulling me into a half-wakeful state with his mysterious outburst before sinking right back into his drunk dreams. The man had been a riddle this entire journey. I was too weary to even lift my eyelids and check on him. My eyes ached with fatigue.

While in the borderlands of sleep and awareness, I heard Shukla's voice: "What happened?"– soft, concerned-followed by the rustling of a zipper. He must've opened his bag to pull something out.

Then came an echo, as if twin voices whispering to me at the same time, "Ahh, Lucknow is the next stop."

It was Ira and Sahoo, speaking at the same time. The synchronicity rang in my head, eerie and gentle, pulling me back with Ira, on our last journey to Lucknow.

"That's exactly what I don't want," I muttered instinctively, my words stumbling out, still lost in the ocean of Ira's eyes.

Ever since I met her, she had been with me– wherever I went, in every season of my life.

After our first encounter in that camp in the Himalayas, we met again, running. The last stretch of the 2012 City Marathon in Lucknow. She came beside me in those final steps, and suddenly, the world wasn't so heavy.

It had been two years since Ma passed. After her, I began running-not out of passion or fitness, but just to wear myself down enough to sleep at night. I wasn't running towards anything; I was simply running away.

But that day-something had changed. Maybe I'd slept better the night before. Maybe I was lighter, like a child chasing a butterfly without reason or end. My body didn't ache. My head wasn't foggy. There was no grief weighing me down. Just the clarity and joy of being utterly alive in that moment– as if nothing more was needed, and nothing else could fit.

I couldn't pinpoint the source of that strange, radiant strength. Maybe it was God's plan, as Benjamin would have said. That day, I wasn't myself-only better. Maybe fate knew we would meet again.

"You know, they're saying this might be the year of doom. Could be our last run," I had said, trying to sound both philosophical and charming. "Would you like to run this final mile together?" Only God knew how I could pull off a pick-up line like that, especially after playing it all dumb in our first meet!

I still remember the way her eyes shifted-first surprised, then amused– and how a smile bloomed slowly across her face, like it had been waiting there all along.

"But it's just February! We've got ten more months to go," she shot back with a mock– serious tone, emphasizing definitely as if she were daring the universe. "And I've definitely got a few more marathons left in me before the scary 21st December 2012."

That smile… it was bright enough to make even the idea of doomsday feel foolish. Witty, full of life, and slightly defiant-like she'd already made peace with everything that could go wrong, and had chosen joy anyway.

We ran the last mile together. And from that moment on, she stayed. Not just in memories or moments, but somewhere deeper. In silence, in crowds, in pain, in joy– I could be anywhere, and she was there too.

I remember how in spring, we would walk past the fields behind my college– the ones where marigolds and lilies grew without anyone tending to them. She'd slow down there, smile at the random bees buzzing around, and sometimes pick a flower or two just to tuck them inside her notebook. The sun would fall on her face like it was meant to. I used to think, maybe the sunflowers were right to follow the sun.

In summer, she would wear her usual light green t-shirt, and we'd take the long road to the lake on Sundays, carrying a bottle of water, Limca, and some extravagant snacks, thanks to her richie-rich roommate. Sitting on the stone slab near the edge, our feet dangling, we'd listen to the soft splashes of water. If water would wet our clothes, first she'd curse, and then laugh. I remember once we found pebbles, smooth ones, and tried skipping them across. I failed every time. She didn't. Man, could she be stronger?

And how in the rain, we would walk under the same black umbrella, the cheap kind that flips in the wind. She'd scold me if I forgot it at home; only, I'd miss it knowingly. Water would splash on our legs from passing scooters, and we'd find shelter under the flyover, waiting for the tea vendor. The tea tasted extra spicy on those days. Sometimes we'd make paper boats, like kids again. Some floated a little, some sank right away. She once said, "Isn't that how people are too?– Some left behind already, some still carrying our journeys together."

In autumn, when the leaves dried up and the wind brought this strange stillness, I saw her eyes become quieter. She'd be wrapped in a shawl, carrying her bag of books, walking beside me but not saying much. In those months when things started falling-flowers, leaves, old friendships-our conversations stayed. We kept talking. That was enough.

And how in winter, we would eat ice cream from a roadside cart, even when our fingers went numb. She liked it that way. I'd ask her to skip it, but she'd say, "This is my rebellion." We'd sit on someone's parked scooter, our backs to the world, her head resting on my shoulder. We wouldn't say anything. Sometimes the quiet said everything.

737 days!

Just like that, 737 days went by. Almost two years. We didn't do anything extravagant. Just walked, talked, fought, laughed, waited, showed up. But maybe that's how it was supposed to be-being there, day after day, in all the seasons. That carelessness when you just come out of teenage life! That confidence you could move mountains.

"I just wish this journey would go on and on," I held her hand tighter. "And this train... it should never stop, ever."

She didn't say a word-just smiled, that soft, knowing smile, her eyes alive like they were holding back laughter and tears all at once.

I turned towards the window, still lost in the warmth of that moment, thinking about what her smile meant. And just then– I felt her closer. Her face was suddenly right there, near mine.

Astonished, unsure if I was dreaming again, I looked into her eyes. There was a silence, but not an empty one– it was full of everything we never said out loud.

Then it happened. The gentlest kiss. Just the corner of her lips brushing the right side of mine, the rest landing somewhere on my cheek, almost like she hadn't decided where to place it– or didn't care.

My skin shivered. Her breath mingled with mine. For a few seconds, the whole world paused. There was no train, no journey, no past or future– just that closeness, just us, suspended in a timeless bubble.

With Ira, I came to believe that saying you loved someone was never just about the words. It wasn't something you said to please the other person– it was something your soul needed to say. Like it pulled some power from the universe and gave it back in those three simple words. And when that feeling came from a place so sacred inside you, it changed everything.

I knew the truth of what I felt for her. And still, there were just these same twenty-six letters– always the same. But no matter how I arranged them, how I grouped them or spun them into sentences, nothing ever seemed enough to capture what I had lived with her. How badly I wanted to shape them differently, mold them into something that could hold even a drop of that magic! The words would come pouring out, but they always felt smaller. Every single time.

"Lovers had loved before, and lovers would love again; but no lover had ever loved, might, could, would, or should ever love, as I loved…" …Ira.

I had read that line a hundred times. But that day, I truly understood what Dickens must have felt when he wrote it. And still– I found even his words a little short for what I carried in my heart.

With nervous smiles, we couldn't even meet each other's eyes for the next few minutes. But in that silence, she kept beating in my chest, moving through my blood. I had even forgotten that Lucknow was close.

"Was it really You, God, who brought us together?" as Benjamin would say.

"You guys are poles apart," Benjamin would often say. "Two different worlds. You must really thank God He got you both in the same story." And maybe he was right. There wasn't a single obvious thing we had in common.

"TJ bhai!" Ganesh woke me up, shaking my head lightly. Sahoo was already up.

"I've got Bhole Baba's Prasada here. Let's touch the pious lands of Lucknow with Lord Shiva's blessings," Ganesh said with that cheesy grin of his, which was basically code for, " This is maal (weed)."

And right then, I heard my friend Shiva's words echoing in my head. He'd always say never to refuse two puffs of 'maal' when a friendship was in the making– and that history itself was witness to how some of the strongest friendships were built on weed and beer-bottle pillars.

I nodded with a half-smile and gave a respectful bow in acceptance.

The three of us made our way to the compartment gate. Ganesh lit it up and offered me the first puff, a warm welcome into their gang. Maybe Shiva was right, after all.

The weather had cleared by then. The stubborn clouds that had been guarding the moon were now nowhere to be seen. By the time I took my third puff, I watched the smoke trail drift back even as the train sped forward, faintly glowing in the moonlight. And with it, the rest of my memories of that journey with Ira seemed to float away, slowly fading into the night.

After that, I didn't sleep. I didn't drift off into that in-between state anymore. No more fatigue. No more swollen eyes or heaviness in the head. Just a strange, quiet kind of peace. Prasada had done its job well.

The last memory I could hold onto from that trip with Ira– right after the kiss– was the way we avoided each other's eyes. I stared out the window, stealing glances through the corner of my eye, trying to decipher everything she wasn't saying. Her face, her silence, her half-smile– they spoke more than words ever could.

All the memories– our laughter, our walk on the platform, our hands intertwined, our first kiss– vanished in an instant. Just like that. Ira Acharya, the woman I had loved more than anyone else.

The smoke from my fourth puff swirled into shapes, first forming my mother's face, then my father's, and finally both of them together, playing with me as a child. Only God and my soul could understand the depth of how much I missed them.

"One last," Ganesh said, passing me the joint. We were all quiet. I wondered what they were thinking about– Ganesh and Sahoo. Did they carry the weight of their own losses and fears, too?

With the fifth and final puff, the memory of my father and his boss, T. Jayadevan, came rushing back. Then I heard his voice, almost as clearly as if he were really speaking: "Are you worthy of my name, T. Jayadevan?" And then, "Who are you, T. Jayadevan?"

Who was I? How was I? The thought held me still, my blink stretching longer than it should.

In that stillness, I wondered how my life had really been in these past five years. And maybe it wasn't just these five years– had I always felt this way? A sense of loss. When everyone was around, I missed things. Now that they are gone, I miss them. Was it just me, always living in this quiet emptiness, and drawing the same from the universe? What if it were true– that I had been hiding behind the lie of playing it safe, when all my soul wanted was to grow?

But like an ignorant grasshopper, I chose to accept my weaknesses and continued living the way I was. I made peace with the idea of being 'less'– settling for a version of myself that wasn't complete. I was okay with being driven by half-felt emotions, with doing things just to get by, without truly experiencing them. I was ready to cheat myself. To let this quiet dishonesty wrap around me like a second skin. And still, I kept asking God not to let me break down under the weight of this separation from my loved ones.

"Let me be happy, God, I would cry."

But monsoon after monsoon, my prayers were washed away like chalk marks in the rain.

And somewhere in between– between when I said the prayers and when they were supposed to be answered– lay the truth. A truth I had probably always known. But I chose to ignore it. I chose to look away. I kept asking instead:

"Why did I have to live like this? Why did all this have to happen?"

And God would calmly ask, "What is it that I am doing?"

Still, I'd stay stuck on my question: "Why have you done this to me?"

And just like that, five years passed. Or maybe, all twenty-nine years of my life did.

Maybe it was fate, written by God. Or maybe it was me– my soul drifting away from the promise it had made to itself: to stay honest. Maybe it was my parents' love, their loss. Maybe it was Ira-her sight, her smile, her hair, her voice-holding me back, refusing to let go of the person I used to be. Keeping me tied to a past I hadn't yet accepted was gone.

Or maybe, it was just me– falling deeper, when I had every chance to rise. As if I had already decided there was no turning back.

Maybe this separation was absolute. Or maybe, I was the one who had been quietly writing this story of disunions-thought by thought, action by action-all along.

I turned back to my old tools-logic reason. I tried to piece it all together. And when that failed, I prayed again, this time harder, more desperately, worn out by the limits of my own human strength. Each day, a part of me still clung to the same questions, "Why me?", while another part whispered, let it go… just breathe, it doesn't matter. But nothing worked. Nothing changed. Not until today.

It's not that I hadn't laughed in the last five years. Not that I hadn't loved what was left of my family– my grandmother and a distant aunt who took care of her, my friends, or all the small things that life offered me daily. I did. Maybe I had found joy in little things too, like everyone else. But this sense of my own identity, this power I used to feel often as a kid– a spark in everything, I missed that. And, it affected everything.

I missed the high I used to feel just before drifting into sleep. I missed that strange tree of knowledge I once felt growing inside my chest. I missed the quiet courage I used to see in the mirror every morning.

All of it had gone. Maybe it started fading long before I even stepped into adulthood, when my parents were right here, with me.

But no one noticed. Because everything that had gone missing… was never outside to begin with.

And not that I would stop missing them-no, I will… always. But now, there was a small difference.

I would know that they were gone. Truly, physically, forever.

And it's not like I hadn't known this before. But now… I was going to be okay with it. I was going to be okay with everything.

Did I really just need those five puffs and the sight of smoke trailing backward to come to this?

Or was it just time? My time, like John, had come too.

Were my parents really meant to leave this world the way they did? Was Ira meant to go too? Was her absence somehow necessary? Did I need to go through this long winding voyage, breathing at every turn of this strange circle?

Did I need to first feel what it was like to have the world… only to then learn what it meant to lose it all?

And did I even know back then that I had the world?

I know nothing about psychology. I've read no books on grief. But these questions and answers came to me all at once, uninvited, while I stood quietly by the compartment gate and weed flowing through my veins. Sahoo and Ganesh were still behind me, finishing the last of the smoke at the other end. And I…

I stood facing the east, imagining how the feeblest rays of dawn would peek through the sky, while it was still entirely dark all around.

The memory dissolved, leaving a quiet ache in its wake. The feeling of having it and not having it at all– it was the story of my life. I had Ira, my parents, a life of blissful ignorance, and then I didn't. Now, I had this mission, this team, this terrifying purpose. I had a chance to understand the 'why' behind the loss. But in having this new life, I had lost the simple peace of being just another passenger on a train, a man with no secrets and no ghosts to chase. The thought hung in the air, heavy and unresolved, as the train continued its journey south, carrying me towards a confrontation that would force me to finally reconcile the two.

Chapter – 21

When Truth Appears

It was past 1:30 AM. High above the plains of Tamil Nadu, the helicopter was a humming beast of steel and shadow, its occupants scanning the darkness below. From their vantage point, the Nagercoil Express was a distant, luminous spine moving across a black expanse. On the ground, the road team, a convoy of dark SUVs, pushed their vehicles to the red. At points where the highway curved close to the railway line, they could hear the faint, rhythmic clatter of the train, a ghost sound that fueled their desperate chase. The train had flown past Karur Junction and was now closing in on Dindigul. The critical patch of track, the one where their only hope lay, was approaching. In the air and on the ground, every nerve was on edge. There was no room for error.

And inside that train, I was floating. The quiet hum of the coach, the gentle sway, the soft snores of the passengers around me– it was a bubble of peace. My mind, free from the immediate pressures of the mission, had rewound to the journey that had changed everything. It felt like a lifetime ago, but it was only yesterday. I was on the verge of a great discovery, not in a lab, but in the cramped corridor of a train, about to come face to face with a truth that would shatter my world and rebuild it all at once. The memory was no longer a flashback; it was the present. I was there…

BULANDSHAHR→ HAPUR → LUCKNOW

(DAY 2, NAUCHANDI EXPRESS)

…"Okay, you guys, take a nap; still an hour to go. With this long night we've all had, one of us MUST stay away from the seat," Sahoo said, still high on the weed, trying on a made-up responsible tone, looking at our exhausted faces. "Go on, I'll wake you up."

Right then, Shukla showed up– probably summoned by nature's ever-urgent call.

"No-no, I've slept enough, guys. You go to sleep. I'm feeling great– fully awake, full of energy," Shukla announced, ruining his statement with an exaggerated, ugly yawn.

"And why wouldn't you be?" Sahoo snapped back, flashing that same sarcastic, nationalist grin. "All you've done is sleep through the entire journey, asshole."

"Ahh, you guys carry on. I'll just use the loo and join in," I said, waving Sahoo and Ganesh off, needing a little time to myself.

By the time I stepped out of the toilet, only Shukla was standing by the gate.

"TJ, here-just a sec!" he called, stopping me as I started walking back to my seat, hoping for a desperately needed nap.

He gestured for me to stay put near the washbasin, and then casually walked to the opposite lavatory door and knocked– "Tak, tak, ta-ta-tak." The rhythm felt odd… deliberate. At first, I thought he was pulling a prank on someone, maybe playing a joke on a co-passenger. I even half-smiled.

But when the door opened instantly from inside, and a big man with his build mirroring my father's, stepped out with a slow, silent nod toward Shukla– chills ran through me. Just for a moment, but enough to freeze time.

How would I have known that this was it?

That I would never be the same again.

"So– how are you, Tarun?"

I turned, numb. Shukla stood near the cabin alley, probably keeping an eye out for the rest of the Fantastic Fours.

It was his voice.

A hundred memories ignited at once. The voice, the presence– I was certain. But how? It made no sense. How could he be here? And Shukla– how the hell did he fit into all this?

"You are T. Jayadevan," I said, the words rolling out slower than I meant them to, more of a breath than a question.

"I am," he replied, that same calm smile resting lightly on his face.

I couldn't speak. My head turned again to Shukla– desperate for answers to fall into place on their own. But he just lit a cigarette, leaned casually near the other gate, and took a drag like nothing out of the ordinary was happening. Every now and then, he peeked down the alley like he was just guarding a secret neither of us had clearance for.

"Tarun, I don't have much time here, Son," T. Jayadevan continued, his voice lowering just enough. "By even being here… I'm breaking rules. Not just protocol-serious ones. I'm putting myself, and this young man helping me, in danger. His entire career. His life."

He paused-long enough for my pulse to start drowning out every sound.

"But it's been five years already… and you need to know this."

My heart pounded in my chest like it wanted to crawl out and listen first. My breathing broke rhythm. I knew it was about my father. But what? Was he still alive? Held somewhere? Was this going to be one of those rare stories I'd heard him talk about– some soldier kept in isolation for decades?

My mind went everywhere, and nowhere, at once.

Then he said it.

"You weren't wrong that day on the platform. And you didn't mistake someone else for your father. It was him."

Two teardrops rolled down my cheeks.

"I'm sorry, son," he said softly.

"He didn't lie to you either. He was supposed to be in Kolkata. He would've been… God, I wish… only if it weren't for this…" He paused, like he was deciding how much truth to let slip. "…this thing we were after."

"What thing?" I asked, baffled. The words sounded like they belonged to some spy thriller. Who was my father? Wasn't he just a Subedar? My head was darting through a maze of questions.

Both he and Shukla raised a hand at the same time, gesturing to me to lower my voice. I hadn't even realized I'd spoken that loud.

"All I can say," Jayadevan said, his voice barely above a whisper now, "is that both your father and mother are very well-known figures-among the top echelons of the Indian Defence Services."

"My mother?" My voice cracked. "Yes. She too," he said, looking straight at me.

"Who were they? And who was she?" I couldn't hold my thoughts together. "If she was this big– why did you let her die?"

"We didn't." He inhaled deeply, almost shaking his head. "We tried everything. God, we had the best on it. But… we just couldn't." He didn't blink. Shukla lit another cigarette and passed it to Jayadevan.

"It was something out of our hands," Jayadevan said, exhaling smoke as he glanced at his watch.

"You know," he continued, slowly, "I was there too. That day."

He took another drag.

"You walked right past me. With two tea cups in your hands."

The words shot a flash through my brain. The loud sounds. The commotion. The chaos.

"And those sounds you remember…" he said, almost reading my thoughts, "…they weren't random. They were some kind of controlled explosions. We still don't fully understand them, even today."

"It was a terrorist attack!" The moment I said it, I felt a surge across my skin– as if ants were crawling inside my bloodstream. A strange kind of static ran over me.

"No," he said firmly. "We don't know."

Flicking ash off the cigarette, his eyes sharpened.

"Your father was our man on the ground," he said. "And your mother– she was his better half… in the lab."

"My mother… lab…?" My eyebrows pulled together in disbelief. I didn't understand anything anymore. But I was listening. With every cell of my body.

"Okay. Let me ask you– why did you take Chemistry for your graduation?" he asked, his voice calm, almost curious.

"No particular reason," I replied. "I didn't know what else to do."

"Still…why Chemistry? Why not Physics?" he pressed, like he already knew something I didn't.

And then– my eyes widened.

Like a light shining through the fog, a forgotten memory rose from the depths. My mother, during my school days, read out chemical compositions from shampoo bottles, sugar packets, medicine strips. How she would quiz me playfully. How I once won the first-and only-prize of my school life in a science exhibition, explaining the effects of different salts on the human body. That model had been her idea. All of it, hers.

Suddenly, I remembered how much I had loved her. How much I had loved them– both of them. When did I grow apart? What happened to me?

My eyes stayed wide open– like doors flung in a storm– and T. Jayadevan noticed. He had seen the recognition land. I had found the thread. Tears followed. I couldn't stop them.

"I'm sorry for Ira, too, Son," he said softly, his gaze dropping to my shoes.

I looked up, trembling. "Do you… do you know where she is? What happened to her? I searched for her… I"

"I know," he interrupted gently, before I could even finish.

"After the train left the station," he said, his voice tightening, "there was one more explosion. Both your father… and Ira… didn't survive it. Nothing about it ever reached the news."

"Ira too…!" Only two words escaped me– dry, cracked, helpless. Tears were the rest.

I had already mourned her once. Accepted her absence like a silent ache. But somewhere deep down, some part of me had still clung to a foolish hope. That I would see her again– maybe in a busy street, having an ice cream, holding a shopping bag with a purple dress folded inside. She looked beautiful in purple. Maybe our eyes would meet. Maybe I would ask her why she left me.

But now, even that sliver of hope is gone. And in its place, just a dull, heavy numbness in my feet.

Jayadevan placed a hand on my shoulder and gave it a gentle squeeze. No words could help now, and he knew it.

"I'm really sorry, Son."

He looked toward the other gate.

"Shukla was in that incident too. We're still surprised he survived. He works for me now."

"That bank PO thing– just a cover," Shukla added the next instant from behind, almost casually, as if dropping the final piece in a puzzle I never knew existed.

Jayadevan looked down. "I just wanted to tell you all this. You deserved to know. It took me five years to gather the courage to face you… and tell you that I am the man who robbed you of both your parents and Ira. Please… forgive me, Son."

I didn't have a single word. Just silence. A long, heavy silence-twenty seconds that felt like they stretched across the entire train.

"Can you get me in?" I said, and for the first time in years, I felt something firm in my chest. Like steel. Like purpose.

"What? What do you mean?" he asked.

"Just like you took in Shukla."

"No. No, no-no way… I can't. I won't. I already carry the weight of losing your parents. To bring you into this mess? It's unimaginable. I'm sorry-no. I can't."

"If you really want to help me, or bless me, or repay anything to me– then get me in. I want to know the truth. The whole truth. Who or what were my parents chasing? What took them away? What took everything from me?"

And then, the dam broke. My body shook, the tears poured out, and I shoved my handkerchief between my teeth, crying like a boy who had been too strong for too long.

Shukla hugged me tight. "Sorry, man…" he whispered, and T. Jayadevan just stood there, gently rubbing my head like a father from his generation would to a crying child.

We stayed like that. Silent again. Like the train held its breath with us.

Finally, he spoke. "Okay. Let me see what I can do."

"Sir, time." Shukla raised his watch to Jayadevan-time for him to go.

Jayadevan turned to me. "Son, your father was so proud of you. Of how you managed everything-your life, your dignity-despite everything. Even though he kept you away from all of this, even with limited means… he loved you. They both did. More than anything."

I nodded, helplessly wiping my tears, wishing they'd stop but knowing they wouldn't.

"Hey, I have to go now. Is there anything else I could help you with?"

"Yes… just this." I sniffled, tried to gather myself, and asked, "What's your first name?"

He smiled. I smiled too in my teary eyes, trying to hide a goodbye behind it.

"That story… of your name!!" He looked out towards the morning sky. "Oh man… I miss you," he whispered to someone who wasn't here, my father. Then he turned to me.

"It's Trishulin."

"Trishulin?" I repeated, unsure if I heard him right.

"Yes. Trishulin. It means Lord Shiva."

The moment he said it, smiling softly, the train gave a gentle screech, slowing mid-way before the scheduled stop at the next station. And before I could say another word, he jumped off, right when the speed was just enough for a man like him to manage.

And just like that, he was gone.

I looked at Shukla-no, stared at him, as if seeing him for the first time.

"You… all this while? A spy? Does anyone else know?"

"No. Nobody knows," he said, calmly, flicking a bit of ash out the window like it was just another morning.

"And do you know anything about my father?" My voice almost cracked.

He exhaled deeply and nodded. "Okay-so, TJ sir asked me to tell you this only if you were to join us and if you asked after he had left. With specific caution that you never heard this, and I never told you anything. And if I did-under no circumstances, should he ever know that you know. Or that I told you."

"What?" I blinked rapidly. "I were to join you? You guys came prepared to… like… recruit me? Was this all a setup? Are you following everything I do?"

"No… not like that." He looked me straight in the eye. "TJ sir didn't want you to. He didn't want this life for you. But we all believe… you're just perfect for this. The only thing we planned was to travel in the same compartment. The rest-us becoming friends, all of it– was coincidence. Pure luck. Or fate, maybe."

"And yes… I do know about your father. And just know…. we all worship him, brother!"

I swallowed. The sound in my throat was louder than the train wheels below.

"He's a highly respected officer in military intelligence," Shukla continued. "And there's this place– a top secret research facility– called IIFPR. Indian Institute of Foreign

Particle Research. Your mother was a consultant scientist there."

"IIFPR..." I repeated, barely able to hold the weight of all this in my mind.

"She was working on a phenomenon, a theory, which-well, we believe– was connected to that train incident. The idea was this: you could control an explosion by controlling a chemical reaction. Basically, when two nanomaterials-let's say a Substrate and a Reagent– are combined, they start a chemical reaction like fire. But here's the twist. You can control where the explosion happens by placing the Reagent material at specific points, even if the Substrate is spilled over a much larger area."

I tried to keep up, but the words were beginning to sound unreal.

"The beauty," he went on, "is that neither of those materials can be detected as explosives on their own. Not by any imaging, not by any scanner-completely invisible. But the real secret... it's in something called a Catalyst. Without it, the materials merely start the fire-like reaction and then stop. But with it... the reaction is deadly. Precise. Controlled. Like detonating only a few tiles on a roof while leaving the rest untouched."

I leaned against the wall, trying to wrap my head around it. "So they were working on a... programmable explosion?"

"Exactly. And we didn't like designing it from zero, out of a blank idea. It was your mother's hypothesis studying a case that involved the death of a very high-profile politician. Each combination of these three materials reacts differently depending on the surface, humidity, even ambient temperature.

Your mother was the one decoding those variables. She was brilliant, Tarun. Way ahead of her time."

"And the train?"

Shukla nodded grimly. "We still don't know who planted it. But the patterns– the reactions, and something we call as energy signals-they match what she was working on. And that's what makes it even worse. Either someone stole her work… or someone on the inside betrayed her."

The train rocked gently, but I didn't feel it anymore. Everything was still.

"And your father… he went after them. After whoever was behind it. He was leaving for Kolkata for routine work. But after dropping you at Hapur that day, they got a lead that the case that haunted the military intelligence for years, was back. TJ sir brought the news themselves. Unfortunately, it involved the train you and Ira were on."

I closed my eyes. The sound of that day came rushing back– the footsteps, the explosions, the cries.

"And Ira?" I asked, expecting an answer to comfort me in some way.

"She wasn't supposed to be there," Shukla said softly. "We don't know if she got involved accidentally or if she was targeted. She might've known something, or maybe she was just in the wrong place. But the explosion that killed them… she somehow carried the same Substrate chemical on her body like I did. That's what we think."

I didn't speak. I couldn't. My world had broken years ago– but this was me standing in its ruins, finally seeing what brought it down.

"We believe there were only two people in the world who held that knowledge. One– someone was involved in the murder of that politician. And the other– your mother, who decoded it. Whoever triggered that first explosion nearly a decade ago never attempted it again. So maybe their intention was limited-targeted to just one person. But then we got intel that one of our own had turned. They had stolen classified documents– your mother's work. The defector was headed toward Nepal, via Lucknow, Gorakhpur… that route. The nanomaterials-Substrate and Reagent– they could still be replicated. But the binding chemical, or the Catalyst– the real key that made it all work… That secret, I'm sorry to say, died with your mother. It's not there in your mother's classified documents. That day, our mission was simple: intercept a potential meeting and extract the mole. No explosion was supposed to happen. We didn't even make contact. But the traces left behind– and the nature of that explosion– confirmed there was more truth to the intel than we'd feared. And now, if someone does have that knowledge, both from those documents and what stayed with your mother… just imagine what that could mean for the world."

"And you were hired because…?"

"Because I was a specimen." Shukla gave a half-smile, like it still felt unreal to say it out loud. "The first two explosions hit the train's wheels-iron-based reactions. The last one… it hit people. Two died. I didn't. I became a case study. They couldn't explain it. But then TJ sir saw something else– he believed I was better suited in the field than strapped to some lab table. Said I had instincts. But honestly? I don't think they were going anywhere with me either."

I looked away for a moment. A thread tugged at something in my memory.

"If we supply the right salts to the human body, along with a binder solution, it could reverse certain organ diseases… The binder just has to be tailored to the person's body and the specific organ under concern."

That wasn't Shukla. That was me. My own voice– my younger self-repeating the words I had read out loud at my school's science exhibition.

It was the theme of my project. "Biology: Ideas of the Future"– written in bright letters on a rough chart paper. A hypothesis. Simple examples. All of it, my mother's ideas.

I suddenly remembered how proud she'd looked that day.

And for the first time in years, I wondered– did I win that first prize because the idea was brilliant… or because no one really understood it?

"IIFPR…! Did my mother die because of that too?"

"It's a possibility," Shukla said slowly, "but we can't be sure. There was no identifiable reaction or trace left on her body. And certainly, no sign of an explosion."

The weight of ambiguity was worse than a definite truth.

"Even that stupid Neel Bandar is true; though we ourselves didn't understand what the hell that thing was. Someone posted a video somewhere. And because it looked FOREIGN to our higher authorities, they gave us the mandate to find it out. Man, we have enough to worry already. So, we just made another video, the morphed version of the original viral so people don't believe in any of it, including the same high-command people, and keep them off our backs" He added more, tapping on his thigh.

"What is– what the hell is-the-you two guys are– what is even happening here?" Ganesh's bewildered voice cut through the stillness like a bad edit in an otherwise seamless reel. He had appeared from behind, rubbing his eyes and blinking at the sight of the two of us deep in conversation.

"Hah, nothing serious," Shukla said quickly, casually flicking his cigarette. "Just needed a smoke. Pulled our new friend here for company."

"Wha…I didn't know you smoke." Ganesh walked over to the small basin, splashing cold water over his face and letting out a long sigh.

"Did you even sleep a wink?" he asked me, wiping his face with the edge of his towel.

Sleep? What value could sleep possibly have, after what I had just uncovered?

For years, I had carried the weight of being ordinary-of being unremarkable. A boy without story, without purpose. No glory to my name. No love that stayed. No memory worth retelling. I lived life like a placeholder, while the real world passed me by.

And suddenly I had stories that stretched across borders and labs, across life and death. Was this mine? Has it always been? Or was it simply borrowed truth now being returned to me?

My father had been proud of me– he thought I had carried everything well, despite knowing so little. But had I? Or had I just survived like a drifting boat in still waters?

Would it have changed anything if I had known all this earlier? If I had grown up knowing my father was more than a Subedar, would my mother be more than a quiet homemaker? Would that truth have turned me into someone else?

And now that I do know… does it really change anything?

Or does it just make me lonelier in the knowing?

What stories do I boast of now? And who do I even share them with?

And share what, really? That my parents were special? That I was special?

But special-why? Because of what I had… or because of what I had lost?

The only feeling that sat quietly in my chest now was the aching absence of three beautiful souls– my father, my mother, and Ira.

But almost in the same breath, something else rose with it.

Their love for me.

The care of my almost forgotten grandmother, my childhood friends– Shiva, Adrien, Chandu, my roommate Benjamin, even when I hadn't fully seen it.

The kindness of these strangers who became companions– Shukla, Ganesh, Sahoo, Verma, drunkard Vajpai Ji, Vet uncle, and even Trishulin Sir, with his quiet, haunted sense of duty.

That was all real. That was what mattered.

I didn't know where I was going from here. I didn't know what lay at the next station, or the one after that.

But for once, I was okay not knowing.

I was okay with what I had left with.

And even with what I had lost.

My eyes snapped open. The hum of the Nagercoil Express filled the silence. The memory, so raw and total, left me breathless. The truth hadn't just appeared; it had detonated, rearranging my entire past. My phone vibrated, a sharp, violent buzz against my leg. I fumbled for it, my heart hammering against my ribs. It was a text from Trishulin Sir.

TJ, high alert. We're close.

The world outside the window was no longer a blur of abstract darkness. Up in that same sky, a helicopter was descending. On the roads below, tires were screeching. The past and the present had collided.

"Sir, I see a deflection in the train's movement!" Chandu's voice crackled through the comms in the helicopter. "Speed dropping… eighty… seventy-five… Ambaturai! Looks like it's going for a stop here! Get ready! Get down, get down!"

The helicopter banked sharply, its searchlight cutting a brilliant, terrifying cone through the night. The ground team's SUVs swerved violently onto a dirt track, narrowly avoiding a collision, their headlights bouncing wildly as they raced to intercept.

The time for memory was over. The truth was here. And it was coming for us all.

Chapter – 22

The Anatomy of a Moving Bomb

The helicopter was a predator in the night sky, its shadow skimming over the dark, sleeping earth. Inside, the roar of the rotors was a palpable roar, a constant, bone-jarring vibration that rattled teeth and matched the staccato beat of their hearts.

"But wait!" Chandu shouted over the noise, his voice laced with a new, sharp confusion, his eyes glued to the data stream. "Speed is constant at sixty-five. By now it should've dropped to max thirty if it were to stop at Ambaturai. I don't understand. But that timestamp was definite!"

Trishulin stared at the grainy infrared image of the train on Chandu's console, a silver serpent slithering through an ocean of black. Ambaturai was a minor station, a ghost stop in the middle of nowhere. It was the perfect place for a quick, untraceable exchange. It was logical. It was efficient. And every instinct in Trishulin's body, honed by decades of chasing shadows, screamed that it was a diversion.

"No," Trishulin's voice was a low command that sliced through the cabin's urgency. "It's a feint. He's playing with us. He wanted us to find the Ambaturai timestamp because he knows we'd anticipate the most logical point. He's drawing us out." He looked at Chandu, his eyes hard as flint. "What's after Ambaturai?"

"Dindigul Junction, sir. A major hub. Much riskier for him, but… the train has a scheduled five-minute halt there."

"That's our window," Trishulin declared, making a bet that felt like it was being placed with his own soul. "He'll use the chaos of a major station as cover. Captain Acharya, get us ahead of the train; buy us as much time as you can and find a quiet place for us to onboard at Dindigul like common passengers!"

They didn't wait to discover whether the train would stop at Ambaturai. The helicopter stirred sharply, surging forward and leaving the twinkling lights of the ghost station behind. On the ground, the road team received the new orders, their tires screeching as they swerved back onto the main highway, gunning their engines to the redline to outpace the train.

Minutes later, the helicopter descended into a dark, fallow field, its landing lights carving a circle of surreal brightness out of the night. The doors slid open, and the team moved out, the rotor whipping at their clothes like a physical assault. They ran, a silent, determined unit, their boots pounding against the dark soil, racing towards the distant, approaching lights of Dindigul station.

The Nagercoil Express rolled into the station with a great sigh of brakes. As passengers began to disembark into the humid night air, Trishulin's team, now joined by six operatives from the road team, emerged from the shadows at the tail end of the train. They boarded with the fluid, unnoticed movements of ghosts, melting into the chaos of families greeting each other and vendors shouting their wares.

"Teams, deploy," Trishulin whispered into his comms. "One operative at each end of coaches S10, S11, and B1. The rest of you, with me. We are moving now."

The six teams fanned out, a network of unseen guardians in the night. The initial sweep was a lesson in growing futility. The coaches were a picture of mundane travel-sleeping families, students hunched over laptops, a group of men animatedly discussing a cricket match. Nothing was out of place. No suspicious packages, no nervous faces, no one betraying the slightest hint of tension. The very normalcy of it was unnerving, an oppressive blanket of calm that felt more threatening than an open confrontation. The Alchemist and his team were here, somewhere, hidden in plain sight. With every passing minute, the knot of dread in Trishulin's stomach tightened. They had made the bet, they were on the train, but it felt like they were searching for a whisper in a hurricane.

The search grew more desperate. The team members, disguised as vendors and passengers, moved through the coaches again and again, their eyes scanning every detail, every interaction. But The Alchemist's operatives knew their game well, their camouflage perfect. Any overt move, any sign of a shakedown, would send them scattering like rats, the mission lost. The minutes bled into an hour. The train left Dindigul, then the next small station, and the next. Hope began to curdle into a cold, hard certainty of failure.

It was Adrien, his mind trained to see patterns in human behavior, who spotted the first crack. In coach B1, he noticed a young man, a student by all appearances, who had a peculiar habit. Every fifteen minutes, like clockwork, he would get up and walk towards the lavatory, not to use it, but to stand by the door, pretending to stretch. It was a nervous tic, perhaps, but it was a repeating pattern in a sea of randomness. Adrien saw it not as a schedule, but as a performance– a poorly rehearsed one.

"Sir," Adrien whispered into his comms, his voice tight with restrained excitement, "B1, seat 17. He's a repeater. The rhythm is off. It's too precise to be natural, too anxious to be casual. He's waiting for something."

Trishulin gave the order. Two operatives, a man and a woman pretending to be a couple arguing over a ticket, intercepted the student on his next trip. The encounter was a blur of silent, brutal efficiency. A staged stumble, a muffled apology, and the student was guided into the narrow space by the lavatory, a needle pricking his neck before he could even register the threat. They dragged his limp body into the bathroom.

The truth serum was fast-acting. His name was Akash. He was a final-year engineering student from a prestigious college, recruited online. He knew nothing of nano-materials or explosions. His job was simple: to act as a mule. He and two others, one in S10 and one in S11, were to receive a package somewhere after Dindigul and simply carry it to Nagercoil.

"The package," Trishulin's voice was ice. "Where is it?"

"I– I don't have it yet," Akash stammered, his eyes wide with a mixture of drugs and terror. "Someone was supposed to deliver it. A bag. Under our seats. Seat 17. All three coaches. After Dindigul."

One of the operatives, a man named Vikram, swore under his breath. "Sir, we're already way past Dindigul; let me take a look."

Vikram moved swiftly to seat 17 in B1. He knelt, his hand reaching under the berth. He pulled out a large, black bag, the kind a musician might use for a Cajon. It was identical to the decoy Adrien had recovered from Kiran's room, only slightly larger, and chained heavily to the seat knob. But no light in it, not active.

A memory sparked in Trishulin's mind-a fleeting glimpse on the crowded Dindigul platform. A man in a simple kurta, his face unremarkable, carrying that exact bag, moving against the flow of the crowd. He had dismissed it as nothing, another face in the sea of humanity. But now, the image returned with chilling clarity. It had to be him. The Alchemist. But where had he gone? He wasn't in any of the three target coaches; Trishulin was certain of it.

The other two students were apprehended just as quietly, their stories identical. And under their seats, 17 in S10 and 17 in S11, were two more identical bags. Three canisters, all accounted for. All chained the same way to the seats. Adrien, his face pale, spat out a mouthful of nervous saliva. The Catalyst was secure.

But as Chandu ran a background check on the three students, a more grim reality surfaced. They were all brilliant, from good families, with no prior records. They had been seduced, seemingly by an ideology, their youthful idealism twisted into a weapon. They knew nothing more. They were disposable.

The question hung heavy in the air of the command coupe. They had the Catalyst. But where were the Substrate and the Reagent? Were there more operatives? Who to look for?

What to search? Kiran's intel about the train not stopping had been wrong. Akash's intel about the delivery being after Dindigul was also wrong. The Alchemist was feeding them contradictory information, keeping them off-balance. Discussing this all, Chandu, Shiva, Adrien, and myself– we had all gathered in the corridor of B2 in a desperate move to get out of the target compartments, to breathe different air, to think. Trishulin Sir's voice echoed again in our comms, "Guys, anything!"

Hearing his voice, we spread across the coaches again, continuing our search. I stood in the corridor of S11, my mind scrambling, trying to connect the science to the reality. My mother's research, the programmable explosions… it all felt so abstract. But now, it was terrifyingly real. I sank into my seat for a sip of water and ran my palm along the wall of the coach, then along the edge of the seat, the rough, synthetic fabric familiar under my fingertips. And then I froze.

The texture. It was almost imperceptibly different. The seats on the Nauchandi Express had been a standard, slightly worn rexine. And so they were in B2 of this train; I had just come from there. This was similar, but it had a faint, almost greasy residue, a subtle stickiness at the inside edge that was completely out of place.

A memory, sharp and electric, flashed in my mind. My mother explained the concept to me for my childhood science fair project. "The binder is the key, TJ. But the impact would differ due to the differences in human bodies." I nodded, only confused, but she continued with her unwavering warmth, "Think of it like different surfaces, a wall, a floor, even the clothes you're wearing. Just like they are visually different, so are the human bodies because of their genetics. Like on the outside, if you apply it as a thin, invisible coating, it becomes part of the environment; very similar is our medicine for the future, it cures patients as required in their own environment."

"Oh my god," I breathed, my voice caught in a choked whisper. I pulled a small, portable spectrometer from my bag, a piece of my own lab equipment I'd brought on instinct. I knelt, pressing the sensor against the seat cushion. The screen flickered, analyzing the material composition. And there it was. A complex polymer chain that had no business being in upholstery. It was laced with a dormant nano-particulate. The Substrate.

I scrambled to my feet, my heart hammering against my ribs. I ran to the next coach, S10, and repeated the test. The same result. Then to B1. The same. And in B2, nothing, like I had expected.

I burst into the command coupe, my face ashen. "Sir," I said, my voice trembling, "it's the seats. The seat cushions. Maybe the walls and the floor too. They're all coated with the Substrate."

Trishulin, Shiva, Adrien, Chandu– they all stared at me, the blood draining from their faces as the horrifying truth of my words landed. The Alchemist hadn't smuggled a bomb onto the train.

The three compartments weren't carrying a bomb. They were the bomb.

Chapter – 23

The Madurai Deception

The train rattled on, each click of the wheels a persistent countdown. The discovery that we were riding inside a bomb had settled over the team like a death shroud. The air in the command coupe was thick with a silence that was heavier than any sound. We had the Catalyst, and we knew the Substrate was everywhere around them, infused into the very fabric of the train. But the Reagent, the final piece of the puzzle, remained a ghost.

As the train began to slow for its scheduled stop at Madurai Junction, a fresh surge of anxiety gripped them. This was it. Maybe another chance for The Alchemist to make a move, to introduce the final element. Will it make its halt here for real? Or is it just another decoy? The team fanned out, their faces grim, their senses on a razor's edge. The train again made its scheduled stop perfectly normal. Kiran's information was established insignificant yet again. We couldn't fathom what to believe and what to not. All pieces of our gathered intelligence were useless. We had to believe in our instincts. "Learn in real time; act fast," Trishulin Sir whispered in his comms. The team watched every passenger who boarded, every bag that was carried on, every interaction on the crowded platform. But there was nothing. No suspicious figures, no clandestine handoffs. The stop was a picture of mundane travel, a chaotic symphony of families and vendors that yielded no clues.

The frustration was a poison, corroding their resolve. Defeated, the four of us– myself, Shiva, Adrien, and Chandu– retreated to the station's 24-hour coffee stall, a small island of fluorescent light in the pre-dawn gloom. The coffee was bitter, but it was hot, and it was something to hold onto.

"This is insane," Chandu muttered, staring into his cup as if the dregs held the answers his algorithms couldn't find. "He's playing with us. He's always ten steps ahead."

"Maybe that's the point," Adrien said, his voice quiet. He looked exhausted, the weight of his potential role in disarming the devices, not one as expected but three, pressing down on him. "It's not just a plan; it's a performance. He wants us to feel this. The helplessness. The frustration." He managed a weak smile. "He's a twisted sort of Romantiologist himself. He's trying to manipulate our emotional state."

The word 'Romantiologist' hung in the air, a strange echo from a different lifetime. "You know," I said, a memory surfacing, "you always had it in you, Adrien. Even as a kid."

A flicker of the old camaraderie, a flash of Pantnagar, entered our small circle. "Remember his 'Law of Reality-Balance'?" I asked, looking at Shiva. "When you were ready to fight that kid for supposedly insulting your mother?"

Shiva grunted, a reluctant smile touching his lips. "And Adrien just calmly points out that my mom is perfectly fine across the field and asks, 'So, is it you who is hurt or your mother?' I didn't know what to say."

"Or the 'Law of Masters and the Slaves'," Chandu added, "when you were fuming about having to do the dishes because the maid didn't show up. We were the slaves to our own thoughts, not the masters of the house."

We shared a small, weary laugh. It was a brief respite, a reminder of a time when our biggest problems were schoolyard squabbles and household chores. Looking at two young fellows distributing some prasadam at the station, we talked about our days collecting old clothes and food for donation drives, a youthful, earnest attempt to make a difference.

"Remember when you almost screwed that up, Chandu?" Adrien chuckled, his voice gaining a little of its old warmth. He perfectly mimicked the stern voice of a neighborhood uncle: "Aren't you going too much for donation, beta? When do you study?"

The memory was sharp and clear. Chandu, hopelessly smitten with a girl, had used the donation drive as an excuse to visit her house three times in one week. And each time, her bemused father had met him at the door. We all laughed, a genuine, shared moment of warmth in the cold, tense night. This is what friends were for. To remind you of who you were, even when you were in the middle of a nightmare.

The train's whistle blew, a sharp, insistent call back to reality. We finished our coffee, the brief moment of peace evaporating as we headed back to the train, the weight of our mission settling back onto our shoulders. We had found nothing. The Alchemist remained a ghost, and the train was ready for its journey further south, a moving bomb hurtling towards a destination unknown.

The train slowly jerked into motion, the brief stop at Madurai having yielded nothing but deeper frustration. We were chasing shadows, playing a game whose rules were constantly changing. As we regrouped in the corridor of coach B2, the failure hung heavy in the air. As we walked back through the target coaches, I noticed several of the passengers who had boarded at Madurai now had the familiar one-kilogram ghee boxes tucked into their luggage.

The sight stopped me in my tracks. I looked at Adrien, and saw the same dawning recognition in his eyes.

"Guys," he said, his voice low, pulling us into a tight huddle. "The ghee. From those guys at the station."

"Adrien, come on," Chandu sighed. "We saw it from that hoarding. It's prasadam from the Meenakshi temple. Some big festival."

"No, that's all fine," Adrien persisted, his eyes narrowed. "But think about it. Who donates ghee at three in the morning? And those guys… they were young, like us. They didn't look like they belonged to the temple. They weren't monks, not priests. And look at that one," he nodded towards the taller of the two through the window, who was stifling a massive yawn. The train paused after a few jerks and the station remained well in sight. "He looked like he hadn't slept in a week. If you're planning a big donation drive at this hour, you prepare. You rest. He looked exhausted." The train started again and sped through the darkness.

A shred of doubt, cold and sharp, pierced the fog of our frustration. We looked at the passengers with their ghee boxes, and this time, we saw what Adrien saw. The act of charity now seemed somehow disturbing, the piety a little too practiced, their smiles a little too bright.

"Sir," I spoke into my comms, my voice tight. "We couldn't find anything at Madurai because maybe there was nothing to find. Maybe the Reagent was just delivered." I quickly explained the situation.

Trishulin Sir's voice returned instantly, devoid of all warmth. "Confirm it. Now. See how many ghee boxes are there in those compartments."

Except for two of his operatives, Trishulin Sir and his team had gone to take a round of the entire train, leaving us four with the responsibilities to find clues for the remaining of the bomb.

The search was quick, discreet, and terrifying. Almost every new passenger who boarded from Madurai in S10, S11, and B1 had a box of the 'blessed' ghee. In fact, few of those already inside, who got up for a coffee or were awake for any reason, got their shares too. The sheer scale of the distribution was staggering. Could The Alchemist's plan really be this deep, this intricate? The question hung in the air, a chilling testament to the mind of the man we were hunting.

The discovery that the ghee had been systematically distributed throughout the target coaches sent a fresh wave of cold dread through the team. The Alchemist wasn't just a terrorist; he was a logistics genius, a puppeteer pulling strings from a distance we couldn't even begin to fathom.

"Guys," Trishulin's voice was a low growl in our earpieces, "I'm on it."

Coming back to the Coach S10, he made a call, bypassing local channels, going straight to a high-level contact in the National Security. The order was clear and absolute: find the two men who were distributing ghee at Madurai Junction. Now.

On the ground, the railway police, jolted into action by a call from the highest echelons, moved with a speed that was a sharp departure from the usual torpor of the night shift. They found the donation table, the banner still up, but the two young men were gone. A frantic search of the station ensued. Ten minutes later, they were found, not in prayer, but smoking cigarettes in the shadows just outside the station entrance.

The interrogation was swift and brutal. The two men, software engineers working for an MNC, crumbled almost immediately. They were part of an online group, a self-styled nationalist organization that promoted acts of civic and religious duty. Their 'Guru,' a man they had never met, had instructed them via an encrypted chat to perform this specific act of charity– to distribute ghee on that platform.

"Was it deliberate? I want specifics." Trishulin's voice crackled through the comms as he relayed the question to the interrogating officer. "Were they told to target those specific coaches and passengers on the Nagercoil Express at 3 AM?"

The answer came back, chilling in its simplicity. "Yes, sir. They were given the coach numbers. S10, S11, and B1."

They knew nothing more. Questioned nothing; just followed what their Guru asked them to. They were just cogs in the machine, their idealism weaponized, their good intentions twisted into a delivery system for a potential atrocity. They were, like the student mules, completely expandable.

The news hit us like a physical blow. We were all gathered in the command coupe, the air thick with the unspoken question. What now?

"Is it possible?" Adrien whispered, his voice barely audible. "Is the Reagent… in the ghee?"

"It's the only thing that makes sense," Shiva said, his face grim. "But we can't be sure. We can't create a panic by confiscating every box. We have to know for sure."

"There's only one way to find out," I said, the words tasting like ash in my mouth. "We have to test it."

The fear in the room was palpable. Test it? How?

"We test it on the Substrate," Shiva said, his voice quiet but firm. "We find a way to get one of the boxes, and we see if it reacts with the coating on the seats."

The risk was astronomical. If we were right, we would be deliberately initiating the very reaction we were trying to prevent. But we were out of time, and out of options. The Alchemist had us trapped, and the only way out was through the maw of the fire.

The decision was made in the silent language of shared desperation. We had to test the ghee.

The plan was as risky as it was necessary. Vikram, the operative who had found the first canister, was tasked with the acquisition. He moved through coach S10, his movements fluid and unnoticed. He identified a target: a passenger who had boarded at Madurai, his box of ghee tucked under his seat, now fast asleep, his snores a gentle counterpoint to the hammering of their hearts. With the deftness of a pickpocket, Vikram slipped the box out from under the berth and retreated.

We chose their laboratory with care: the small, unoccupied space near the lavatory at the end of the AC coach, where extra pillows and blankets were stored. It was isolated, and crucially, it had a door that opened to the outside.

Adrien, his hands now encased in the heavy leather gloves he carried in his magician's kit, took the box. His face was a mask of concentration, every ounce of his being focused on the task at hand. He held the box out over the open doorway, the wind whipping at his clothes. If anything went wrong, he would drop it into the rushing darkness below.

With a deep breath, he broke the seal and opened the box. Inside, it looked completely normal. The ghee was a pale, creamy yellow, its scent rich and familiar. A fragile flicker of relief washed over us all.

"I'll take a sample," Shiva said, stepping forward with a small spoon that came as extra along with coffees at Madurai Junction.

He carefully extracted a small potion and brought it right over the seat. The seat, like the others in the target coaches, was coated with the invisible Substrate. With a hand that was surprisingly steady, he let the drop of ghee fall onto the blue rexine.

We waited. One second. Two. Five. Ten. Nothing happened. The drop of ghee simply sat there, a glistening bead on the surface of the seat.

A collective sigh of relief and a renewed wave of despair filled the small space. We were wrong. The ghee was just ghee. The Reagent was still out there, a ghost we couldn't find.

"It doesn't make sense," Shiva muttered, his voice thick with frustration.

Adrien, his face a mix of defeat and grim resignation, began to tilt the ghee box, letting the contents pour out into the night air, an offering to a universe that seemed to be mocking them. He was halfway through when he stopped.

"Wait," he said, his voice sharp.

Something had shifted inside the box. He tilted it again, and a small, black, plastic box, no bigger than a matchbox, slid out from the bottom, coated in ghee.

"What the hell is that?" Chandu breathed.

Adrien looked at the side of the ghee box. In small print, under the brand name, was a promotional slogan: "A golden surprise in every box! Lucky winners will find a gold coin inside!"

A hysterical laugh escaped Adrien's lips. "A gold coin. Of course. My lucky day."

He threw the rest of the ghee out into the night, then quickly washed the small black box in the lavatory sink. As he wiped it dry, a faint, acrid smell, like acid, hit his nostrils. He became cautious. Pulling his leather gloves back on, he carefully pried the box open.

Inside, a thick, corrosive acid was fuming, having already eaten through half of the plastic.

Before we could process this new horror, a sharp hiss came from behind us. We spun around.

On the seat where Shiva had placed the single drop of ghee, a faint, almost invisible smoke was rising. The ghee itself, now that it had been exposed to the air for a few minutes, was reacting with the Substrate on the seat, a slow, sinister burn that was just beginning.

The hypothesis was correct. The ghee was the Reagent. The acid was the timer. It was designed to eat through the plastic box, spilling the ghee onto whatever surface it was on, initiating the reaction. Add the aerosolized Catalyst to this equation, and the result would be a catastrophic explosion.

The truth, in its full, terrifying scope, was finally revealed. We stood in the narrow corridor of the moving train, the pieces of the puzzle clicking into place, forming a picture of almost unimaginable horror. The coated seats were the Substrate. The ghee, now slowly, inexorably spilling from dozens of boxes throughout the three coaches, was the Reagent. And the canisters, chained under the seats of the three student mules, held the Catalyst, the final element that would turn this chemical reaction into a devastating explosion.

The Alchemist had designed a bomb with a distributed, delayed-action timer. The acid eating through the small black boxes was the fuse, ensuring that the Reagent would be released gradually, creating a widespread, undetectable threat. All that was needed was the introduction of the Catalyst.

Just as this horrifying realization settled over us, a new voice, sharp with panic, crackled through our earpieces. It was Vikram, the operative guarding the command coupe.

"Sir! We have a problem! There's a light active on the canisters! It just appeared. The timer light is still off but the other light, Green, just went on as I tried to pull the chains out!"

The Alchemist had made his final move. The canisters, we now realized, must have been equipped with a pressure sensor or a remote trigger. The act of moving them, of cutting them from their chains, had activated the final countdown.

The race was on.

We all were trapped in a metal tube hurtling through the night, surrounded by sleeping passengers, sitting on a bomb of The Alchemist's own ingenious design. We had all the components, we deciphered the mechanism, but we were no closer to stopping it. The spilled ghee that would start the slow burn any moment now was the terrifying reminder of the fire that was to come. And now, the clock was ticking. Only the Alchemist had the countdown until the Catalyst was released, until the three coaches became a raging inferno. The time for discovery was over. The endgame had begun.

Chapter –24

Alchemist's Gambit

Hope flickered like a dying ember. The green light on the Catalyst canisters, coupled with the insidious sizzle of ghee reacting on the seat behind us, drowned the team into hopelessness. The command coupe air thickened with metallic fear, a stench now eclipsed by acrid fumes rising from the coaches. For seasoned operatives, it was the cold, familiar dread of a mission spiraling; for us civilians, a primal terror: the paralyzing certainty of imminent death, clawing at the throat, stealing breath.

My own mind, a whirlwind of scientific possibilities moments before, went utterly blank. Equations, structures, theories–all dissolved into a raw, emotional void. In that terrifying void, a kaleidoscope of small, perfect life moments flashed: my mother's gentle smile over her teacup, my father's solid hand on my shoulder before Lucknow, Ira's unreal kiss on a rainy platform. Not a cinematic reel, but intimate fragments, sharp, beautiful pangs, desperate anchors against encroaching oblivion.

Shiva, usually a fortress of calm logic, was a caged animal, pacing the cramped confines of the coupe. Fists clenched, lips thin, he muttered molecular bonds, his scientific mind a desperate, crumbling citadel against terror. Chandu stared at his console, face ashen, data streams a meaningless pixel river, a mocking reminder of helplessness. Even Adrien, master of his craft, the illusionist who could charm away any fear, had a visible tremor in his hands, a clear signal that even his practiced calm was fracturing under the weight of their collective doom. He closed his eyes for a fleeting second, and I imagined he saw the faces of his audience, the cheering crowds, the applause that now seemed like a distant, impossible dream.

It was in this crucible of fear, this shared plummet into hopelessness, that Trishulin Sir found him. Moving through the chaos of coach S10, his eyes, usually cold, burned with desperate intensity, scanning disoriented faces. Then he saw him: the man from the Dindigul platform. The man with the Cajon bag. He was sitting calmly, almost serenely, reading something on his phone, a picture of detached normalcy amidst the rising panic. He was just another traveler, heading home, or so he seemed. But when he looked up, his cold, intelligent eyes met Trishulin Sir's, and in them, there was a flicker of something chilling: a knowing amusement, a silent acknowledgment of the trap he had sprung. It was him. The Alchemist.

Trishulin Sir, his face a mask of grim determination, signaled two operatives. Their movements were swift, silent, and practiced. The Alchemist offered no resistance, a ghost in their hands. Cold steel clicked on his wrists. A thin, cruel smile touched his lips-triumph, a game perfectly played. He subtly tapped his watch. In the command coupe, a new alert flashed on the catalyst canister, a malevolent red glow against the green.

"Sir!" Chandu's voice choked, raw with disbelief. "The timer… it's active. Forty-one minutes!"

The Alchemist had waited. He'd let them chase shadows, piece fragments, and believe they gained ground. Then, at their greatest despair, with ghee already burning, he revealed himself. He turned their small victory into a terrifying trap. This wasn't just a bomb; it was psychological warfare, designed to break their spirit before their bodies.

"The train cannot be stopped," The Alchemist said, calm, conversational, as they secured him in an empty S11 bay. He settled, cuffed hands resting easily on his back, gaze sweeping their desperate faces. "And you cannot get off. A beautiful, elegant design, don't you think? A testament to true ingenuity." His words taunted, a celebration of twisted brilliance.

Panic, a wild, untamed beast, rippled through the coaches. The team's urgent, hushed movements, their strained whispers, hadn't gone unnoticed by the now-waking passengers. The slow burning smell, though no fire yet, raised concern. A murmur grew into hysteria, then a full-blown roar. Trishulin Sir, grim-faced, knew they had no choice. "Evacuate the coaches. Now," he commanded, cutting through the din.

It was a controlled stampede, as controlled as possible. The team, a human chain, a desperate barrier against surging fear, moved passengers from S10, S11, and B1 into adjacent coaches. Simultaneously, a new, frantic race against time erupted. The corrosive acid, the bomb's insidious fuse, was unforgiving. It had eaten through countless ghee boxes. Now, as the team plunged hands in, it burned exposed skin. Without a single moment's hesitation, without thought for gloves, they frantically gathered remnants of ruined boxes, hands searing, and hurled them, box by ruined box, out the open gates. It was a desperate, haphazard cleansing, a chaotic purge of the spreading danger, but their only hope. No matter how fast, how many burning boxes, significant ghee had already spilled, a slick, oily film coating everywhere. The reagent met the substrate. Faint, acrid smoke curled up, a terrifying prelude in all three coaches.

In the relative quiet of the now-empty S11, air thick with fear and burning chemicals, Trishulin Sir faced his nemesis. The Alchemist, seemingly unfazed by the chaos he had unleashed, maintained his serene, almost beatific smile. "Your son," he said softly, cutting through tension like a razor. "How is he?"

The question, personal, intimate, utterly out of place, was emotional combat. Designed to disarm, wound, exploit a father's deepest vulnerability. Trishulin Sir's face was a mask of stone, betraying nothing. "He is in custody," he replied, flat.

"A pity! I had hoped you would save him," The Alchemist sighed theatrically. "He has a brilliant mind. Exceptional intellect. He understands, as you do not, that sometimes, a fever is necessary to burn out a disease. That true healing requires a painful, transformative fire." He spoke of a corrupted world, failed systems, and necessary destruction. Not just a terrorist; a prophet of chaos, a preacher of annihilation.

The two men shared a moment of silence, on opposite sides of a war for the future, the fate of hundreds of lives ticking away on a timer that could not be stopped.

"How did you even find him, my son?" Trishulin Sir asked him, voice low, a flicker of the father beneath the commander, desperate to understand his child's precipice.

Before he could answer, Shiva called from the back. "Sir, come fast." They gathered in the now-empty AC coach, B1, air thick with ozone and despair, a silent testament to impossible odds.

"We have a plan," Shiva said, voice a low growl, raw with urgency. "But we need your help to mobilize a few things," I added immediately.

"Can we put water on this fire?" Trishulin Sir interrupted abruptly, voice strained, pragmatism battling panic. "If we can flood the coaches, can we wash away the substrate? Dilute the reaction?"

"No," Shiva and I said in unison, scientific instincts overriding fear. "Water doesn't absorb ghee; no impact. In fact, worse," Shiva explained, sharp, mind racing. "The reaction could accelerate, spread faster. Not worth the chance."

"But we need something similar," he continued. "We don't need to remove the substrate. It is a losing battle. Neutralize the Reagent, the ghee that has already spilled. We need an emulsifier. Something that can bond with the ghee, encapsulate it, and make it soluble in water, so we can wash it away, render it inert."

For the next three minutes, which felt like a decade, Shiva and I worked in frantic, desperate synergy, explaining our attempt to Trishulin Sir.

Meanwhile, Adrien and Chandu hunched over the Catalyst canister from B1, grim, fingers flying with desperate precision. The Alchemist's round key opened thc outer casing, revealing not wires, but a complex, multi-layered puzzle lock. A masterpiece of intricate design, a cruel joke from a master manipulator.

"It's a recursive algorithm," Chandu muttered, fingers flying across his tablet, mapping connections, logic gates, self-referential loops. "A logic loop designed to trap you. One wrong move, one misplaced touch, and it locks permanently, triggering detonation. I can build a digital twin, map the sequence, and understand the logic. But the processing power... Sir, we can only attempt it for one. And even then, if we make a single mistake, it will lock permanently." His voice was tight.

"Then focus on this one," Trishulin commanded, strategic mind cutting chaos like a scalpel. B1's closed windows, being an AC coach, made any potential blast more dangerous, more contained, turning it into a pressure cooker of destruction.

While the two teams battled, Trishulin Sir returned to S11, to the puppet master. The Alchemist sat with a tranquil smile, hands cuffed behind him, eyes gleaming with chilling satisfaction.

"You asked how I found your son," he said, casual, polite, not a bomb confrontation. "Simple. We don't find them– they find us." He leaned back, gaze sweeping empty seats, faint smoke. He spoke of a digital ecosystem: a vast, dark web of academic forums, encrypted chats, hidden online communities for disillusioned intellectuals. "We monitor them," he explained softly. "Listen to frustrations, anger at a failed system, stifled brilliance, hunger for purpose. We praise their work. Validate their pain. Give bitterness purpose. Kiran was a star, burning with righteous fire, yearning for recognition, that too by his own father, and a cause, bigger than himself. All we did was give him a target for the flames, a direction for his righteous fury." He paused, a faint, almost imperceptible tremor. "We identify the vulnerable, the brilliant, the broken. We hack university servers, monitor academic publications, and track online discussions. We find minds too sharp for your mundane world, too sensitive for your callous systems. Then, we offer them a new path, a new purpose. A cleansing."

His words, a chilling testament to new warfare: battle for minds of brilliant and broken, twisting idealism into terror. In quiet rage, a single phrase escaped, a whisper almost lost in the train's hum, a confession meant only for himself. "… so that no more Hiltons will have to leave their children dying of hunger…"

Trishulin sir's eyes narrowed, sharp recognition flashing. He caught it. A flicker of a name, a ghost from his past, a personal wound buried beneath false layers of his pseudo ideology. The Alchemist, usually controlled, saw recognition. His serene mask cracked, revealing raw pain, a glimpse of human fuel for his monstrous crusade. He'd said it to himself, private agony. But Trishulin, years of observation, his uncanny ability to read lips, captured it. The Alchemist's eyes widened, surprise, then dawning horror. He knew. Trishulin had heard him. How? Said it only to himself. His own anger, rage, had betrayed him this time.

Twenty minutes. Catalyst timer glowed malevolent red, a relentless heartbeat to oblivion. In B1, Adrien, deep in trance-like concentration, hands hovering, fingers dancing over intricate mechanisms. Every click is a small victory. But each step solved a new, more complex challenge, a fresh layer of the Alchemist's twisted genius. He was a performer on the ultimate stage, his audience death, stakes hundreds of lives.

Fifteen minutes. Chandu, face bathed in cold blue console light, looked up, eyes bright with desperate triumph. "I'm in. Mapped final sequence. Pressure points, specific rhythm. Incredibly precise, almost musical." He turned to Adrien, voice strained. "It's your show."

Adrien nodded, pale but clear-eyed, focused, burning with supernatural intensity. "Leave me," he said, quiet but firm, cutting through rising tension. "I need to do this alone." He closed his eyes. The world fell away. Train roar, acrid smell, ticking clock-all faded to distant hum. Romantiology laws, strange, beautiful philosophies, no longer abstract. Tools, keys, only things to solve impossible puzzles, bring order to chaos. Laws of "in-between," "reality-balance," "creator and created"-not just theories, but living instructions, guiding trembling hands.

Chandu retreated to S11, joining the rest of us, gaze fixed on the Alchemist. The Alchemist watched him come, his eyes, usually cold and calculating, now tracing the subtle shifts in our collective posture, the unspoken understanding that passed between us. The Alchemist recognized Chandu. He was also among the ones, the brilliant and the broken. But as fate would have it, he stopped following his tale after only the first two interactions. Chandu didn't know what horror he had dodged. But the Alchemist knew that he had failed himself once. The only final-shortlisted candidate who the Alchemist couldn't tame to join his pseudo world. As the minutes bled away, a trace of fear, raw and unmasked, became visible on his face. It wasn't merely the chilling dread of his own demise, though that too must have gnawed at him. It was the dawning horror of a man who had gambled everything on the predictable chaos of human nature, only to find himself confronted by an unpredictable, unified will. He had been so certain of his victory, so confident in the elegant design of his chaos, in the inevitability of his triumph.

But he had utterly underestimated them. He had underestimated the illogical, indomitable power of human connection, of friendship forged in fire, of a father's love that defied all reason. He had planned for individuals, for their self-preservation, for their breaking points. Instead, he saw them, every single one, standing together, a unified front against his meticulously crafted destruction, their faces grim but resolute, ready to face even death to save strangers. In their unwavering unity, in their shared willingness to sacrifice, he saw not just his own vulnerability, but the profound, terrifying flaw in his entire anti-growth philosophy. His mission, the grand design he believed was bigger than any single life, was no longer merely threatened; it was about to consume him, dragging him down into the very inferno he had so carefully planned for others, a victim of the very humanity he sought to eradicate.

"You think you can win?" he snarled, voice a low growl, laced with desperate fury. Serene mask gone, replaced by contorted rage. "You and your government, you build your towers of 'growth,' your monuments to progress. But what is the result? Filth. Pollution. Cancer. Diseases. You have created a world where the rich grow fat while the poor starve. Where nature is raped and plundered for your insatiable greed. My vision: cleanse, destroy symbols of your failure! Make Nature thrive! Return to how God created humanity, in harmony with Earth. Slowly, I'll destroy the very symbols of what you call Growth!" His voice rose to a fever pitch, a manic crescendo of righteous anger.

The train slowed, rhythmic clatter softening, air brakes hissing. "You can't stop it!" The Alchemist screamed, voice cracking with rage and terror, eyes darting between Trishulin Sir and slowing landscape. "Stop it, and you'll blast the whole train! Fools!"

"We're not stopping," Trishulin Sir said, calm, faint smile. "Just reducing speed."

As the train passed deserted Satur station, a desolate stretch bathed in pale moonlight, it happened. From darkness outside, multiple jet streams of liquid erupted, arcing, pouring through open windows of S10 and S11. The Alchemist, instantly drenched, laughed, wild, desperate, spitting water. "Fools! Water can't stop it! It's mixed in ghee and a coating! It's oil and polymer, you imbeciles!"

But his laughter died. He smelled it. Faint, unmistakable, nutty aroma. Soy. Eyes wide with dawning horror, locked onto Trishulin's. His victory was once again taken. The scent, a silent confession, chemical signature of his undoing.

Shiva and I, faces streaked with sweat and grime, found the solution. Soya lecithin. An emulsifier. It wouldn't remove the Substrate coating-too ingrained. But mixed with water, it encapsulated ghee, rendering reagent inert, preventing reaction. Slow burn on seats sputtered, died. Acrid smoke dissipated. The timer still showed 2 minutes on the catalyst canisters. But S10 and S11 were safe.

"But what about B1?" Chandu asked with urgency.

Just as the words left his lips, a soft click. B1's empty AC coach door slid open with gentle hiss. Adrien stood there, face streaked with sweat, hands trembling. In them, he held the diffused Catalyst canister. Inert. Malevolent red light extinguished. He'd done it. Solved an impossible puzzle. Disarmed bomb.

Game over.

The sight of the diffused canister, symbol of ultimate defeat, broke something in The Alchemist. Eyes burning with pure, unadulterated hatred, locked onto Adrien, then swept to Trishulin Sir. Facade shattered, revealing raw, primal fury. He clicked again on his watch, and the remaining two canisters became inert too, along with the bombs that were synced to the train's speed. Then, with a sudden, impossible surge of strength, a movement so fluid and unexpected it defied the very notion of his cuffed hands, he snapped the restraints that bound him. The cuffs, which had seemed so secure moments before, lay discarded on the floor, as if they had never held him. Before anyone could react, before a single thought could form, he lunged for the open door and, with the grace of a phantom, leaped out into the darkness, vanishing into the rushing night. He was gone.

A stunned silence filled the coach, broken only by the rhythmic clatter of the slowing train. It felt as if he had been free all along. The realization hit them with the force of a physical blow. Why had he stayed? Why had he engaged in the conversation, the debate, the philosophical rant? Why had he allowed himself to be captured, to be taunted, to witness his own defeat? The question hung in the air, a final, unsettling mystery, a chilling testament to the depth of his manipulation.

The timers on the remaining two Catalyst canisters had run down to zero. No detonation. Even if there was a detonation, it would cause no harm as the reagent was already diffused.

Vikram and his team, grim but relieved, brought the two canisters from S10 and S11. No timer visible. But instead of a countdown or expected explosion, the small digital screens now displayed a simple, mocking message, glowing with malevolent green: "Ha ha ha… You lose."

Decoys. The entire threat, the elaborate, three-part bomb, the student mules, the ghee, the acid-all a performance. A grand, terrifying act of misdirection, designed to draw their attention, consume resources, fixate on a single, contained threat.

"He said it slowly but I'm certain, he had said it," Trishulin Sir murmured, the words from the Alchemist's lips echoing, a chilling whisper. "…so that no more Hiltons have to leave their children dying of hunger…"

Confused, a new, unsettling dread coiling in their stomachs, we all looked at each other. The victory, hard-won, now felt hollow, tainted by this final, cryptic message. Chandu, fingers flying across his laptop, began a frantic search, a desperate attempt to find meaning in the Alchemist's final taunt.

"Sir," Chandu said– a quiet whisper– eyes wide with dawning horror, staring at his laptop. "The Hiltons."

Trishulin turned, face etched with fresh apprehension. "What about them?"

"Anthony and Sana Hilton," Chandu read, barely audible, words heavy. "The first two activists and fishermen killed during the anti-Kudankulam Nuclear Power Plant protests in the early-nineties. They were survived by a twelve-year-old son."

The age matched. A cold, hard certainty settled over Trishulin Sir. A further, frantic search confirmed it. A man with the same name, the same age, a brilliant, troubled orphan who had earned a double PhD from Harvard in Chemistry and Computer Science. The pieces clicked, forming a picture of chilling clarity.

"This is it, Sir," I said, a sudden jolt of excitement in my voice. "The Kudankulam connection. This means his target is the plant itself! It has to be!" My voice, usually reserved, cracked with a blend of triumph and dread. The pieces seemed to fall into place with a terrifying precision, a narrative so compelling it felt undeniable. "His parents died there, he blames the 'growth' it represents. The method, the scale... it all fits. This is his ultimate revenge."

Shiva nodded, his eyes gleaming with scientific curiosity, caught in the same logical trap. "It's the most logical conclusion. The plant symbolizes everything he despises. The distributed nature of the substrate, the aerosolized catalyst... it's a perfect, insidious attack on a massive symbol of industrial growth."

But Adrien, who had been listening silently, his gaze fixed on the distant, receding lights of the train, shook his head. His expression was troubled, a subtle shift in his usually composed features. "No. It's too obvious. And it doesn't fit him." He looked at Trishulin Sir, his voice gaining a quiet conviction. "His anger, his philosophy... it's about cleansing, about making nature thrive, about returning to a purer state. Would he truly destroy a nuclear plant, knowing it would devastate his own village, his own people who are the last memory of his parents? That's not cleansing; that's indiscriminate destruction. His ideology is incompatible with that."

Just then, Trishulin Sir's secure comms crackled with a new, urgent report, cutting through Adrien's words like a knife. RAW had just received intelligence from multiple, highly sensitive channels. The external affairs, naval intelligence, had also intercepted the similar chatter from offshore surveillance that India's coastal cities were in danger. Someone was planning something big. No intelligence agency from any source had any clue about it till about forty-five minutes ago. Then suddenly, every phone in every office rang to spread this fear from the unknown that the thousands of kilometers of India's coastal line was no longer secure. The sheer volume and disparate sources of the intel made it undeniable.

The intel also suggested some external involvement, potentially a state-sponsored terrorist attack on key coastal cities, and dependent on a trigger at an offshore location near Kanyakumari.

The moment he heard Kanyakumari, his mind raced whether it was related to the Alchemist in any conceivable way. His counterparts, still reeling from the train incident's initial reports, were completely unaware of its true resolution. This new, massive threat was too big, too new, too sensitive to be shared over a quick phone call.

Trishulin Sir's face tightened, a grim visage of apprehension. He looked at us, his team, the only ones who truly understood the Alchemist's methods. "This is getting way more dangerous than we imagined," he muttered, almost to himself, his gaze sweeping the empty S11 coach as if searching for answers in the air. "RAW believes foreign powers are involved. We don't even know which other countries are behind this, or for whom this Alchemist truly works. China, Pakistan, or even North Korea, for God's sake... we can't say." The weight of this new, external threat settled heavily on his shoulders, a stark contrast to the internal, philosophical war he'd just fought on the train.

"Sir," Chandu interjected, his fingers already flying across his tablet, a new intensity in his eyes. "I've been experimenting with a GenAI scenario builder for certain business use cases. It's designed to predict complex outcomes based on vast datasets. Not sure it would work here, given the human element, but let me try. I'll feed in all this new intel– the RAW reports, the Alchemist's profile, his known targets, the Kanyakumari location, the coastal threat, the foreign involvement parameters..."

He typed furiously for a few moments, the tablet's screen a blur of algorithms and data streams. Then, a series of complex scenarios began to populate the display, each outlining a potential threat. Adrien leaned in, his eyes scanning the first scenario, a chilling depiction of a coastal radar station being compromised. And just as he read the words, Trishulin Sir, coming out of his own deep thought, verbalized them too, his voice matching Adrien's in a chilling synchronicity, as if their minds had converged on the same terrifying conclusion. "Integrated Coastal Surveillance System."

We all looked at Trishulin Sir, surprised by his immediate grasp, his intuition cutting through the digital noise. Maybe that's why my father was a big fan, I thought, a quiet awe settling over me, recognizing the same uncanny foresight my father had always revered.

"Yes, it has to be the coastal surveillance system that DRDO had built," Trishulin Sir continued, his voice firm, his gaze now fixed on the tablet. "That would essentially make our coastal defense go blind. This Alchemist has once again defeated us in our way of thinking. What could be his plans once that system is destroyed? It could mean the security of our key ports, cities like Mumbai, Chennai, Vizag would be at stake. It's getting way more dangerous than we had imagined. We don't even know which other countries are involved or for whom this Alchemist works."

The Nagercoil Express, still hurtling through the night, became our strategic command center. The next looming threat was at Kanyakumari, and staying on course on this very train was the most effective way to reach there faster than any other transport. The train, now a silent arrow aimed south, would not be stopped until Nagercoil Junction, its final destination, ensuring Trishulin Sir and team maintained their precious lead.

Chapter – 25

Shifting Sands

The Nagercoil Express, a steel and human missile, tore through the pre-dawn darkness. The rhythmic thump-thump of the wheels became a frantic drumbeat, each revolution a feverish tick closer to catastrophe. The train, usually a leisurely traveler, arrived at Nagercoil Junction at 5:50 AM, a full hour and a half earlier than its scheduled time. The abrupt, unscheduled arrival startled the platform staff, but for us, it was a desperate victory, buying precious minutes. All government authorities were now getting into action, their focus narrowed onto the Coastal Surveillance Station near Kanyakumari.

The moment the train hissed to a halt, a maelstrom of action erupted. There was no time for explanations, no time for doubt. Our mission had shifted from defusing a train bomb to preventing what was perceived as a state-sponsored attack on India's critical coastal defense. The frantic race against time had truly begun, a desperate dash from the Nagercoil railhead to the very tip of the Indian subcontinent, Kanyakumari, where the land met three oceans.

As we disembarked, Trishulin Sir, his face a mask of grim resolve, barked orders into his comms. A convoy of unmarked vehicles, already pre-positioned by the NSA's rapid response team, waited on the deserted road outside the station. We piled in, the tires screeching as we accelerated into the pale, nascent light of dawn.

Chandu, already hunched over his laptop in the back seat, furious flurry of motion. His fingers flew across the keyboard, analyzing possible escape routes The Alchemist could take from his jump point on the train, and cross-referencing them with potential access points to the Coastal Surveillance Station. Meanwhile, Trishulin Sir, continually on the secure line, coordinated with the NSA. A local team, already dispatched, was making their way into the Integrated Coastal Surveillance System's main control room, tasked with an internal sweep, unaware that the true threat might loom from the outside, or that their very focus might be another layer of the Alchemist's deception.

Shiva and I, our minds locked in frantic scientific synergy, began to piece together the new potential detonation plan for the radar station. If the methodology of the bomb remained the same, then the substrate must already be applied there.

"The Substrate," Shiva murmured, his voice tight with concentration, "it has to be pre-deployed. A coating, a paint, something applied in advance. It's the only way to bypass high security in real-time."

I nodded, a chilling realization dawning on me. "And the Reagent and Catalyst? They must be delivered separately, and fresh, for the reaction to initiate and accelerate."

Trishulin Sir, listening intently, suddenly interjected. "Team, is there any record of recent repair work inside the Coastal Surveillance Station?" He had a direct line connected to the higher authorities at the DRDO facility, a line now crackling with their urgent, coded requests.

The answer came back, a chilling confirmation that plunged us into a fresh wave of dread. "Yes, Sir. Some structural repairs were completed on the radar dish mounts and the main antenna housing over the last two months."

"Did it involve any specialized coating or sealant work too?"

"Yes, Sir. An anti-corrosion coating was applied to the metal structures, and some sealant for the electronics housing."

The revelation hit us like a physical blow. It was a stunning, terrifying confirmation. The Substrate. It wasn't just a hypothetical paint. We were sure it was already there, meticulously applied by the Alchemist's team, a dormant poison waiting to be activated. The Alchemist had been planning this for months, perhaps years. A message was relayed to send the IDs of all involved in the repair work at all levels.

The chilling question remained, a cold knot in our stomachs: how would the Alchemist bring the Reagent and the Catalyst into such high-security, in real-time, for the reaction to start and accelerate? And what could happen if India's coastal surveillance system was dead? Which cities to defend? How to deploy defence resources of this stature and this quick? India had never faced such a threat on its water fronts... not once... along its massive 11000 kilometer long stretch of coastal line. What type of war was waiting on us, no one knew. We weren't even sure whether the attack on the radar system was planned the very same day or the next day or next week or next month.

It was a catastrophic Intelligence failure. Trishulin Sir and his NSA counterparts agreed, our best chance to avoid such a war was to stop the trigger attack at the Kanyakumari Surveillance Station, or worst case, delay it. Trishulin Sir knew that the Alchemist wouldn't have planned such a precise attack on the Nagercoil Express if his next attack were not to happen the very next day. He wanted to create a master distraction to conclude his ultimate agenda. If Trishulin Sir's guts were to be trusted, he had either already reached Kanyakumari or he was on his way or his team would've already been there. The scale of the problem dwarfed anything we had faced on the train.

The drive from Nagercoil to Kanyakumari was a blur of speed and escalating tension. The sun, a nascent orange sphere, was just beginning to paint the eastern sky as we sped towards the very tip of the Indian subcontinent. The air, thick with the scent of salt and damp earth, felt heavy with unspoken dread. Reaching the Kanyakumari beach, we onboarded a jetty, and sailed past the iconic silhouette of the Thiruvalluvar Statue, its majestic form rising from the sea, and the Vivekananda Rock Memorial, serene and timeless. The morning sun, now showering its gentle, golden rays across the landscape, cast a deceptive calm over the scene, a stark contrast to the storm brewing within us.

The beauty of the dawn, the spiritual weight of Kanyakumari, usually a source of profound peace, felt almost mocking in its serenity. Our minds were not on contemplation, but on catastrophe. The realization that the local team dispatched earlier was now inside the Coastal Surveillance Station, meticulously sweeping for an internal threat, while the real danger loomed from outside, was a bitter pill to swallow. They were blind to the true nature of the attack, a meticulously crafted deception that had consumed our every resource.

We arrived at the coast near the Integrated Coastal Surveillance System, a sprawling complex of antennae, domes, and electronic towers that now seemed less like a symbol of progress and more like a colossal, fragile target. The air here was heavy, charged with an unseen energy. Our eyes instinctively scanned the horizon, searching for any anomaly, any sign of the Alchemist's next move.

And then we saw it. A faint, dark smudge against the brightening sky, just above the shimmering expanse of the ocean. It was too uniform to be a cloud, too deliberate to be smoke from a distant fire. As we drew closer, the smudge coalesced into a fleet of sophisticated drones, their sleek forms glinting in the rising sun. They hovered with an unnerving precision, their rotors a faint, almost imperceptible hum against the roar of the waves. And from their undersides, a fine, smoke-like mist was being released.

"Drones," Trishulin Sir breathed, his voice tight. "Releasing something."

The drones, silent harbingers of destruction, hung suspended against the dawn sky, their faint hum lost in the rhythmic crash of waves. From their undersides, a fine

mist drifted, caught by the steady sea breeze and carried inland, a deadly, unseen current flowing towards the Coastal Surveillance Station's main radar arrays and control buildings.

Chandu, already pulling up the station's blueprints on his tablet, zoomed in on the coastal area. His fingers danced across the screen, overlaying real-time atmospheric data, wind speeds, and thermal imaging onto the complex schematics. The Alchemist's plan, initially a terrifying enigma, began to unravel with chilling clarity.

"Sir," Chandu's voice was strained, a tight whisper barely audible above the wind. "The drones are seemingly releasing the aerosolized Catalyst. And the prevailing sea breeze… it's a perfect vector. It's carrying the aerosol directly towards the radar dish mounts and the delicate electronic housing."

My blood ran cold. The radar systems. I knew enough about their operation to understand the terrifying implication. These weren't just metal structures; they were the eyes and ears of India's maritime defense, drawing in vast quantities of air for cooling and maintaining atmospheric pressure within their sensitive electronics.

"And those systems," Shiva added, his voice grim, finishing my unspoken thought, "are directly connected to the internal cooling mechanisms and power conduits. The area where the repair work was completed just a few weeks ago. The area where the substrate was laid painted on all its walls, undetected to this very day."

The realization hit us with the force of a physical blow, a collective intake of breath, a shared horror. The Alchemist wasn't targeting the core of the station directly. He was targeting its lifeblood. He planned to blow the critical electronic components, destabilizing it. This wasn't about a direct explosion; it was about a controlled, insidious failure, a slow, agonizing meltdown triggered by a cascade of chemical reactions, blinding India's coastal defenses.

We were consumed by helplessness. The puzzle was repeating with new, terrifying stakes, with new variables and a bigger threat. RAW's initial fears of international involvement now seemed terrifyingly plausible. Has he corrupted bright minds working at the DRDO itself? This was becoming bigger and bigger, and all government parties would need to be informed.

But a crucial piece of the puzzle remained missing, a question that clawed at our minds: how would the Alchemist bring the Reagent into such high-security, in real-time, in the massive quantities needed to trigger a station-wide catastrophe? The station was a fortress, its perimeter bristling with checkpoints. The answer to that question, we knew, would be the final, terrifying piece of the Alchemist's meticulously crafted masterpiece.

Chapter – 26

The Ultimate Deception

A terrifying energy crackled in the air, a palpable tension that mirrored the invisible chemical reactions now accelerating within the Integrated Coastal Surveillance System. The drones, having completed their deadly ballet, were mere specks vanishing into the vast morning sky. The sea breeze, once a gentle caress, was now a relentless, unseen hand, pushing the aerosolized Catalyst into the station's vulnerable cooling and ventilation systems. Every second was a hammer blow against the fragile shield of our hope. We didn't know what was truly unfolding inside the station, or precisely where. No one had truly grasped what the Alchemist was after.

More defence personnel continued to flow in at the coast. We four were mere spectators. Trishulin Sir, his face etched with grim resolve, was a whirlwind of commands. His voice, usually a controlled growl, now carried a raw urgency as he coordinated with the NSA, the Air Force, and the Naval command. Two helicopters screamed overhead, their contrails slashing across the pristine blue, preparing to unleash an absorption agent which the DRDO scientists had recommended, drawing inspiration from the train incident a few hours ago. Four small Naval boats, their sirens silent, cut through the choppy waters, deploying specialized buoys designed to disperse multiple potential counter-chemicals into the ocean, hoping to neutralize the Reagent as soon as they found what and where that could be in a preparatory move. It was a desperate, unprecedented mobilization, a last-ditch effort to fight an invisible enemy on multiple fronts.

Shiva, his mind a maelstrom of chemical equations, watched furiously on Chandu's laptop, his fingers flying across the screen as he analyzed the real-time data streaming from the station's compromised electronic systems. The temperature readings were spiking. "The reaction is starting, Sir!" Shiva shouted over the roar of the helicopters. "But how? What is the reagent? Where?" His voice was laced with the chilling certainty of scientific prediction.

One of the government's top computer security experts was working frantically alongside Chandu. His job was to try and break into the radar station's old computer systems. He needed to find a way to shut down only the parts of the radar that were under attack. But the way these old systems were built was very complex and tightly linked; you couldn't just fix them with a quick software update.

Every emergency shutdown procedure they tried failed because turning off one part would also accidentally shut down another vital part of the radar, rendering the entire system to shut down and in turn triggering the very thing we were there to save from getting triggered. Meanwhile, the special coating on the radar's surfaces had already started to mildly burn, but the source remained a mystery. We knew the catalyst was being blown in by the sea breeze, but the 'reagent' that would cause a full explosion was still missing. Everyone's fear was at its pinnacle; a detonation seemed imminent. Death felt imminent.

The local team inside the station, now fully aware of the external threat, moved with a desperate urgency, evacuating non-essential personnel, their faces pale with terror. Navy received orders to follow war-time measures along the coast and were alarmed for a full-blown emergency scenario. Everything unfolded so quickly, from nothing couple of hour ago to war-time measures, the entire system of the government felt under utter shock and panic.

I stood by Trishulin Sir, my eyes fixed on the station, then on the distant drones, then on the churning ocean. The sheer scale of the Alchemist's plan, its meticulous orchestration, its reliance on natural elements– it was a horrifying masterpiece. He had not only understood the science of destruction but the psychology of distraction. He had used our own intelligence against us, forcing us to chase shadows while he set his true stage.

"He's not here," Trishulin Sir muttered, his voice hollow, his gaze sweeping the horizon. "He never intended to be. This was always about the Coastal Surveillance System. He used us, used my son, used the train… to buy himself time, to ensure our focus was elsewhere." The bitter realization was a fresh wound, a betrayal that cut deeper than any physical blow.

The drones, their mission complete, were now mere specks disappearing into the vastness of the sky. The sea breeze, a chilling reminder of the Alchemist's cunning, continued to carry the deadly Catalyst towards its target. The station's hum, once a symbol of power, now sounded like a death rattle.

The final countdown had begun. The battle for the Coastal Surveillance System, for the very future of the nation, was no longer a theoretical exercise. It was here. And we were standing at ground zero, watching the unraveling of a meticulously planned catastrophe.

Yet, even as Shiva's data screamed of accelerating reactions, a nagging doubt began to gnaw at me. The train incident, the Alchemist's final, mocking message– "Ha ha ha… You lose."– it echoed in my mind. The timers on the decoy canisters had run down to zero, and nothing had happened. Was this entire spectacle– the drones, the complex chemical delivery, the sheer audacity-all worth it? Was the efficiency of this reaction truly on the scale we were imagining?

Could this catalyst, so far from its intended coupling place over the walls inside the radar infrastructure, really be transported by the sea breeze through the ventilation system and still create an explosion to the scale we were all dreading? Were we giving too much credit to this Alchemist, believing he possessed knowledge far beyond the combined intelligence of so many DRDO scientists? What if the real threat was something simpler, not so scientifically grand, but profoundly human? Psychological, perhaps? Like he loved to play with people's minds.

Adrien, who had been watching this all silently, his role in this scenario seemingly sidelined, suddenly spoke, his voice cutting through the frantic calculations. "Hold on a moment. Someone so angry that his parents died, someone who became what he is because of that pain… would he truly destroy a coastal radar station and then handover these coasts to foreign powers knowing it would impact his own village too? His people who probably are the last memory of his parents? His 'anti-growth' ideology doesn't sync with this 'anti-national' attempts. He'll not let that happen." Adrien paused, a wry, almost sad smile touching his lips. "This seems off for someone like him. He cares for his own, not knowing… that we are all his own too. Not different. We are all just one." Benjamin's words, a quiet echo from a different life, resonated in my mind.

Then Shiva said it, his voice laced with doubt, "TJ, what if there's no reagent at all? Or no catalyst– I don't care which is which. What if there's only one? And the substrate. Then the reaction can't be of the scale that it could turn into an explosion. What if it is meant to only be like this? Like the experiment we conducted on the train seat– a mild and slow burning that is only enough to raise the temperature a little bit. What if whatever this catalyst aerosol is, this is only acting as a reagent, reaching the substrate already with the sea breeze, and creating this very mild burning? What if this is all that is supposed to happen here?"

Shiva and I, who until this moment had been racking our brains for available absorbents or emulsifiers, debating what to ask Trishulin Sir, what to do if the Reagent turned out to be this or that– we suddenly looked at everything in doubt. The grand show of drones, the complex chemical delivery, the entire terrifying spectacle… was it all just a massive, elaborate misdirection?

The chilling realization settled over us: The Alchemist wasn't just a master of chemistry. He was a master of the human mind.

"Guys, I'm counting on you to solve this bigger problem here, and not think like teenagers and solve a puzzle," Trishulin Sir's voice cut through our dawning realization, his gaze sweeping over the frantic activity around the station. He was still focused on the immediate, visible threat.

"Sir, please trust us!" Shiva shouted back, the urgency in his voice overriding all protocol. "This is all a fluke! The real threat is somewhere else, not here."

He paused, his eyes meeting mine for a fleeting second, a silent acknowledgment of my plea, before turning back to the drones and the unfolding chaos. Do what you have to, his gaze seemed to say.

Chandu, with unlimited data access from Trishulin Sir and the government, was already a blur of motion. He pulled up the details of the four third-party agencies involved in the radar system repair work from two months ago, listing all their 31–manpower crew. Two potential anomalies identified– Joy and Niro. Both belonged to separate agencies but their Adhaar was linked to account numbers having transactions with similar digital traces as Bengaluru.

Chandu searched these agencies, and there it was: both were long-time contractors for government key infrastructure maintenance, e.g., coastal, deep sea, and hydro powerplants. But the real twist lay in their leadership. Both agencies shared a director with the same surname, Mani, and first names that were seemingly Christian: Hayden and Jayden. It didn't sound like luck. The financial traces between the two agencies were identified, again matching the Bengaluru connection. And it turned out that the same pattern followed in three more government contractors' databases.

Adrien leaned over to Chandu's screen. "Is there a way to know where these agencies are working now? Where are these specific people at this very moment?"

Upon close search, with help from the government team, Shiva, Adrien, and I-all fixated on Chandu's laptop-found it. Joy actually worked for a Submarine Cable company out of Cochin. He was also a data centre expert, writing India's digital economy story. Niro was a facility management expert in HVAC systems. Coincidently, both agencies carried maintenance work at two different places: Chennai and Cochin, both at the cable landing stations in these cities.

But then, Chandu's eyes widened, catching something even more familiar. He looked at the ID of another junior technician from the agency that had applied the anti-corrosion coating to the radar mounts. The name: Rahul Sharma. And listed as his residential address: Chandu's own college address. Chandu saw the face and was surprised to see it was the son of his own hostel warden. A really bright guy. But how could he be working in maintenance jobs, he was a computer and data science mastermind.

What appeared then as a coincidence was far from mere luck.

A frantic search for the warden's son, Rahul, revealed he was currently in Mumbai at a Submarine Networks conference on the rise of data centres in India. As it turned out, he was working for another large tele-communication company that managed the cable landing station in Mumbai and Cochin. The other person– Niro, from the initial list– was at Trivandrum at the Local CLS there. And when the full scope of all five contractors– those initial two, and the three others linked by their common, shadowy director– was finally laid bare, the true, horrifying nature of the threat became devastatingly clear. It was a plot beyond anything any of us could have possibly imagined, meticulously designed to cripple the very fabric of the Indian economy.

India's digital services, a sector contributing hundreds of billion dollars to its GDP, stood on the precipice of annihilation. The success, the very pulse of this services sector, was utterly dependent on an invisible thread, a silent, omnipresent force we all now took for granted: the internet. Life, as we knew it, was simply unimaginable without its constant hum. How would families communicate across continents, their voices silenced, their faces unseen? How would businesses conduct trade, their digital arteries severed? How would basic needs, even healthcare, remain accessible, with telehealth services, emergency communications, and vital supply chains instantly paralyzed?

Shutting down these five major submarine cable landing stations– Trivandrum, Mumbai, Cochin, Chennai, and Tuticorin– would not merely bring an entire nation to its knees; it would plunge India into a digital dark age, a terrifying isolation. And the ripple effect would extend far beyond its borders, impacting the entire modern civilization, a world so intricately connected that its very existence hinged on these unseen cables. The thought was a cold, creeping dread: a return to an era before the digital breath, a favor, as the Alchemist had chillingly stated, to 'Mother Nature,' a brutal, forced regression to the old ways."

"I will do a favor to Mother Nature," the Alchemist had said, "going back to the old days how things were." Was this what he meant?

Trishulin Sir, still focused on the immediate, visible threat at the radar station, shouted at us, "Guys, this is not the time to make stories! Try and assess how we can stop this potential explosion at the Integrated Radar Surveillance System!"

"Sir, we know where the actual target is!" I yelled back, pointing frantically at the map of India on Chandu's tablet, highlighting all five cities with key cable-landing stations. "The real threat is here!"

There was no time to align everyone. A decision had to be made.

And believing us, Trishulin Sir– with a decisive roar into his comms– immediately deployed the resources stationed near the coasts of those five cities to the cable-landing stations themselves, which were not far away. The higher-ups in RAW and elsewhere were still converging on the radar stations.

At those five critical locations, the teams found one or two men from each contractor engaged in something deeply out of place: planting bombs designed to sever the internet cables– to black out communication, cutting India off from the world and the world from India.

Within an hour, all five landing stations were secured.

No one at the radar station yet understood what had changed, but the comms crackled with the same words again and again:

"We're safe, guys. We're safe."

This had been the Alchemist's ultimate deception: drawing all forces to the right cities but the wrong locations, focused on an external target, while the true strike was always internal– an attack on the digital nervous system of the nation, timed so that no agency could possibly track what was happening at all five stations simultaneously.

The Alchemist, watching the operation unfold from the Coastal Surveillance Station– his drones now flying too high to remain inconspicuous– felt the ground shift beneath him. He saw the teams make no further attempt to defend the radar station, at least not from what his drone camera could capture, positioned near the base of the Thiruvalluvar statue.

Startled, he began calling his operatives at all five sites.

No answer on the first ring.

On the second, the line connected– not to his men, but to Trishulin Sir.

"Hello, Cyril. Cyril Hilton," Trishulin Sir said calmly, not even waiting to confirm the identity on the other end.

"We met on the train. You remember."

Cyril Hilton– the Alchemist's real name– clenched his fists, fury flooding through him. No words came.

"This is not over…" he finally growled.

"And yet," Trishulin Sir replied, steady as steel, "I will stop it again– until it is."

The line went dead.

Epilogue

The immediate aftermath was a blur of exhausted relief. The sun, now fully risen, painted the sky in hues of triumphant orange and soft, hopeful blue. Standing at the coast near the surveillance station– a place of immense natural and man-made power– we watched a rocket tear through the sky, shedding clouds as it arced gracefully into the heavens, a silent testament to human ambition and ingenuity.

We stood there, a small, grimy group, watching it disappear, the weight of the last twenty-four hours slowly lifting. The roar of the ocean, once a terrifying accomplice, now sounded like gentle applause. We had faced a phantom, outmanoeuvred a genius, and saved a nation from a threat it never even knew existed. The victory was immense– a quiet, profound triumph that settled deep in our bones.

Just as the last trace of the rocket vanished, Adrien's phone buzzed. His face, still etched with the remnants of tension, softened as he listened. It was Ishan.

"What happened? None of you picked up the phone last night," Ishan's voice, clear and relieved, cut through the static.

"Ah, nothing…All well," he said, with an exhausted smile, looking at all of us, as if meaning where to even start from to answer what all had happened.

"And Kai? Any news on his health?" Adrien asked, instantly remembering him.

Trishulin Sir let out a long, slow breath, a sound that was half-sigh, half-chuckle, just as he hung up another call. "Phew, again," he muttered, a wry smile touching his lips, a shared glance passing between us. "Another thing to worry about, another puzzle waiting."

We all shared a laugh, a genuine, unburdened sound that, for a precious moment, made us forget that the Alchemist, Cyril Hilton, remained on the run.

Ishan then requested Trishulin Sir, his voice low and urgent, if they could keep Kai's existence a secret. Kai was willing to cooperate with their studies, but he was searching for a cure for his entire planet, and if news of his existence were to get out, his body would be carved across laboratory tables–dissected, examined, his very being reduced to a scientific specimen.

Trishulin Sir, his face grim, promised Kai's safety, assuring Ishan that his existence would remain hidden.

It was then that Kai spoke. His voice was weak, but it carried a weight that stilled the room.

"You are different. Thank you."

He paused, as if searching for words that no longer came easily.

"My world chased more. Always more. Bigger. Faster. Advanced."

Another pause.

"We called it progress."

He looked at us then, not accusing, not pleading. Just tired.

"I hope you do not become what we once believed we were becoming."

It was not a threat. It was a warning.

One born from a world that had already paid the price for unexamined growth.

In its quiet way, it echoed the Alchemist's creed, yet differed entirely in spirit.

Where the Alchemist spoke from fracture, this came from loss without bitterness.

From knowing, not rage.

And so the question remained.

Was the Alchemist trying to save the world from itself, or merely replaying his own wound on a grander scale?

No answer arrived.

Only the unsettling realization that conviction and consequence do not always travel together.

Right then, as the weight in the air began to settle, Shiva stirred, as if a thought had finally found its way out of his restless mind. He lifted his hand, measuring the air, and asked, "Hey Kai. Just one last thing. A sharp blue monkey, about this big, with golden patches. Do you know him?"

Kai's eyes widened.

"Zeilo," he said urgently. "Have you seen him? I've been looking for him for months. Sir, please, he's harmless. I saw a video about him. That was all a lie."

Trishulin Sir let out a soft breath, the corner of his mouth lifting.

"There you go," he murmured. "Another complication."

Then, more gently, "Don't worry. We'll find him."

"An alien monkey," Shiva said, blinking.

I leaned toward Adrien and pinched his arm lightly. "Tell me this is still real."

Adrien broke into a grin. "I'm calling him I.B. Mon," he said. "The Indian Blue Monkey."

The call went silent.

"The Alchemist," Adrien sighed, the name settling differently now, shaped by a deeper understanding.

"He's still out there," Trishulin Sir said, his voice regaining its usual steel, "and we don't know how many more brilliant minds are under his grasp. But we'll find them. This is a long way from what we'll call a true victory. For now, let's get you guys home."

He looked at us all– his team, his friends, his unlikely heroes.

The Alchemist's audacious gambit had been thwarted, but we knew the real war had only just begun.

The rest of the team and Trishulin Sir moved away, absorbed in their comms, leaving only the four of us behind.

The same small gang from Pantnagar.

A profound silence fell over us, not of exhaustion, but of a strange, almost disorienting calm. The adrenaline that had fueled us for twenty-four hours drained away, leaving behind a vast emptiness. The world, which moments ago had been a ticking time bomb, now felt… too quiet.

We looked at each other, our faces streaked with sweat and grime, a shared understanding passing between us. We had defused the immediate threat– but where did we go from here?

It was a question that hung heavy in the air, a sudden, unsettling void after the relentless urgency. It had been only a day on this journey, yet it felt as if it had been our entire lives. Our minds, conditioned by the relentless pursuit of a singular objective, now struggled to comprehend what came next… what was normal.

Shiva, ever the pragmatist, was the first to break the silence, a weary smile touching his lips. "Well, my flight back to Europe leaves in a few hours. I suppose molecular bonds await."

Adrien, though visibly drained, managed a theatrical sigh. "And I, my friends, have a show in Chandigarh. The illusion must go on, even after facing the ultimate illusionist."

And Chandu, usually so self-assured, hesitated, his gaze flickering between Trishulin Sir and the vast ocean. He asked, almost shyly, if there was a way he could join Trishulin Sir's team.

I immediately called him over and passed on Chandu's request. Trishulin Sir's eyes held a knowing glint as he looked at Chandu, then at me.

"Let me see what I can do," he said, the same words he had spoken to me just twenty-four hours ago, a quiet promise now shaped by shared experience.

I smiled, a genuine, unburdened smile.

"The kind of threat we just witnessed," Trishulin Sir continued, his voice turning serious, "suggests we will need new machinery in our defence system."

"Our old brains couldn't process what we were truly up against," he said quietly.

"So, thank you very much, young men. Perhaps this is the flipped version of intelligence: how one is ready to engulf the world, and how others are ready to die to save it."

Before leaving, we all stood for a moment, watching the vastness of the sea, its endless horizon mirroring the new possibilities stretching before us.

We promised to meet again in the coming summer, in Pantnagar, the place where we had grown up, where the seeds of our unlikely camaraderie were first sown.

And then Adrien, the man who would one day be known as the Romantiologist, leaned in, his voice soft.

"Don't miss coming to Pantnagar," he said. "Stay at my place."

It struck me then, how often I had been the one to abandon plans like this, and how strange it felt now, knowing there was little left for me in Pantnagar, except them.

His hug was tighter than any magic trick, a physical confession that the curtain made of his own skin had finally been pulled back. He whispered, "Vaise bhi, Bahut din huye dil halka kiye (It's been a while since we've unburdened our hearts anyway)."

He didn't have to say more. After five years of me ditching them, those words and that look held the entire weight of all the time lost.

Then Shiva and Chandu followed, their hugs tighter, lingering for just a moment longer– a quiet acknowledgment that there was still so much left unsaid between us.

With a final nod, we parted for our respective destinations. Dawn had fully broken by then, and with it, something else had begun.

By the time I reached Lucknow, the city appeared as a hazy collage of familiar streets and half-remembered corners. On the way from the airport, my auto-rickshaw passed the Charbagh Railway Station, and a sudden wave of nostalgia caught me off guard.

Just the previous morning, I had stood there with my newly made companions– the Fantastic Four (Sahoo, Ganesh, Shukla, and Verma)– after seeing off Mr. Vajpai Ji to Prayagraj.

It felt impossibly distant now. As if it belonged to another life.

As I watched the station recede in the auto's side mirror, my phone buzzed. It was Shukla. "How was your first day on duty?" he asked, his voice laced with his usual dry wit.

All I could do was laugh. Just then, Ganesh also called. "TJ bhai… aap bhool na jao, to humne call kiya (so you don't forget... that's why I called)." His voice, cheerful and familiar, brought another smile.

"It's important to speak sooner than later," he added, then chuckled. "Doctor Sahiba se bhi mil lijiyega… jaldi milna bhi zaroori hota hai (Do meet the Lady doctor... it's even more important to meet sooner than later)." He laughed again, and I suddenly remembered what he meant.

The Nauchandi Express. The previous morning, at Charbagh Junction, the roly-poly Mrs. Gupta from Bulandshahr had climbed down from her air-conditioned coach– still loud, still majestic in her own delightful way.

"How was the journey, beta?" she smiled. "You had almost missed your train, ha! Glad you made it!"

"Yes, thank you, Aunty. Bas bach gaya kal to (Just barely survived yesterday)," I said. "I got lost just standing there at the platform."

"Hmm… I understand," she chuckled, her laughter shaking her belly in rhythm. "Ye umra hi aisi hoti hai. The mind never stays still (This age is like that)." She jerked her hands dismissively. "My daughter's the same. Look-she was supposed to pick me up an hour ago! Still not here. Thankfully, the train was running late, or I'd have been waiting alone for so long."

"Oh, your daughter! Does she live in Lucknow too?" I asked, trying to keep the conversation going.

"Oh no, no-she's a doctor. Government doctor," she said, proudly emphasizing Government, flashing her wide gums. "Just got posted at Barabanki Hospital. I'm going there with her." She picked up the corner of her saree and held it out to me. "She sent this with her first salary last month. Although it's a bit uncomfortable sleeping in it on a train, I wore it today to surprise her."

"That's lovely," I smiled. "You must be so proud." I said, almost compulsively, as Ganesh kept staring at me, his eyes shouting, "let's go!"

"Haan… proud to hoon (Yes… I am proud)," she said, then paused for a moment. "But she doesn't have time for me the way she used to." Then, brightening again, she added, "But who am I to complain? Her life's started now. She has to go where it takes her. Yahi to zindagi hai (That's life)– the old things stay behind, and new things come."

"What do you do here in Lucknow?" she asked, shifting the spotlight back to me. By now, I'd realized she wasn't going to leave me alone until

either her daughter showed up or someone else joined her to chat.

"Oh, I work as a-" I had just started, when her daughter appeared.

"Maa… Maa… over here!"

"Sorry I got late," she said, slightly out of breath, eyes squinting in apology. "There was a late shift at the hospital yesterday. Come on, now-I've got to report by sharp nine."

"Arre, at least stop for a breath," Aunty said, trying to calm her down.

"No, no, Mamma. No time. Let's talk in the car."

Then Mrs. Gupta turned to me and smiled faintly. "Okay then, beta," she said, looking at me warmly, "I'll take your leave."

It was only then that the daughter noticed me standing beside her mother. We exchanged a small nod-no questions, no curiosity-just a brief acknowledgment. And just like that, she gently but firmly began to drag her mother away, walking fast.

I watched them go, smiling silently and thanking aunty in my heart-for saving my journey, for being a character in this new adventure of a lifetime. I saw her lift her dupatta and place it carefully in her daughter's hand, as I watched them go from behind. And in that exact moment, the daughter turned to look back at me-five deliberate seconds of eye contact. Maybe she was about to ask her mother who I was. Maybe not. I lifted my hand to wave, almost instinctively, though I'm not sure why. But she turned away just after I did. I wondered if she even saw it. That sheepish feeling of embarrassment! And just like that, another set of strangers had come and gone.

This was the lady doctor Ganesh referred to, the one with whom I exchanged five eternal seconds of eyes.

Walking towards the exit, Ganesh and I had exchanged numbers, while all debated over who made the best Golgappas in Ganj, argued about chicken in Aminabad, praised the Lassi at Qaisar Bagh, and planned an imaginary, aimless visit to the Imambara. Just anything and everything. There, that was happiness.

In minutes, we had already reached the auto-rickshaw stand. And that's where Anand Mishra Ji picked me up, and I was on my way to my hostel.... when I got the call from Trishulin Sir.. amidst the sweet voice of Anand Mishra Ji, singing...

"diwaanaa huaa baadal,

saawan kee ghataa chhaayee,

ye dekh ke dil zoomaa,

Li pyaar ne angadaayee..."

So much had happened, so much, in but a single day– a life remade, so profoundly, I could scarcely recall the ghost of who I was a mere sunrise ago. It was as if every quiet moment, every hidden grief, every unnoticed breath of my past, had been a meticulous preparation for this very dawn.

Is this the way of it? That once life begins to heal your own wounds, a quiet pull turns you toward the wounds of others? Or is it a sacred, strange truth: that you can only see the world's sorrow when you've finally found the strength to face your own? I do not know which comes first, which truth makes the other possible.

But I thought of Chandu, his quiet battles fought in the shadows of algorithms, yet now, a profound happiness bloomed in his eyes before our goodbyes– as if his own time had come, a quiet unveiling. And Adrien, Shiva, Ishan... their lives, seemingly ordinary, yet each probably a universe of silent struggles and whispered dreams. And Trishulin Sir, the man who remained a mystery my entire life, a pillar of unwavering duty; he may have saved a nation from unseen threats, yet a long, lasting, and deeply personal battle awaited him in the cold, sterile confines of the Bengaluru Command interrogation room, a father's heart aching for a son he could not save.

Kai– with his entire planet suffering, a world dying of unchecked 'growth' – hadn't found the cure he sought on Earth, but at least, he now knew the insidious cause of 'The Stillness.' Perhaps, in that, God had heard their distant cries, sent a fleeting, fragile hope. *Which God would they follow on Sone'Vora?* I chuckled softly, a tear tracing its own path, remembering Benjamin and his boundless belief in the divine in every drop of water, every human soul.

Life… it is indeed so much like the clouds. One moment, a clear sky– vast and unburdened; the next, a gathering storm, heavy with unspoken promise or sorrow. We never truly know where it will take us, what shadows it will cast upon our path, or what fleeting, radiant light it will release.

But as I stand here, trying to grasp the boundless, chaotic beauty of it all, maybe… just maybe, this journey, so wild and unpredictable, is only a passage inward. A tender, relentless unfolding of who we truly are, destined to bring forth tears not of pain, but of profound, aching understanding, right when the time is right.

Still sitting with all that had happened, I shifted my gaze between the three mirrors of the auto-rickshaw.

In the right-side mirror, the station traffic slowly faded into the distance.

In the middle, though I didn't ask his name, a different Mishra Ji's cheerful face beamed, humming lightly under his breath, maybe a different song.

And on the left, despite its little jumps from the road's bumps, I caught a glimpse of a smile I hadn't seen in a long, long time.

It was mine.

Passengers we all are, going out in this open, wide wide world, only to discover in the end that…It has always been the journey within!

– Vineet

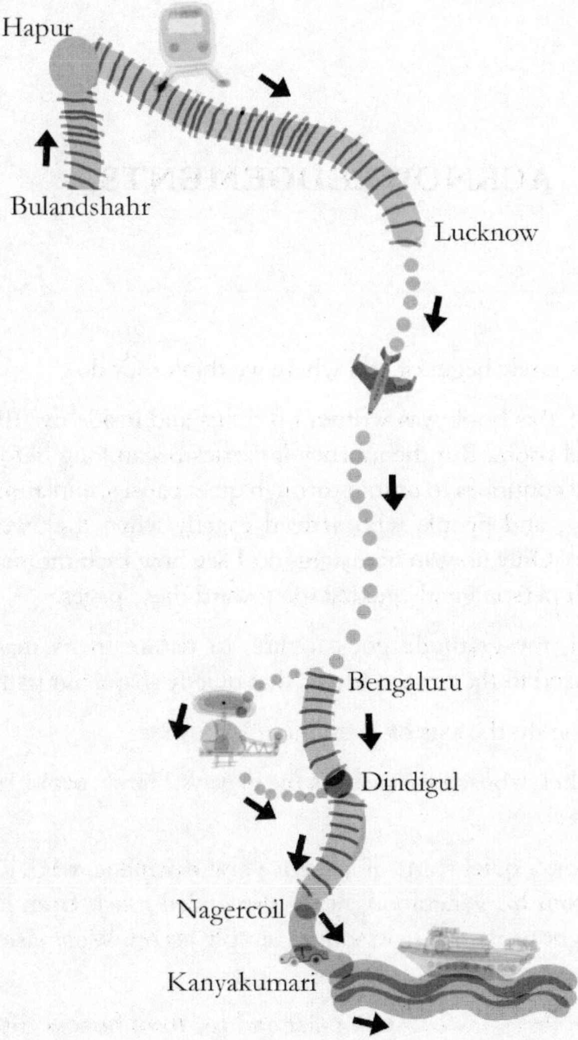
Hapur
Bulandshahr
Lucknow
Bengaluru
Dindigul
Nagercoil
Kanyakumari

ACKNOWLEDGEMENTS

Journeys rarely begin or end where we think they do.

Much of this book was written on trains and inside my 10× 10 hostel room. But the journey it carries began long before that, and continues to unfold through quiet pauses, unplanned crossings, and people who arrived exactly when they were meant to. Only now, in hindsight, do I see how each moment and each person gently guided me toward these pages.

For that, my gratitude goes to life, to nature in its many moods, and to the unseen forces that quietly shape our paths.

To my family, the axis of everything I know:

My mother, whose love steadies me in ways I rarely name, but always feel.

My father, a quiet spirit of patience and discipline, who, like many from his generation, never demanded much from life and taught us its truest lesson: to simply go on. What else is there anyway?

My wife, Priya, my constant pillar and my most honest critic, who gave me courage to every step I doubted.

To Pradeep Singh, a steady presence in difficult early days.

To Prof. Mrinalini Shah, who has taught me as much about living as about management.

To my cousin and childhood mentor, Brajesh Singh Rawat, for offering light when I needed it most.

To my earliest guides, Y. P. Singh and Amit Jindal, and to my mentors, Tushara Nair and Rohit Pillai, for teaching me humility.

To Clay Heinz, who began as a colleague and became a mentor and friend.

To my Guru, **Swami Yogendra Muni Ji**, Peethadheeshwar of Shree Nityeshwar Dham, Kanpur, Uttar Pradesh, for your divine blessings and guidance.

To the Gayatri Pariwar, Haridwar, and to my schools, Saraswati Shishu Mandir and Vidya Mandir, and to all my teachers who gave me the foundation I stand on today.

And finally, to my village, my community, for your quiet love and steady support.

Thank you, from the depths of my heart.

–Vineet

To my brother, my cousins, and the large, warm family I am blessed with, for always keeping me grounded in where I belong.

To my friends who have walked beside me:

Rohit Rajora, for being the rare reader who listens deeply and challenges thoughtfully.

Neeraj, a writer whose insight I value profoundly.

And Sudhira, among the earliest to believe in this story.

To Muskan and Sadrashya, my nieces, who grew up in my arms and later taught me more than I taught them. Every milestone of this book carries a part of you.

To Anupama Ma'am, for your patient guidance through the maze of publishing.

To the team behind this book:

Ashish and Sylph, my editor, for your clarity and calm.

Nisha and Pankaj Kumbharkar, for giving this story its visual life.

And Alind, for your trust and for standing by this manuscript from the beginning.

My respect and gratitude to my Gurus and teachers.

To Prof. P. K. Singh 'Pranav', whose spiritual writing sparked my desire to write more than two decades ago.

To the late Prof. V. K. Singh, whose guidance shaped a key turning point in my life.

To Rakesh Dwivedi, a legal professional, academic writer, and a lifelong teacher, mentor, and guide, who helped me think beyond my own confines and see the world with a wider, braver lens.